The Book of Tomorrow

ALSO BY CECELIA AHERN

The Gift
Thanks for the Memories
There's No Place Like Here
If You Could See Me Now
Love, Rosie
P.S. I Love You

The Book of Tomorrow

a novel

Cecelia Ahern

HARPER

An Imprint of HarperCollins*Publishers*
www.harpercollins.com

Originally published in a slightly different form in 2009 in Great Britain by HarperCollins UK.

FIRST U.S. EDITION

Designed by Eric Butler

Library of Congress Cataloging-in-Publication Data
    Ahern, Cecelia, 1981–
        The book of tomorrow : novel / Cecelia Ahern. — 1st ed.
            p.   cm.
        "Originally published in 2009 in Great Britain, in a slightly different form, by HarperCollins UK."
        ISBN: 978-0-06-170630-1
        1. Children of the rich—Ireland—Fiction. 2. Fatherless families—Ireland—Fiction. I. Title.
    PR6101.H47B66   2010
    823'.92—dc22   2010017858

11   12   13   14   15   OV/BVG   10   9   8   7   6   5   4   3   2   1

For Marianne,
who moves so silently but causes a right clatter

For my readers,
thank you for trusting me

CHAPTER ONE

Field of Buds

They say a story loses something with each telling. If that is the case, this story has lost nothing, for it's the first time it's been told.

This story is one for which some people will have to suspend their disbelief. And, if it didn't happen to me, I would be one of those people.

Many won't struggle to believe it though, for their minds have been opened; unlocked by whatever kind of key causes people to believe. They're either born that way or, as babies, their little bud-like minds are nurtured until their petals slowly open and prepare for the very nature of life to feed them. As the rain falls and the sun shines, they grow, grow, grow; minds so open they go through life aware and accepting, seeing light where there's dark, seeing possibility in dead ends, tasting victory as others spit out failure, questioning when others accept. Just a little less jaded, a little less cynical. A little less likely to throw in the towel. Some people's minds open later in life, through tragedy or triumph, either thing acting as the key to unlatch and lift the lid on that know-it-all box, to accept the unknown, to say good-bye to pragmatism and straight lines.

But then there are those whose minds are merely a bouquet of stalks that bud as they learn new information—a new bud for each new fact—but yet they never open, never flourish. They are the people of capital letters and full stops but never of question marks and ellipses . . .

My parents were these latter kinds of people. The know-it-all kind. The if-it's-not-in-a-book-or-I-haven't-heard-it-anywhere-before-then-don't-be-ridiculous kind. Straight thinkers with heads filled with the most beautifully colored buds, so neatly manicured and so sweetly scented, but which never opened, were never light or dainty enough to dance in the breeze; upright and rigid, so matter-of-fact, they were buds till the day they died.

Well, my mother isn't dead.

Not yet. Not medically, but if she is not dead, she is certainly not living. She's like a walking corpse that hums every once in a while as though testing herself to see if she's still alive. From far away you'd think she's fine. Up close you can see that the bright pink lipstick is a touch uneven, her eyes are tired and soulless, her body like one of those TV show houses on studio lots—all façade, nothing of substance behind. She moves around the house, drifting from room to room in a dressing gown with loosely flapping bell sleeves, as though she's a Southern belle on a mansion ranch in *Gone with the Wind*, worrying about worrying about it all tomorrow. Despite her graceful, swanlike room-to-room drifts, she's kicking furiously beneath the surface, thrashing around trying to keep her head up, flashing us the occasional panicked smile to let us know she's still here, though it does nothing to convince us.

Oh, I don't blame her. What a luxury it must be to disappear as she has, leaving everyone else to sweep up the mess and salvage whatever fragments of life are left.

I haven't told you a thing yet; you must be very confused.

My name is Tamara Goodwin. Goodwin. One of those awful phrases I despise. It's either a win or it's not. Like "bad loss," "hot sun," or "very dead." Two words that come together unnecessarily to say whatever could be said solely by the second. Sometimes when telling people my name I drop a syllable: Tamara Good, which is ironic as I've never been anything of the sort, or Tamara Win, which mockingly suggests good luck that just isn't so.

I'm sixteen years old, or so they tell me. I question my age now because I feel twice it. At fourteen, I felt fourteen. I acted eleven and wanted to be eighteen. But in the past few months I've aged a few years. Is that possible? Closed buds would shake their heads no, opened minds would say possibly. Anything is possible, they would say. Well, it's not. *Anything* is not.

It is not possible to bring my dad back to life. I tried, when I found him lying dead on the floor of his office—very dead, in fact—blue in the face with an empty pill container by his side and an empty bottle of whiskey on the desk. I didn't know what I was doing but I pressed my lips to his regardless, and pumped up and down on his chest furiously. That didn't work.

Nor did it work when my mother dived on his coffin at the graveyard during his burial and started howling and clawing at the varnished wood as he was lowered into the ground—which, by the way, was rather patronizingly covered by fake green grass as though it wasn't the maggoty soil he was being lowered into for the rest of eternity. Though I admire Mum for trying.

Nor did the endless stories about my dad that were shared afterward at the "Who Knows George Best" storytelling competition, where friends and family had their fingers on the buzzers, ready to jump in with "You think that's funny, wait till you hear this . . ."; "One time George and I . . ."; "I'll never forget the time George said . . ." All were so eager, they ended up talking over one another, spilling tears and red wine on Mum's new Persian rug in the process. They tried their best, you could tell, and in a way he was *almost* in the room, but their stories didn't bring him back.

Nor did it work when Mum discovered Dad's personal finances were about as healthy as he. He was bankrupt; the bank had already started repossession of our house and all the other properties he owned, which left Mum to sell everything—*everything*—that we owned to pay back the debts. Dad didn't come back to help us then either. So I knew then that he was gone. He was really gone. I figured if he was going to let us go through all of that on our own, let me blow air into his dead body, let Mum scratch at his coffin in front of everybody, and then watch us be stripped of everything we'd ever owned, I was pretty sure he was gone for good.

It was good thinking on his part not to stick around for it all. It was all about as awful and as humiliating as I'm sure he feared.

If my parents had flowering buds, then maybe, just maybe, they could have avoided all that. But there were no other possibilities, no other ways of doing things for them. They considered themselves practical people, but there was no practical solution for the situation. Only faith and hope and some sort of belief could have seen my father through it. But he didn't have any of that, and so when he did what he did, he effectively pulled us all into that grave with him.

It intrigues me how death, so dark and final, can shine a light on the character of a person. The lovely stories I heard about Dad during those weeks were endless and touching. They were comforting and I liked getting lost in those tales, but to be perfectly honest, I doubted if they were true. I loved him, of course, but I know my dad wasn't a good man. He and I rarely spoke and when we did, it was to argue over something, or he was giving me money to get rid of me. He was prickly, he snapped often, and he had a temper that flared easily. He forced his opinions on others and was rather arrogant. He made people feel uncomfortable, and inferior, and he enjoyed that. He would send his steak back three or four times in a restaurant just to watch the waiter sweat. He would order the most expensive bottle of wine and then claim it was corked just to annoy the restaurateur. He would complain to the police about noise levels of house parties on our street that we couldn't even hear, and he'd have them shut down just because we weren't invited.

I didn't say any of this at his funeral or at the little party at our house afterward. In fact, I didn't say anything at all. I drank a bottle of red wine all by myself and ended up vomiting on the floor by Dad's desk where he'd died. Mum found me there and slapped me across the face. She said I'd ruined it. I wasn't sure if she meant the rug or Dad's memory, but either way I was pretty sure that he'd fucked up both of them all by himself.

I'm not just heaping all the hate on my dad here. I too wasn't the best daughter. My parents gave me everything and I rarely said thank you. Or if I said it, I don't think I ever meant it. I don't actually think that I knew what it meant. "Thank you" is a sign of appreciation. Mum and Dad continually told me about the starving babies in Africa, as if that was a way to make me appreciate anything. Looking back on it, I realize the best way to make me appreciate anything was probably not to have given me everything.

We lived in a seven-thousand-square-foot, six-bedroom contemporary mansion with a swimming pool, tennis court, and private beach in Killiney, County Dublin, Ireland. My room was on the opposite side of the house to my parents' and it had a balcony overlooking the beach that I hardly looked out at. It had a private bathroom with a shower and Jacuzzi bath, with a plasma TV— TileVision, to be precise—in the wall above the bath. I also had a wardrobe full of designer clothes and handbags, a top-of-the-line computer, a PlayStation, and a four-poster bed. Lucky me.

In truth, I wasn't just ungrateful; I was a nightmare daughter. I was rude, I answered back, I expected everything, and even worse, I thought I deserved all these things just because everybody else I knew had them. It didn't occur to me for one moment that they didn't particularly deserve them either.

I figured out a way to escape my bedroom at night and sneak outside to meet with my friends; a climb from my bedroom balcony and down the piping, onto the roof of the swimming pool, then a few easy steps to the ground. There was an area on our private beach where my friends and I went drinking. The girls mostly drank Dolly Mixtures: the contents of our parents' drinks cabinets all in one plastic bottle. We took just a couple inches from each bottle so they wouldn't suspect anything. The guys preferred to drink whatever hard cider they could get their hands on. They also had whichever girl they could get their hands on. That person was mostly me. There was a boy, Johnny, who I stole from my best friend, Zoey, whose dad was a famous actor and so—I'll be honest—just because of that I used to let him put his hand up my skirt for about a half hour every night. I figured that one day I'd get to meet his dad. But I never did.

My parents felt it was important for me to know how fortunate I was to be living in my big house by the sea. So to help me appreciate the world, and to see how other people live, we spent our summers in our villa in Marbella, Christmas in our Verbier chalet, and Easter at the New York Ritz. There was a pink convertible MINI Cooper with my name on it waiting for me for my seventeenth birthday, and a friend of my dad's, who had a recording studio, was waiting to hear me sing and possibly sign me up. Though after I felt his hand on my arse, I never wanted to spend a moment alone in a room with him. Not even to be famous.

Mum and Dad attended charity functions throughout the year.

Mum would spend more money on her dresses than the actual cost of the tables, and twice a year she'd hand down the impulse buys she never wore to her sister-in-law, Rosaleen, who lived down in the country—in case Rosaleen ever felt the need to milk cows in a Pucci sundress.

I know now—now that we're out of the world we once lived in—that the three of us weren't very nice people. I think somewhere beneath the current nonresponsive surface of my mother she knows it too. We weren't evil people, we just weren't *nice*. We didn't offer anything to anybody in the world but we took an awful lot.

But. We didn't deserve this.

Before, I never thought of tomorrow. I lived in the now. I wanted this now, I wanted that now. The last time I saw my father I shouted at him and told him I hated him and then I slammed the door in his face. I never took a step back or a step outside of my little world to think about what on earth I was doing or saying, and how it was hurting anybody else. I told Dad I never wanted to see him again, and I never did. I never thought about the possibility that those would be my final words to him and that *that* would be my final moment with him. That's a lot to have to deal with. I have a lot to forgive myself for. It's going to take time.

But now, because of Dad's death and because of the story I have yet to share with you, I have no choice but to think of tomorrow and all the people that tomorrow affects. Now I'm glad when I wake up in the morning that there is a tomorrow.

I lost my dad. He lost his tomorrows and I lost all my tomorrows with him. You could say that now I appreciate them when they come. Now I want to make them the best they can possibly be.

Two Bluebottles

In order for ants to find the safest route to food, one goes out on its own. When that lone ant has found the path, it leaves a chemical trail for the others to follow. When you stamp on a line of ants or, less psychotically, if you interfere in their chemical trail in any way, it drives them crazy. The ones that have been left behind crawl around frantically in a panic, trying to regain the trail. I like watching them totally disoriented at first, running around bumping into one another while trying to figure out which way to go, then regrouping, reorganizing, and eventually crossing the pathway back in their straight line as if nothing had ever happened.

Their panic reminds me of Mum and me. Somebody broke our line, took out our leader, ruined our trail, and our lives descended into utter chaos. I think—*I hope*—that with time, we'll find the right way to go again. It takes one to lead the rest. I think, seeing as Mum is sitting this one out, that it's up to me to go out front alone.

I was watching a bluebottle fly yesterday. In an effort to escape the living room, he kept flying against the window, hitting his head against the glass over and over. Then he stopped launching himself at it like a missile and stuck to one little windowpane, buzzing about like he was having a panic attack. It was frustrating to watch, especially because if he'd just flown up a little bit higher toward the top of the window, which was open, he'd have been free. But he just kept doing the same thing over and over again. I could imagine his frustration of being able to see the trees, the flowers, the sky, just on the other side of the glass, yet not being able to get to them. I tried to help him a few times, to guide him toward the open window, but he flew away from me and continued his manic flying around the room. He'd eventually come back to the same window and I could almost hear him: "Well, this is the way I came in . . ."

I wondered if my watching him from the armchair is what it's like to be God, if there is a God. He sits back and sees the big picture, just as I could see that if the bluebottle just moved up a few inches, he'd be free. He wasn't really trapped at all, he was just looking in the wrong place. I wondered if God could see a way out for me and Mum. If I can see the open window for the bluebottle, maybe God can see the tomorrows for me and Mum. That idea brings me comfort. Well, it *did*, until I left the room and returned a few hours later to see a dead bluebottle on the windowsill. Then to show you where my mind is right now, I started crying . . . Then I got mad at God because in my head the death of that bluebottle meant Mum and I might never find our way out of this mess. What good is it being so far back you can see everything and yet not do anything to help?

Then I realized this: I had tried to help the bluebottle, but it wouldn't let me. And then I felt sorry for God because I understood how it must be frustrating for him. He offers people a helping hand, but it often gets pushed away. People always want to help themselves first.

I never used to think about these things before; God, bluebottles, ants. I'd rather have been caught dead than be seen sitting in an armchair with a book in my hand and staring at a dirty fly tapping against a window on a Saturday. Maybe that's what Dad had thought in his final moments: *I'd rather be caught dead here in my study than go through the humiliation of having everything taken from me.* My Saturdays used to be spent at Topshop with my friends, trying on absolutely everything and laughing nervously while Zoey stuffed as many accessories down her pants as she could manage before leaving the store. If we weren't at Topshop we'd spend the day sitting in Starbucks having grande gingersnap lattes and banana honey muffins. I'm sure that's what they're all doing now.

I haven't heard from anyone since the first week I got here, except a text from Laura before my phone was cut off, filling me in on all the gossip, the biggest of all being that Zoey and Johnny got back together and did it in Zoey's house when her parents were away in Monte Carlo for the weekend. Her dad has a gambling problem, which Zoey and the rest of us loved because it meant when we all stayed over at her house, her parents would come home much later than everybody else's. Anyway, apparently Zoey said that sex with Johnny hurt worse than the time the lesbian from the Sutton hockey team hit her between the legs with the stick, which was really bad, believe me—I *saw*—and she isn't in a rush to do it again. Meanwhile Laura told me not to tell anyone but she herself was meeting Johnny this weekend to do it. She hopes I don't mind and please don't tell Zoey. As if I could tell anyone if I wanted to, where I am.

Where I am. I haven't told you that yet, have I? I've mentioned my mum's sister-in-law, Rosaleen, already. She's the one my mum used to empty her wardrobe of all her unworn impulse buys for, sending them down in black sacks with the tags still on. Rosaleen's married to my uncle Arthur, who is my mum's brother. They live in a gatehouse in the country in a place called Meath in the middle of nowhere with hardly anybody else around. We visited them only a few times in my life and I was always bored to death. It took us an hour and fifteen minutes to get there and the buildup was always a letdown. I thought they were hicks in the middle of the sticks. I used to call them the Deliverance Duo. That's the only time I remember Dad laughing at one of my jokes. He never came with us when we visited Rosaleen and Arthur. I don't think they ever had an argument or anything, but like penguins and polar bears, they were just too far apart to be able to spend any time near one another. Anyway, that's where my mum and I live now. In the gatehouse with the Deliverance Duo.

It's a sweet house, a quarter of the size of our old one, which is no bad thing, and it reminds me of the one in "Hansel and Gretel." It's built from limestone and the wood around the windows and roof is painted olive green. There are three bedrooms upstairs and a kitchen and a living room downstairs. Mum has a private bathroom but Rosaleen, Arthur, and I all share a bathroom on the second floor. Used to having my own bathroom, I think this is gross, particularly when I have to go in there after my uncle Arthur and his daily newspaper-reading session. Rosaleen is a neat freak, obsessively tidy; she never ever sits down. She's always moving things, cleaning things, spraying chemicals in the air, and saying stuff about God and his will. I said to her once that I hoped God's will was better than the one Dad left behind for us. She looked at me, horrified, and scuttled off to dust somewhere else.

Rosaleen has the depth of a shot glass. Everything she talks about is totally irrelevant, unnecessary. The weather. The sad news about a poor person on the other side of the world. Her friend down the road who has broken her arm, or who has a father with two months to live, or somebody's daughter who married a dick who is leaving her with two children. Everything is doom and gloom and followed by some sort of utterance about God, like "God love them," or "God is gracious," or "Let God be good to them." Not that I talk about anything important, but if I ever try to discuss any of these things in more detail, to get to the root of the problem, Rosaleen is totally incapable of carrying on. She only wants to talk about the sad problem, and she's not interested in talking about why it happened, nor in the solution. She shushes me with her God phrases, makes me feel like I'm speaking out of turn or as though I'm so young I couldn't possibly take the reality. I think it's the other way around. I think she brings things up so that she doesn't feel like she's avoiding them, and once they're out of the way, she doesn't talk about them ever again.

Before we came to live here, I think I'd heard my uncle Arthur speak about five words total. It's as though Mum had gone through her life speaking for both of them—not that he would have shared her views on anything she said. These days Arthur speaks more than Mum. He has an entire language of his own, which I've slowly but surely learned to decipher. He speaks in grunts, nods, and snot-snorts; a kind of mucous inhale, which is something he does when he disagrees with something. A mere "Ah," and a throw back of the head means he's not bothered by something. For example, here is how a typical breakfast conversation would go.

Arthur and I are sitting at the kitchen table and Rosaleen as usual is buzzing about the place with crockery piled with toast and little dishes of homemade jam, honey, and marmalade. The radio is blaring so loudly I could hear every word the newscaster was saying from my bedroom before coming to the table; some annoying miserable man talking in monotone about the terrible things happening in the world. And so Rosaleen comes to the table with the teapot.

"Tea, Arthur."

Arthur throws back his head like a horse trying to rid his mane of a fly. He wants tea.

And the man on the radio talks about how another factory in Ireland has closed and one hundred people are losing their jobs.

Arthur inhales and a load of mucus is sucked up through his nose and then down his throat. He doesn't like this.

Rosaleen appears at the table with another plate of toast piled high. "Oh, isn't that terrible, God love their families. And the little ones now with their daddies out of work."

"Their mothers too, you know," I say, taking a slice of toast.

Rosaleen watches me bite into the toast and her green eyes widen as I chew. She always watches me eat and it freaks me out. It's as though she is the witch from "Hansel and Gretel," watching for me to become plump enough so that she can throw me into the stove with my hands tied behind my back and an apple stuffed in my gob. I wouldn't mind an apple. It would have the fewest calories of anything she'd ever fed me.

I swallow what's in my mouth and put the rest of my toast down on my plate.

She leaves the table again, disappointed.

On the news they talk about some new government tax increase and Arthur inhales more mucus. If he hears any more bad news, he'll have no room for his breakfast with all that mucus. He's only in his forties but he looks and acts older. From the shoulders up he reminds me of a king prawn, always bent over something, whether it's his food or his work.

Rosaleen returns with a plate of Irish breakfast enough to feed all the children of the one hundred factory workers who have just lost their jobs.

Arthur throws his head back again. He's happy about this.

Rosaleen stands beside me and pours me tea. I'd love nothing more than a gingersnap latte but I tip the milk into the strong tea and sip it all the same. Her eyes watch me and don't look away till I swallow.

I don't know how old Rosaleen is exactly but I'm guessing somewhere in her early to mid-forties, and if this makes sense, I'm sure whatever age she really is, she looks ten years older. She looks like she's from the 1940s in her floral tea dresses buttoned down the middle, with a slip underneath. My mum never wore slips; she barely wore underwear. Rosaleen has mouse-brown hair, always worn down, parted sharply in the center of her head, revealing gray roots, and it's short, to her chin. She always tucks her hair behind both ears, pink little mouse ears peeping out. She never wears earrings. Or makeup. She wears a gold crucifix on a thin gold chain around her neck. She's the kind of woman that my friend Zoey would say looks like she's never had an orgasm in her life, and I wonder, while cutting the fat off the bacon and as Rosaleen's eyes widen at me doing this, if Zoey had an orgasm when she did it with Johnny. Then I visualized the damage the hockey stick did to her and I instantly doubted it.

Across the road from the gatehouse is a bungalow. I have no idea who lives in it—I haven't bothered to ask—but Rosaleen pops back and forth every day with little parcels of food. Two miles down the road is a post office, which is operated from somebody's house, and across the road from that is the smallest school I've ever seen, which, unlike my school at home which has activities every hour throughout the year, is completely empty during the summer. I asked if they offered any yoga classes or anything and Rosaleen told me she'd show me how to make yogurt herself. She seemed so happy by her offer that I couldn't correct her. In the first week I watched her make strawberry yogurt. In the second week, I was still eating it.

The gatehouse that is Arthur and Rosaleen's house once protected the side entrance to Kilsaney Castle in the 1700s. The castle's main entrance has a disused scary-looking gothic entrance—I imagine I see severed heads hanging out of it every time we pass. The castle was built as a towered fortification of the Norman Pale—that was the area with Norman and English control in the East of Ireland established after Strongbow invaded—sometime between 1100 and 1200, which, when you think about it, is a bit vague. It's the difference between me or my half-human, half-robot great-great-great-great-great grandchildren building something. Anyway, it was built for a Norman warlord, so that's why I think of the severed heads, because they did that, didn't they?

The area it's in is called County Meath. It used to be East Meath and, along with Westmeath—surprise surprise—it made up a separate and fifth province in Ireland, which was the territory of the High King. The former seat of the High Kings, the Hill of Tara, is only a few kilometers away. I know all of this because the castle's in the news all the time now because they're building a motorway nearby. We had to debate the issue at school a few months ago. I was "for" the motorway being built because I thought the King would have liked to have one in his day, as it would have made it easier for him to get to his office instead of having to go through the shitty fields. Imagine the filth of his sandals. I also said it would be more accessible for tourists. They could drive right up to it or take photographs from open-top buses going one hundred and twenty kilometers on the motorway. I was only joking, but our substitute teacher went crazy, thinking I actually meant it. I found out later that she was on a committee to try and prevent the motorway from being built. It's so easy to give substitute teachers nervous breakdowns. Especially the ones who believe they can do some good for the students. I told you I was nasty.

After the Norman psycho, various lords and ladies lived in the castle. They built stables and outhouses around the place. Controversially one lord even converted to Catholicism after marrying a Catholic, and built a chapel there as a treat for the family. Me and Mum got a swimming pool as our treat, but to each his own. The demesne is surrounded by a famine wall, which was a project to provide work for the starving during the potato famine. It runs right along Arthur and Rosaleen's garden and house, and creeps me out every time I see it. If Rosaleen had ever visited our house for dinner she'd probably have started building a wall around us, because none of us eats carbs. At least we never used to eat carbs, now I'm eating so much I could fuel all the factories they're closing down.

Kilsaney descendants continued to live in the castle until the 1920s, when some arsonists didn't get the memo that the inhabitants were Catholic and they burned them out. After that they could only live in a small section of the castle because they couldn't afford to fix it up and heat it, and then they eventually moved out in the nineties. I don't know who owns it now but it's fallen into disrepair: no roof, fallen down walls, no stairs, you get the idea. There's loads of stuff growing inside it and whatever else that scutters around. I once had to do a project on the castle and Mum suggested I stay with Rosaleen and Arthur for the weekend and do some research. She and Dad had the biggest fight I'd ever seen or heard over that. The atmosphere was so bad that I was happy to leave them. But as soon as I got there, I wasn't really interested in snooping around and finding out the history of the place. I just about managed to stay with Rosaleen and Arthur for lunch, and then went to the toilet to call my nanny, Mae—who we've since had to send back home— and made her pick me up and bring me home. I told Rosaleen I had stomach cramps and tried not to laugh when she asked me if I thought it was the apple pie.

I ended up copying an essay about the castle from the Internet. Then I was called to the principal's office and she failed me for plagiarism, which was ridiculous because Zoey did her project on Malahide Castle, stole everything from the Internet, changed a few words and dates around, got the words and dates *wrong* to make it look like she didn't copy it, and she still got a higher score than me. Where's the justice in that?

Surrounding the castle is one hundred acres of land. Arthur is the groundskeeper and, with one hundred acres to look after, he's out first thing in the morning and back at five-thirty on the button, as dirty as a coal miner. He never complains, he never groans about the weather, he just gets up, eats his breakfast while deafening himself with the radio, and then goes out to work. Rosaleen gives him a flask of tea and a few sandwiches to keep him going and he rarely comes back during the day, except to get something from the garage that he forgot, or to go to the toilet. He seems like a simple man, only I don't really believe that. Nobody who says as little as he does is as simple as you'd think. It takes a lot to not say a lot, because when you're not talking, you're thinking, and he thinks *a lot*. My mum and dad talked all the time. Talkers don't think much; their words drown out any possibility of hearing their subconscious asking, *Why did you say that? What do you really think?*

I used to stay in bed for as long as possible on school mornings and on weekends until Mae dragged me out kicking and screaming. But here I wake up early. Surrounded by so many gigantic trees, the place is swarming with birds. They're so loud they wake me up. I'm always up by seven, which is nothing short of miraculous for me. Mae would be so proud. But it's not easy keeping myself busy during the daylight. That's an awful lot of hours for an awful lot of nothing to do.

Dad decided to end his life in May, right before my Junior Certificate exams, which was a little unfair as, up until then, I thought I was the one who was supposed to want to off myself. I did my exams anyway. I probably failed them but I don't really care and I don't think anybody else does either. I'll find out those results in September. My entire class came to Dad's funeral, which I'm sure they loved because they got a day off school. Can you believe I was actually embarrassed about crying in front of them? I did it anyway, which started off Zoey and then Laura. A girl in my class called Fiona, who nobody ever talked to, hugged me really tight and gave me a card from her family saying that they were all thinking of me. Fiona gave me her mobile number and her favorite book, and said she'd be there for me if I ever needed somebody to talk to. At the time I thought it was a bit lame, her trying to get in with me at my dad's funeral, but thinking about it after—which is something I do now—it was the kindest thing anybody did or said to me that day.

I started reading the book in the first week I moved to Meath. It was kind of a ghost story about a girl who was invisible to everybody in the world, including her family and friends, even though they knew she existed. She was just born invisible. I won't give away the rest but she eventually becomes friends with someone who does see her. I liked the idea and thought Fiona was trying to send me some kind of message, but when I stayed overnight at Zoey's house and told her and Laura, they thought it was the weirdest thing they'd ever heard and that Fiona was even more of a freak. So I dropped it. You know what, I'm finding it increasingly hard to understand Zoey and Laura lately.

After the first week we moved here Arthur drove me to Dublin so that I could stay overnight at Zoey's house. The car ride was over an hour and we never spoke once. The only thing he said was, "Radio?" and then when I nodded he turned it on to one of those channels that just talk about the problems in the country and don't play music and he snot-snorted his way through it. But at least it was better than silence. Then, after spending the night with Zoey and Laura—and bitching about him all night—I was feeling confident. Back to my old self. We all agreed that he and Rosaleen definitely lived up to being called the Deliverance Duo and that I shouldn't allow them to pull me into their weirdo existence. That meant that I should be able to listen to whatever the hell I wanted in the car. But the next day, when he picked me up in his filthy dirty Land Rover, which Zoey and Laura so obviously couldn't stop laughing at, I felt bad for Arthur. I felt really bad.

Having to go back to a house that wasn't mine, in a car that wasn't mine, to sleep in a room that wasn't mine, to try to talk to a mother that didn't feel like mine, made me want to hold on to at least one thing that was familiar. Who I used to be. Maybe it wasn't necessarily the right thing to hold on to, but it was something. So I kicked up a fuss in the car and told Arthur that I wanted to listen to something else. He put my favorite radio station on for one song and then he got so frustrated listening to the Pussycat Dolls singing about wanting boobies, he grumbled and changed it back to the talk channel. I stared out the window in a huff, hating him and hating myself both at the same time. For half an hour we listened to a woman crying on the phone to the show's host about how her husband had lost his job in a computer factory, couldn't find another, and they had four children to look after. My hair was down across my face and all I could do was hope that Arthur didn't see me crying. Sad stuff really gets to me now. I heard this kind of stuff before but I was kind of numb to it. Before, it just didn't happen to me.

I don't know how long we're going to live here. Nobody will answer that question for me. Arthur simply doesn't talk, my mum isn't communicating, and Rosaleen isn't able to cope with a question of that magnitude.

Needless to say, my life right now is not going as I planned. I'm sixteen and by now I should have had sex with Johnny, I should be in our villa in Marbella swimming every day, eating barbecued dinners, clubbing every night at Angels & Demons, and finding guy number two to fancy and sleep with. If the first person I sleep with ends up being the man I marry, I think I'll die. Instead I'm living in hicksville, in a gatehouse with three crazy people, the nearest things to us being a bungalow housing people who knows who, a post office that's practically in somebody's living room, an empty school, and a ruined castle. I have absolutely nothing to do here.

Or so I thought.

Let me start the story from when I arrived here . . .

CHAPTER THREE

The Beginning Began

My mum's best friend, Barbara, drove us to our new life in Meath. Mum didn't say a word the whole way. Not one word. Even when asked a question. Now that's a hard thing to do. I got so frustrated that I shouted at her in the car; this was back when I was still trying to get her to respond.

The fight happened because Barbara got lost. The GPS in her BMW X5 failed to recognize Rosaleen and Arthur's address and so we just headed to the nearest town it could locate. When we got to the town, a place called Ratoath, Barbara had to rely on her own brain and not the equipment in her SUV. As it turns out, Barbara's not a thinker. After we spent ten minutes driving down country roads spotted with houses and no signposts, I could tell Barbara was starting to get nervous. We were driving down roads which, according to the GPS, didn't exist. I should have taken this as a sign. Used to going *somewhere*, and not down invisible roads, Barbara began to make mistakes, driving blindly through crossroads, veering dangerously onto the other side of the road. I'd only been to Meath a handful of times over the years and so I was no help but the plan was this: for me to look on the left-hand side for gate-houses and for Barbara to look on the right-hand side. She snapped at me at one point for not concentrating, but really, I could see that there were no gates for at least a mile, so there was absolutely no use in looking. This, I shared with her. Finally she snapped, "Feck all," seeing as we were already driving down "fecking roads that don't exist," she couldn't see why there couldn't be "a fecking house without a fecking gate." Hearing the word "fecking" come out of Barbara's mouth was a big deal considering her usual expression of annoyance was "fiddlesticks."

Mum could have helped us but she just sat in the front seat smiling as she looked out the window. So, trying to help matters, I leaned forward and—okay, it wasn't right and it wasn't clever, but it was what I did, regardless—I shouted in her ear, the loudest possible scream that I could summon up. Mum jumped with fright, blocked her ears, and then when her shock had died down, with two hands she swatted me across the head over and over again as though I were a swarm of bees. It really hurt. She pulled at my hair, scratched me, slapped me, and I couldn't escape her grip. Barbara pulled the car over and had to pry Mum's hands off me. Then Barbara got out of the car and paced up and down the side of the road, crying. I was crying too and my head was pounding from where Mum had pulled and scratched at it. It's fashionable where I'm from to have a hairstyle like a haystack but Mum just ruined it; she'd made me look like somebody from an insane asylum. We both left her in the car, looking straight ahead and angry.

"Come here to me, sweetheart," Barbara said between tears, and she reached her arms out to me.

I didn't need to be asked twice for a hug. I longed for a hug. Even when Mum was on form, she wasn't a hugger. She was bony, always dieting, had the same relationship with food as she had with

Dad. Loved it but didn't want it most of the time because she felt it was bad for her. I know this because I overheard a conversation she had with a friend at two A.M. on returning from a ladies' lunch. But regarding the hugging, I think she just felt awkward having somebody physically so close. She wasn't a comfortable person and so had no comfort to give anybody else. It's like words of advice; you can't give them unless you have them. I don't think it meant she didn't care. I never felt she didn't care. Well, okay, maybe I did a few times.

Barbara and I stood on the side of the road embracing and crying while she apologized to me over and over again about how unfair this all was for me. When she'd pulled over, she'd left the car's ass sticking out on the road and so every car that came around the corner blasted us with its horn, but we ignored them.

The tension was released somewhat after that. You know the way storm clouds gather when there's going to be rain—that's what had been happening with us all the way from Killiney. It was all building, and finally it exploded. So feeling like we'd all had the chance to release at least a portion of our woes, we prepared ourselves for what lay ahead. Only we didn't have time because as soon as we rounded the next turn we were there. Home sweet home. On the right-hand side stood a gate, and just inside it on the left was a house. Rosaleen and Arthur were standing by the little green gate of their "Hansel and Gretel" house and God knows how long they'd been waiting there. We were almost an hour late. If they were pretending not to look worried about the whole thing, then it must have been near impossible for them to keep up the ruse when they saw our faces. Not knowing we were so close to the house we hadn't enough time to compose ourselves. My and Barbara's eyes were red raw from crying, my hair was high in tatters—well, more tattered than usual—and Mum was in the front seat with a look of thunder on her face and I never thought about how difficult that moment must have been for Arthur and Rosaleen. I was so busy thinking about myself and how much I didn't want to be there, I didn't once think about how they were opening their home to two people they had no relationship with. It must have been so unbelievably nerve-racking for them and I didn't thank them once.

Barbara and I got out of the car. She went to the trunk to sort out the bags, and I assume give us all a moment to greet each other. That didn't quite happen. I stood there looking at Arthur and Rosaleen, who were still standing behind the little green swinging gate, and I immediately wished I'd dropped bread crumbs all the way from Killiney so I could find my way home.

Rosaleen looked from one of us to another like a meerkat, trying to take in the SUV, Mum, me, Barbara, all at once. She clasped her hands at her front, but kept unlocking them to smooth down her dress as though she were at a Lovely Girl competition in a country *feis*. Mum finally opened the door and got out of the car. She stepped onto the gravel and looked up at the house. Then her anger disappeared and she smiled, revealing puce lipstick on her front teeth.

"Arthur." She held out her arms as though she had just opened the door to her home and was welcoming him to a dinner party.

He snot-snorted, inhaling the mucus—the first time I'd heard it—which made my lip curl in disgust. He stepped toward Mum and she took his hands and looked at him, her head tilted, that strange smile still pulling at her lips like a bad facelift. In an awkward movement she leaned forward and rested her forehead against his. Arthur stayed there a millisecond longer than I thought he would, then patted the back of her neck and pulled away from her. He patted me hard on the head as if I was his faithful collie, which messed my hair even more, and then made his way to the trunk to help Barbara with the bags. So that left me and Mum staring at Rosaleen, only Mum wasn't staring at her. She was inhaling the fresh air deeply, her eyes closed, smiling. Despite the depressing situation, I had a feeling then that this stay could be good for Mum.

I wasn't as worried about her then as I am now. It had only been a month since Dad's funeral and we were both feeling numb and unable to say much to each other or to anybody else for that matter. People were so busy talking to us, saying nice things, tactless things, whatever things popped into their heads—almost looking for us to console them and not the other way around—that Mum's odd behavior wasn't so noticeable. She was just sighing along with everybody else every now and again, and saying little words here and there. A funeral is like a game, really. You have to just play along and say the right thing and behave the right way until it's over. Be pleasant but don't smile too much; be sad but don't overdo it or the family will feel worse than they already do. Be hopeful but don't let your optimism be taken as a lack of empathy or an inability to deal with the reality. Because if anybody was to be truly honest there would be a lot of arguments, finger-pointing, tears, snot, and screaming.

That's what I thought Mum was doing, just playing along, being the good widow, but then afterward when her behavior didn't change, when it felt like she didn't actually know what was going on and she was using those same little words and sighs in every conversation, I wondered then if she was bluffing. I'm still wondering how much of her is actually with us and how much she's pretending just so she doesn't have to deal with it. There was a crack in her immediately after Dad died, quite understandably, but when people stopped looking at her and went back to their own lives, the crack kept growing, and it seemed like I was the only person who could see it.

It wasn't the bank that was being exceptionally unreasonable by turfing us out on our ear. They had already given Dad the repossession date but, along with a good-bye, it was just another message he'd forgotten to pass on to us. So even though they'd let us all stay for much longer than they'd threatened, we had to leave after a certain point. Mum and I stayed in the back of Barbara's house, in her nanny's mews, for a week. Eventually we had to leave there too because Barbara had to go to their house in St. Tropez for the summer and gave us the hint. Maybe she was afraid we'd steal the silver.

Though I wasn't as worried about Mum then, when we first arrived at the gatehouse, it doesn't mean I wasn't concerned at all. Before we arrived here I thought she should go see a doctor, whereas now I'm thinking she should check herself into one of those places where people wear white bumless smocks all day and rock back and forth in the hallways. It was to Barbara that I suggested Mum should visit the doctor. Barbara just patronizingly sat me down in her kitchen and told me that Mum was doing what is called "grieving." At sixteen years old, you can imagine how delightful it was to learn that word for the first time. And then I settled down, preparing myself for a lecture about heavy petting. But Barbara didn't go there. Instead she asked if I minded sitting on her suitcase while she zipped it shut. As I sat on her bulging Louis Vuitton suitcase that held her zebra-print bikinis, gold thong sandals, and ridiculous hats, I made a wish for it to burst open on the conveyer belt at the airport in St. Tropez, and for her vibrator to fall out and buzz around for everybody to see.

So there we were, on the first day of the rest of my life, outside the gatehouse, Mum with her eyes closed, Rosaleen staring at me with excited wide green eyes and her little pink tongue licking her lips now and then, Arthur snot-snorting at Barbara, which meant he didn't want her to carry any bags, and Barbara watching him with bewilderment and probably trying not to gag at his snot snort-ing, Barbara in her loose tracksuit, flip-flops, and Oompa-Loompa orange face. She'd just had a spray tan that morning.

"Jennifer." Rosaleen finally broke the silence over on our side.

Mum opened her eyes and smiled brightly and it seemed to me that she recognized Rosaleen and knew exactly what she was doing. If you hadn't spent every second of the last month with her as I had, you'd think she was okay. She was bluffing rather well.

"Welcome." Rosaleen smiled.

"Yes. Thank you." Mum chose a correct response from her little words file.

"Come in, come in, and we'll get you some tea," Rosaleen said with urgency in her voice, as though we were all going to die unless we had some tea right that minute.

I didn't want to follow them. I didn't want to go in because then that would mean that it all had to start. Reality, that is. No more in-betweenness of funeral arrangements or Barbara's mews. This was our new life and it had to begin.

Arthur, the king prawn, rushed by me and up the garden path laden down with bags. He was stronger than he looked.

Then the car trunk slammed and I spun around. Barbara was fidgeting with her car keys and shifting from one Louis Vuitton flip-flopped foot to the other. It was only then that I noticed she had cotton wool between her toes. She looked at me, awkwardly, in a heavy silence while she figured out how to tell me she was now leaving me.

"I didn't realize you had a pedicure done too," I said to fill the silence.

"Yes." She looked down and wriggled her toes as if to confirm it. Jewels glistened from her big toes. And then she added, "Danielle's invited us to a drinks party on her yacht tomorrow evening."

Most people would think those two sentences were unrelated, but I understood. You can't wear shoes on Danielle's yacht, therefore competition of the jewels and white tips would be fierce. Those women would find ways to accessorize their patellas if they were the only parts showing.

We stared at each other in silence. She was dying to go. I wanted to go with her. I too wanted to be shoeless on the Mediterranean coast while Danielle floated around the guests holding a martini glass daintily between her squared French tips, a plunging Cavalli dress revealing tits as pert as the pimento-stuffed olive floating in her glass, and on her head a tilted sea captain's hat, making her look like Captain Birdseye in drag. I wanted to be a part of all that.

"You'll be all right here, sweetheart," Barbara said, and I heard sincerity in her voice. "With family."

I looked back uncertainly at the "Hansel and Gretel" house and wanted to cry again.

"Oh, sweetheart," she said, sensing this, and came at me again with her arms held out. She was really good at hugging, she obviously felt comfortable with it. That, or her implants suitably assisted in cushioning my head. I squeezed her tightly again and closed my eyes, but she let go a little sooner than I wanted and I was plunged back into reality.

"Okay." She inched her way toward the car and placed her hand on the door handle. "I don't want to disturb them inside so please tell them—"

"Come in, come in," Rosaleen's voice sang out from the shadow of the front doorstep, stopping Barbara on her way back to her jeep. "Hello, there," Rosaleen called again. "Won't you come in for a cup of tea? I'm sorry I don't know your name, Jennifer didn't say."

She'd have to get used to that. There was a lot Jennifer wasn't going to say.

"Barbara," Barbara replied, and I noticed her grip tightening on the door handle.

"Barbara." Rosaleen's green eyes glowed like a cat's. "A cup of tea before you hit the road, Barbara? There's some fresh scones and homemade strawberry jam there too."

Barbara's face was frozen in a smile as she thought hard for an excuse.

"She can't come in," I responded for her. Barbara looked at me gratefully, and then guiltily.

"Oh . . ." Rosaleen's face fell, as though I'd ruined her tea party.

"She has to go home and wash her fake tan off," I added. I told you, I'm a horrible, horrible person, and in my eyes, even though I was none of Barbara's business and she had a life of her own which she needed to get back to, she was still leaving me behind. "And her toes are still wet." I shrugged.

"Oh." Rosaleen looked confused, as though I'd spoken some odd Celtic Tiger language. "Coffee then?"

I burst out laughing and Rosaleen looked hurt. I heard Barbara flip-flopping behind me and she passed by without looking at me. I'd made it easier for her to leave. I looked back at Rosaleen, who was gazing at me hopefully. I still couldn't bring myself to go inside.

"I'm going to have a look around," I said.

She seemed disappointed, as though I'd denied her something precious. I waited for her to go back into the house, to disappear into the darkness of the house front hallway, which was like another dimension, but she didn't move. She stood at the porch, watching me, and I realized I'd have to move first. With her eyes searing into me, I looked around. Which way to go? To my left was the house, behind me was the open gate leading to the main road, in front of me trees, and to my right, a small pathway that led into the darkness of even more trees. I started walking down the main road. I didn't turn around, not once—I didn't want to know if she was still there. But the farther I walked, it wasn't just Rosaleen that I felt was watching me. I felt revealed, as though beyond the majestic trees somebody else was watching. Just that feeling you get when you intrude on nature's world, where you're not supposed to be, not without an invitation. The trees that lined the road all turned their heads to watch me.

If men dressed in armor had come galloping toward me on horseback, waving swords, they wouldn't have seemed out of place here. The estate was steeped in history, crowded with ghosts of the past, and now here I was, just another person ready to begin my story. The trees had seen it all, yet still I held their interest, and as the light summer breeze blew, the leaves swished to one another making the sounds of gossiping lips, never growing bored of another generation's journey.

I followed the main road until finally the trees, which were cleverly landscaped to conceal the castle, fell away. Even though it was me that was moving toward it, it felt like it was the castle that suddenly came upon me, as though it had sneaked toward me without my noticing, a whole pile of sneaky stone and mortar on its tiptoes with a finger across its lips, as if it hadn't had a bit of fun for the past few hundred years. I stopped walking when it came in sight. Little me before a big castle. It looked more domineering, more commanding as a ruin than as a castle because there it stood before me with its scars revealed, all wounded and bloody from battle. And I stood before it, feeling a shadow of who I used to be, with my own scars revealed. We instantly bonded.

We studied one another and then I walked toward it, and it didn't blink once.

Though I could have walked into the castle through the gaping hole in the side wall, I felt it would be more respectful to enter through what used to be the front entrance. Respectful to whom, I don't exactly know, but I think I was trying to appeal to the softer side of the castle. I paused at the door, a respectful pause, and then went inside. There was a lot of green inside, a lot of rubble. It was eerily quiet within the walls, and I felt as though I was intruding on somebody's house. The weeds, the dandelions, the nettles, all stopped what they were doing to look up. I don't know why, but it was then I started crying.

Just as I'd felt sad for the bluebottle, I felt sad for the castle, but realistically, I think I felt those things because I was mostly sad for myself. I felt like I could hear the castle moan and whine as it was left to stand here, falling apart, while the trees around it continued to grow. I moved over to one of the walls, the stones so rough and so large I could imagine the strength of the hands that had carried, or that had been forced to carry, them. I hunkered down in the corner, pressed my ear against the stone, and closed my eyes. I don't know what I was listening for, I don't really know what I was doing—trying to comfort a wall?—but it's what I did anyway.

If I'd told Zoey and Laura what I'd done they'd have carted me off to the fashion house of bumless smocks for sure, but I felt like I'd connected to the building in some way. I don't know, maybe because I'd lost my home and I felt that I had nothing that was truly mine, coming across this building that wasn't anybody's, I instantly wanted to make it mine. Or maybe it was just that when people are lonely they cling to anything not to feel that way anymore. For me, that anything was the castle.

I don't know how long I stayed there but eventually the sun was going down behind the trees, casting a sprinkle of sparkling light on the ruin every time the trees swished from side to side. I watched it for a while and then I realized the surroundings were heading toward dusk. It must have been long after dinner.

My legs were stiff from being in the same position for so long as I slowly rose to my feet. From the corner of my eye, I thought I saw something move. A shadow. A figure. Not an animal, yet it darted. I wasn't sure. Not wanting whoever or whatever it was to come up behind me, I kept my back to the castle entrance and moved backward quickly. Then I heard another noise—an owl or something squawked—and I jumped out of my skin and got ready to run. Unable to see the ground underneath the growth, I tripped over a rock and fell backward to the ground. I smacked my head, whimpered, and I could hear the panic in my voice as I fell into the disgusting overgrowth with God knows what living in it. My vision blurred a little, black spots appearing in place of the line of the ruined roof against the indigo sky. I climbed to my feet, used my hands to push myself up, scraped against the pebbles and rocks, which cut into my skin, and I didn't look back as I ran as fast as my Uggs would take me. It felt like forever until the house came into sight, as though the road and the trees were conspiring to keep me away from it.

Finally the house came into view. The absence of Barbara's SUV was confirmation that I'd been completely cut off from my former life. The drawbridge had been lifted. The front door of the house opened and Rosaleen stood watching me, as though she had been standing there waiting since the moment I left.

"Come in, come in," she said with urgency in her voice.

I finally stepped over the threshold and into my new life, and the beginning began. My once-clean pink Uggs were now filthy from the castle walk. The house was deathly quiet.

"Let's have a look at you," Rosaleen said, holding my wrists tightly, and took a step back to give me the once-over. But her once-over went twice, then three times . . . I tugged away from her and her grip instinctively tightened, but then as though she realized what she'd done, or she saw how my face changed, she finally let go.

Her voice was sweeter. "I'll darn those for you. Leave them in the basket by the armchair in the sitting room."

"Darn what?"

"Your trousers."

"They're jeans. They're supposed to be like this." I looked down at my ripped jeans, so torn apart that there was hardly any denim visible at all. The holes revealed my leopard-print tights underneath, which was the idea. "They're not supposed to be dirty, though."

"Oh. Well, you can leave them in the basket in the kitchen."

"You have a lot of baskets."

"Just two."

I'm not sure if what I'd said was a joke or a smart comment but she missed it either way.

"Okay. Well, I'm going to my room . . ." I waited for her to guide me but she just stared at me. "Where is it?"

"What about a cuppa? I made an apple tart." Her tone was almost pleading.

"Eh, no, thanks, I'm not very hungry." I felt my stomach grumble in response and hoped she wouldn't hear it.

"Of course. Of course you're not," she berated herself silently.

"So which way is my room?"

"Up the stairs, the second door on the left. Your mum is the last room on the right."

"Okay, I'll go see her." I began to make my way upstairs.

"No, child," Rosaleen said quickly. "Leave her. She's resting."

"I'd just like to say good night to her." I smiled tightly.

"No, no, you must leave her," she said firmly.

I swallowed. "Okay."

I slowly backed away and went upstairs, each step creaking under my foot. From the landing I could still see the hallway, Rosaleen still standing there watching me. I smiled tightly and went into my room, closed the door firmly behind me, and leaned against it, my heart pounding.

I stood in the same spot for five minutes, barely taking in the room, knowing I had enough time ahead of me to come to terms with my new space, but first I needed to see my mother. When I opened the door again slowly, I peeped my head out and looked down from the landing balcony and into the hallway. Rosaleen was gone. I opened the door wider and stepped outside. I jumped. There she was, Rosaleen, standing outside Mum's bedroom door like a guard dog.

"I just checked on her," she whispered, her green eyes glowing. "She's sleeping. You best go and get some rest now."

I hate being told what to do. I used to never do what I was told, but something about Rosaleen's voice, about the look in her eye, about the feel of the house and the way she was standing, told me that I wasn't in control now. Without another word I went back into my room and closed the door.

Later that night, when the house was so thick with darkness I couldn't make out any shapes—I woke up thinking there was some-one in the room with me. I heard breathing above my bed and smelled a soapy lavender smell, and so I scrunched my eyes shut and pretended to be asleep. I don't know how long Rosaleen stayed there watching me but it felt like an eternity. Even after I heard her leave the room, clicking the door gently shut, I kept my eyes tightly closed, my heart pounding so loudly I was afraid she would hear it, until I eventually fell asleep.

CHAPTER FOUR

The Elephant in the Room

I awoke the next morning around six A.M. to the sound of the birds calling to one another. Their constant whistling and chatter made me feel as though the house had been airlifted in the middle of the night and transported up to the trees. Their noisy banter reminded me of the builders we'd once had working on our swimming pool, who went about their business loudly and cockily, as though we weren't still living in the house. There was one guy, Steve, who kept trying to get a look at me in my bedroom while I was getting dressed. So one morning I really gave him something to look at. Don't get the wrong impression; I took three hairpieces and pinned them to my bikini—you can guess where—and I took off my bathrobe and paraded around my room like Chewbacca, pretending I didn't know he was looking. He never looked again after that, but a few of the others used to stare at me whenever I passed by, so I can only assume he told them, dirty little bugger. Well, there would be no such games here, unless I wanted to send a red squirrel flying off his branch in shock.

The blue-and-white-checked curtains in my room did little to keep out the sunlight. It was fully lit like a bar at closing time; all blemishes, drunkards, and cheaters revealed. I lay in bed, wide awake, and stared at the room that was now *my* room. It didn't seem very *my*; I wondered if it would ever feel *my*. It was a simple room, surprisingly warm. Not just from the morning sun streaming in, but it was cozy warm, in an authentic Laura Ashley way, and though I usually hated all that twee stuff, it worked here. Where it didn't work was in my friend Zoey's bedroom, which her mum decorated to suit a ten-year-old in an obvious attempt to convince herself her daughter was still sweet and innocent. That room was the equivalent of sticking her daughter into a pickle jar. It was never going to work. It wasn't so much that the lid came off when her mother wasn't looking, but more that Zoey liked pickles a little too much.

The bedrooms here were in the eaves of the house, the ceilings sloping toward the windows. There was a cracked white-painted wooden chair in one corner of my room with an old blue-and-white-checked pillow on it. The walls were a pale blue, but they didn't feel cold. There was a white-painted freestanding wardrobe that was just big enough to hold my underwear. My bed had a metal frame, white linen, and a blue floral duvet cover with a duck-egg-blue cashmere throw at the foot of it. Above the door hung a simple St. Bridget's cross. On the windowsill was a vase of fresh wildflowers—lavender, bluebells, other things I couldn't recognize. Rosaleen had gone to a lot of trouble.

There was a noise coming from downstairs. Plates were clanging, water was running, a kettle whistled, and there was the sizzle of food on a pan, and eventually the smell of fry drifted upstairs and into my room. I realized that I hadn't eaten since lunch at Barbara's yesterday, when we had divine sashimi. I also hadn't been to the toilet yet and so my full bladder conspired to get me out of bed.

Just as I thought of it, through the paper-thin walls I heard the door next to my room close and lock. I heard the toilet lid lift and then the trickle of urine as it splashed against the bottom of the bowl. It was falling from a height, so unless Rosaleen pissed while on stilts, I knew it was Arthur.

Judging by the sounds coming from both the kitchen and the bathroom, I guessed my mother wasn't in either room. Now would be my chance to see her. I stepped into my pink Uggs, still filthy from yesterday's romp, wrapped the duck-egg-blue blanket around my shoulders, and sneaked down the hall to Mum's room.

Despite my lightness of foot, the floorboards creaked with every step. Hearing the toilet flush in the bathroom, I ran down the hall and entered Mum's room without knocking. I don't know what I expected but I suppose something closer to the sight that had greeted me each morning over the previous two weeks: a dark, cavelike room, and buried somewhere beneath a heavy duvet would be Mum. But I was pleasantly surprised that morning. Her room was even brighter than mine—a kind of buttery yellow, fresh and clean. Her vase on the windowsill was filled with buttercups and dandelions, long green grasses all tied together in yellow ribbon. Her room must have been directly above the living room as there was an open fireplace along the wall with a photograph of the Pope above it, which made me shudder. It wasn't the Pope—though I'd rather Zac Efron were on my wall—but the fire that made me uncomfortable. I've just never liked them. The fireplace had white molding with black paint inside, and it looked as though it had plenty of use, which I thought was weird for a spare bedroom. Rosaleen and Arthur must have had a lot of guests, though they didn't strike me as the sociable entertaining type. Then I noticed the private bathroom and realized Rosaleen and Arthur must have given Mum their bedroom.

Mum was sitting in a white rocking chair, not rocking, and she was facing the window, which looked out over the back garden. Her hair was pinned back neatly, and she was dressed in an apricot-colored floaty silk robe. She was wearing the same puce lipstick she'd had on since the day of Dad's funeral. She wore a small smile, so tiny, but it was there, and she looked like she was intently studying something out the window. When I came near her, she looked up and her smile grew.

"Good morning, Mum." I gave her a kiss on her forehead and sat down beside her on the edge of her already made bed. "Did you sleep well?"

"Yes, thank you," she said happily, and my heart lifted.

"I did too," I realized as I spoke. "It's so quiet here, isn't it?" I decided not to mention anything about Rosaleen being in my bedroom last night, in case I'd dreamed it. It would be so embarrassing to accuse somebody of that, until I had further evidence.

"Yes, it is," Mum said again.

We sat together, looking out into the back garden. In the middle of the one-acre garden stood an oak tree, its branches veering out in all directions, just begging to be climbed. A beautiful tree, it rose up to the sky grandly, its arms filled with green. It was sturdy and solid and I understood why Mum kept looking at it. It was safe and secure, and if it had stood there for a few hundred years, you could trust it was going to stay there for a bit longer. Stability in our rocky lives right now. A robin hopped from one branch to the other, seeming excited to have the entire tree to itself, like a child who was playing musical chairs alone. That was something I'd never have cared to look at before: a tree with a bird. And even if I'd seen it, I'd never have compared it to a child who was playing musical chairs. Zoey and Laura would seriously have a problem with me right now.

I was beginning to have problems with me. Thinking of them suddenly gave me pangs for home.

"I don't like it here, Mum," I finally said, and realized my voice was shaking and I was close to tears. "Can't we stay in Dublin? With friends?"

Mum looked at me and smiled warmly. "Oh, we'll be okay here. It will all be okay."

For a moment I was relieved to hear her say that, to hear the confidence in her words. But I wasn't convinced.

"But how long are we going to stay here? What's our plan? Where am I going to school in September? Can I still go to St. Mary's?"

Mum looked away from me then, keeping her smile but gazing back out the window. "We'll be okay here. It will all be okay."

"I know, Mum," I said, getting frustrated but trying to keep my tone soft. "You just said that, but for how long?"

She was quiet.

"Mum?" My tone hardened.

"We'll be okay here," she repeated. "It will all be okay."

I'm a good person, but only when I want to be, and so I leaned up close to her ear and just as I was about to say something so truly horrible that I can't even write it, there was a light knock on the door and it was quickly opened by Rosaleen.

"*There* you both are," she said, as though she'd been searching high and low for us.

I quickly moved my mouth away from Mum's ear and sat back down on the bed. Rosaleen stared at me as though she could read my mind. Then her face softened and she entered the room with a silver breakfast tray in her hand, wearing a new tea dress that exposed her flesh-colored slip down by her knees.

"Now, Jennifer, I hope you had a lovely rest last night."

"Yes, lovely." Mum looked at her and smiled and I felt so angry at her for fooling everybody else when she wasn't fooling me.

"That's great. I've made you some breakfast, just a few little bites to keep you going . . ." Rosaleen continued, nattering like that as she moved around the room, pulling furniture, dragging chairs, plumping pillows, while I watched her.

A few bites, she'd said. A few bites for a few hundred people. The tray was loaded with food. Slices of fruit, cereal, a plate piled with toast, two boiled eggs, a little bowl of what looked like honey, another bowl of strawberry jam, and another of marmalade. Also on the tray was a teapot, a jug of milk, a bowl of sugar, all sorts of cutlery and napkins. For somebody who normally just had a breakfast bar and an espresso in the morning, and only because she felt she had to, Mum had a task on her hands.

"Lovely," Mum said, addressing the tray before her on the little wooden table and not looking at Rosaleen at all. "Thank you."

I wondered then if Mum knew that what had been placed in front of her was to be eaten by her, and wasn't just a work of art. "You're very welcome. Now is there anything else you want at all?"

"Her house back, the love of her life . . ." I said sarcastically. I didn't aim the joke at Rosaleen, I was just letting off some steam. But I think Rosaleen took it personally. She looked shaken and— oh, I don't know—maybe even embarrassed or angry. She looked at Mum to make sure she wouldn't be broken by my words.

"Don't worry, she can't hear me," I said, bored and examining the split ends of my dark brown hair. I pretended I wasn't bothered but really Rosaleen's response to my comments was causing my heart to beat wildly in my chest.

"Of course she can hear you, child," Rosaleen half scolded me while continuing to move about the room fixing things, wiping things, adjusting things.

"You think?" I raised an eyebrow. "What do you think, Mum, will we be okay here?"

Mum looked up at me and smiled. "Of course we'll be okay." I joined in on her second sentence, imitating Mum's hauntingly chirpy voice so that we spoke in perfect unison, which I think chilled Rosaleen. It definitely chilled me as we said, "It will all be okay."

Rosaleen stopped dusting to watch me.

"That's right, Mum. It will all be okay." My voice trembled. I decided to go a step further. "And look at the elephant in the bedroom, isn't that nice?"

Mum stared at the tree in the garden, the same small smile on her pink lips. "Yes. That's nice."

"I thought you'd think so." I swallowed hard, trying not to cry as I looked to Rosaleen. I was supposed to feel satisfaction, but I didn't, I just felt more lost. Up to that point it was all in my head that Mum wasn't right. Now I'd proven it and I didn't like it.

Perhaps *now* Mum would be sent to a therapist or a counselor and get herself fixed so that we could start moving on with our chemical trail.

"Your breakfast is on the table, Tamara," Rosaleen said simply, then turned her back on me and left the room.

And that is how the Goodwin problems were always fixed. Fix them on the surface but don't go to the root, always ignoring the elephant in the room. I think that morning was when I realized I'd grown up with an elephant in every room of my life. It was practically our family pet.

CHAPTER FIVE

Grève

I took my time getting showered and dressed, knowing that there was very little else I was going to do that day. I stood shivering in the avocado-colored bath as the hot water trickled down with all the power of baby drool, and I longed for my pink iridescent mosaic-tiled wet room with six power-shower jets and a plasma TV in the wall.

By the time I had managed to wash out all of the shampoo—I couldn't be bothered battling with conditioner—and dried my hair and arrived downstairs for breakfast, Arthur was scraping the last of the food from his plate. I wondered if Rosaleen had told him about what happened in Mum's bedroom. Probably not, because if he was in any way a decent brother, he'd be doing something about it. I don't think tipping the base of a teacup into his oversized nose was going to fix much.

"Morning, Arthur," I said.

"Morning," he said, into the bottom of his teacup.

Rosaleen, the busy domestic bee, immediately jumped into action and came at me with giant oven gloves on her hands.

I lightly boxed each of her hands. She didn't get the joke. But without a word, or a twitch, or a movement of any kind in Arthur's face, I sensed he got it.

"I'll just have cereal, please, Rosaleen," I said, looking around. "I'll get it, if you tell me where it is." I started opening the cupboards, trying to find the cereal, then had to take a step back when I came across a double cupboard filled from top to bottom with jars of honey. There must have been over a hundred jars.

"Whoa." I stepped back from the opened cupboards. "Have you got, like, honey OCD?"

Rosaleen looked confused, but smiled and handed me a cup of tea. "Sit yourself down there, I'll bring you your breakfast. Sister Ignatius gives the honey to me," she said with a smile.

I was unfortunately taking a sip of tea when she said that, and I choked as I started laughing. Tea came spurting out my nose. Arthur handed me a napkin and looked at me with amusement.

"You've a sister called Ignatius?" I laughed loudly. "She's totally got a man's name. Is she a tranny?" I shook my head, still giggling.

"A tranny?" Rosaleen asked, forehead crumpled.

I burst out laughing again, then stopped abruptly when her smile immediately faded and she closed the kitchen cabinets and went to the Aga for my breakfast. She placed a plate piled high with bacon, sausages, eggs, beans, pudding, and mushrooms in the middle of the table. I hoped her sister Ignatius was going to join me for breakfast because there was no way I was going to finish this alone. Then Rosaleen disappeared, flitted about behind me, and came back with another plate piled high with toast.

"Oh, no, that's okay. I don't eat carbs," I said as politely as I could.

"Carbs?" Rosaleen asked.

"Carbohydrates," I explained. "They bloat me."

Arthur placed his cup on the saucer and looked out at me from under his bushy eyebrows.

"Arthur," I said, changing the subject. "You don't look anything like Mum at all."

Rosaleen dropped a jar of honey on the floor tiles, which made me and Arthur jump and turn around. Surprisingly, it didn't smash. Rosaleen, at top speed, continued on and placed jam, honey, and marmalade before me, along with a plate of scones.

"You're a growing girl, you need your food."

"The only growing I want right now is here." I gestured at my 34B chest. "And unless I stuff my bra with black-and-white pudding, this breakfast isn't going to make that happen."

It was Arthur's turn to choke on his tea. Not wanting to insult them any further, I took a slice of bacon, a sausage, and a tomato.

"Go on, have more," Rosaleen said, watching my plate.

I looked at Arthur in horror.

"Give her time to eat that," Arthur said quietly, getting to his feet with his plates in his hands.

"Leave that down." Rosaleen fussed around him, and I felt like grabbing a fly swatter and attacking her. "You get on now to work."

"Arthur, does anybody work in the castle?" I asked.

"The ruin?" Rosaleen asked.

"The castle," I responded, and immediately felt defensive on its behalf. If we were going to start name calling we may as well start with Mum. She was clearly a broken woman yet we weren't referring to her as a ruin. She was still a woman. The castle was not as it once had been, but it was still a castle. My conviction settled, I knew from then on I was never going to call it a ruin.

"Why do you ask?" Arthur asked, as he slipped his arms into a lumberjack shirt and then put a padded vest over it.

"I was taking a look around there yesterday and just thought I saw someone. No big deal," I said quickly, taking a bite of bacon and hoping that my comment wouldn't make them stop me from going there again.

"Could have been a rat," Rosaleen said, looking at Arthur.

"Wow, that makes me feel better." I looked to Arthur for more but he was silent.

"You shouldn't go wandering about there on your own," Rosaleen said, pushing my plate of food closer to me.

"Why?"

Neither of them said anything.

"Right," I said, ignoring the plate. "That's settled. It was a giant, human-sized rat. So if I can't go there, what's there to do around here?" I asked.

There was more silence. "In what way?" Rosaleen finally asked, seeming afraid.

"Like, for me, to do. What is there? Are there shops? Clothes shops? Coffee shops? Anything nearby?"

"Nearest town is fifteen minutes," Rosaleen replied.

"Cool. I'll walk there after breakfast. Work this off." I smiled and bit into a sausage.

Rosaleen smiled happily and leaned her chin on her hand as she watched me.

"So which way is it?" I asked, swallowing the sausage and opening my mouth to show Rosaleen it was gone.

"Which way is what?" She got the hint and stopped watching.

"The town. I go out the gates and turn left or right?"

"Oh no, you can't walk it. It's fifteen minutes in the car. Arthur will drive you. Where do you need to go?"

"Well, nowhere in particular. I just wanted to have a look around."

"Arthur will drive you and collect you when you're ready."

"How long will you be?" Arthur asked, zipping up his vest.

"I don't know," I replied, looking from one to the other, feeling frustrated.

"Twenty minutes? An hour? If it's a short time he can wait there for you," Rosaleen added.

"I don't know how long I'll be. How can I? I don't know what's in the town, or what there is for me to do."

They looked at me blankly.

"I'll just hop on a bus or something and come back when I'm ready."

Rosaleen looked at Arthur nervously. "There's no buses along this way."

"What?" My jaw dropped. "How are you supposed to get anywhere?"

"Drive," Arthur responded.

"But I can't drive."

"Arthur will drive you," Rosaleen repeated. "Or he'll pick up whatever it is that you need. Have you anything in mind? Arthur will get it, won't you, Arthur?"

Arthur snot-snorted.

"What is it you need?" Rosaleen asked again, eagerly, leaning forward.

"Tampons," I spat out, feeling so frustrated now.

I just don't know why I do it.

Well, I do know. Rosaleen and Arthur were both annoying me. I was used to so much freedom at home, not the Spanish Inquisition. I was used to coming and going whenever I pleased, at my own pace, for however long I liked. Even my own parents never asked me so many questions.

They were quiet. I shoved another bit of sausage into my mouth.

Rosaleen fiddled with the doily underneath the scones. Arthur was hovering near the door, waiting with bated breath to hear whether or not he was being sent out on a tampon run. I knew I had to now clear the air.

"It doesn't matter," I said, calming down. "I'll have a look around here today. Maybe I'll go into town tomorrow." Something to look forward to.

"I'll be off then," Arthur said, and nodded to Rosaleen.

She jumped up out of her chair as though a finger had poked up through the straw seat. "Don't forget your flask." She hurried about the kitchen as though there was a time bomb ticking. "Here you go." She handed him a flask and a lunch box.

I couldn't help but smile, watching that. It should have been weird, her treating him like a child going off to school, but it wasn't. It was nice.

"Do you want some of this for your lunch box?" I asked, pointing at the plate of food before me. "There's no way in the world I'm going to eat it."

I meant that comment to be nice. I meant that I couldn't eat it all because of the quantity, not because of the taste, but it came out wrong. Or it came out right but was taken up wrong, evidenced by the hurt look on Rosaleen's face. I don't know. Anyway, I didn't want to waste the food. I wanted to share it with Arthur for his cute little lunch box, but it was as though I'd punched Rosaleen in the stomach again.

"Ara go on, I'll have some of it so," Arthur said, and I felt like he was saying it just to make Rosaleen happy.

Rosaleen's cheeks pinked as she fussed around in a drawer for another Tupperware box.

"It's really lovely, Rosaleen, honestly, but I just don't eat this much breakfast usually." I couldn't believe such an issue was being made of breakfast.

"Of course, of course." She nodded emphatically, as though she was so stupid not to have known this. She scooped it up and put it into the little plastic tub. And then Arthur was gone.

While I was still sitting at the table trying to get through the three thousand slices of toast that could easily have been used to rebuild the castle, Rosaleen collected the tray from Mum's room. The food hadn't been touched. Head down, Rosaleen brought it straight to the bin and started scraping it into the bag. After the earlier scene, I knew this hurt her.

"We're just not breakfast people," I explained, as gently as I could. "Mum usually grabs a breakfast bar and an espresso in the morning."

Rosaleen straightened up and turned around, ears alert to food talk. "A breakfast bar?"

"You know, one of those bars made of cereal and raisins and yogurt and things."

"Like this." She showed me a bowl of cereal and raisins and a little bowl of yogurt.

"Yes, but . . . in a bar."

"But what's the difference?"

"Well, you bite into the bar."

Rosaleen frowned.

"It's faster. You can eat it on the go." I tried to explain further. "While you're driving to work or running out the door, you know?"

"But what kind of breakfast is that? A bar in a car?"

I tried so hard not to laugh at that. "It's just, you know, to . . . save time in the morning."

She looked at me like I'd ten heads, then went quiet as she cleaned the kitchen.

"What do you think of Mum?" I asked after a long silence.

Rosaleen kept cleaning the counters with her back to me.

"Rosaleen? What do you think about the way my mum's behaving?"

"She's grieving, child," she said quickly.

"I don't think that's the proper way to grieve, do you? Thinking an elephant is in the room?"

"Ah, she didn't hear you right," she said lightly. "Her head is elsewhere, is all."

"It's in cuckoo land, is where," I mumbled.

Because people keep throwing this "grieving" comment at me, as if I was born yesterday, I've since read a lot on grief. All online, but still. What I've learned is that there's no proper way to grieve, no wrong or right way. I don't know if I agree with that. I think Mum's grief is the wrong way. The word "grief" comes from the old French word *grève* which means heavy burden. The idea is that grief weighs you down with sorrow and a lot of other emotions. I feel that way: heavier, like I have to drag myself around, like everything is an effort, is dark and crap. It's as though my head is continually filled with thoughts I'd never had before, which gives me a headache.

But oddly, Mum seems lighter. Grief doesn't seem to be weighing her down at all. Instead, it feels like she's flying away, like she's halfway in the air and nobody else cares or notices, and I'm the only one standing beneath her, at her ankles, trying to pull her back down.

CHAPTER SIX

The Bus of Books

The kitchen had been cleared and cleaned; scrubbed to within an inch of its life, and the only thing left that wasn't stacked away on a shelf somewhere was me.

I had never seen a woman clean with such vigor, with such purpose, as if her life depended on it. Rosaleen rolled up her sleeves and sweated as she scrubbed, biceps and triceps astonishingly well formed, wiping away every trace of life that ever existed in the place. So I sat watching her in fascination, and I admit with a hint of patronizing pity too, at the unnecessary act of such intense polishing and cleaning.

She left the house carrying a parcel of freshly baked brown bread that smelled so good it sent my taste buds and my already full stomach into spasms. I watched her from the front living room window power-walking across the road to the bungalow. I waited by the window, intrigued to see who would answer the door, but she went around the back and spoiled my fun.

I took the opportunity to wander around the house without

Rosaleen breathing down my neck and explaining the history behind every single thing I laid my eyes on as she'd done all morning.

"Oh, that's the cabinet. Oak, it is. A tree came down hard one winter, thunder and lightning, we'd no electricity for days. Arthur couldn't rescue it—the tree that is, not the electricity; we got that back." Nervous giggle. "He made that cabinet out of the tree. Great for storing things in."

"That could be a good little business for Arthur."

"Oh no." Rosaleen looked at me as though I'd just blasphemed. "It's a hobby, not a moneymaking scheme."

"It's not a scheme, it's a business. There's nothing wrong with that," I explained.

Rosaleen tut-tutted at this.

Hearing myself, I sounded like my dad, and even though I had always hated this about him—his desire to turn everything into a business—it gave me a nice warm feeling. As a child if I brought home paintings from school he'd suddenly think I could be an artist, but only an artist who could demand millions for my works. If I argued a point strongly, I was suddenly a lawyer, but only a lawyer who demanded hundreds per hour. I have a good singing voice, and at one point I was going to record in his friend's studio and be the next big thing. But it wasn't just me he did that with, it was everything around him. For him life was full of opportunities, and that wasn't necessarily a bad thing, but I think he wanted to grab at them for all the wrong reasons. He wasn't passionate about art, he didn't care about lawyers helping people, he didn't even care about my singing voice. It was all for more money. And so I suppose it was fitting that it was the loss of all his money that killed him in the end. The pills and the whiskey were just the nails in the coffin.

"Is it that photo you've got your eye on?" Rosaleen would continue as my eyes roamed the room. "That was taken by himself when we visited the Giant's Causeway. It rained the entire day and we got a flat tire on the way up."

And on she went.

"I see you're looking at the curtains. They need a bit of a clean. I'll take them down tomorrow and do them. I bought the fabric from a woman doing door-to-door. I never usually but she was a foreign woman, hadn't much English or money, but she had all this fabric. I like the flowers in it. I think it matches the cushion there, what do you think? I've lots left in the garage down the back."

Then I looked to the garage down the back and she'd said, "Arthur built that himself. Wasn't here when I moved in."

It struck me as odd phrasing. *When* I *moved in*. "Who lived here before?"

Rosaleen looked at me then, with those wide, curious eyes she'd previously reserved for when I was eating, and she didn't say anything. She does that a lot, at the most random times. Dropping in and out of our conversations with looks and pauses as though she loses the signal on her brain connection.

She freaked me out so much that I looked away, down at the rug that was given to her by somebody for something, I don't know . . . But anyway, later that morning when I was finally alone and didn't have her nervous jabbering interfering with my thoughts, I was able to look around properly.

The living room was cozy, I suppose, if not a little old. Well, a lot old, not like my house, which is—was—modern and clean, crisp lines and everything symmetrical. This room had things all over the place. Art that didn't match the couches, funny-looking ornaments, tables and chairs with spindly legs and animal claws, two couches with totally different fabrics—one blue-and-ivory floral, the other multicolored as if a cat had thrown up on it—and a coffee table that doubled as a chessboard. The floor felt like it was uneven, sloping from the fireplace to the bookshelves, making me feel a little seasick. The busiest area seemed to be around the fireplace; an open fire that made me shudder with its contraptions that looked like something out of a medieval torture chamber: wrought-iron pokers with animal heads, coal shovels of different sizes, an ancient bellows, a black cast-iron fireguard with an animal of some sort emblazoned on the front. I turned my back on the fireplace and concentrated on the floor-to-ceiling bookcase, with a ladder running the length of the wall. It was filled with books, photos, tins, keepsake boxes, useless trinkets, that kind of thing. Most of the books were on gardening and cooking, very specific, not at all to my taste. They were old and well-read, some ripped apart, some missing their covers with yellowing pages, and some that looked water damaged—but not a speck of dust was to be seen. There was a huge red-bound book, which looked so ancient the pages were black with the red dye running into them. It was *Lloyd's Register of Shipping 1919–1920, Volume 2.* Inside were hundreds of pages of the alphabetically arranged names of vessels, showing the deadweight and capacities of holds and permanent bunkers. I slid it back into place and wiped my hands on my clothes, not wanting the bacteria of 1919 to infest me. Another book was about faiths of the world, which had on the cover a gold emblem of a cross dug into the ground with a snake twisted around it. Then beside it was a book on Greek cooking, though I doubted very much that there'd be a place for souvlaki next to Rosaleen's Aga. The next book was *The Complete Book of the Horse*, though it mustn't have been, for there were twelve more on the subject.

I'd read only the first chapter of the book Fiona gave me at my dad's funeral, and already that was the most I'd read in a year, so the books stuffed onto these shelves didn't particularly interest me.

What did interest me was a photo album filed alongside them all. It was in the large book section, beside the dictionaries, encyclopedia, world atlas, and that kind of thing. An old-fashioned album, it had the look of a printed book, or at least its spine had. It had a red velvet cover and was embossed by a frame of gold, and when I took it out and ran my finger across the front, I left a darkened trail on the velvet. I curled up in the leather-studded armchair, looking forward to getting lost in somebody else's memories. As soon as I opened the first page, the doorbell rang, long and shrill. It broke the silence and made me jump.

I waited, almost expected Rosaleen to come sprinting across the road with her tea dress hitched up to her thighs, revealing hamstrings so tight Jimi Hendrix could play on them. But she didn't. Instead there was silence. There wasn't a peep upstairs from Mum. The doorbell rang again and so I placed the photo album down on the table and made my way to the front door, the house feeling a little more like home as I did so.

Through the obscure stained glass, I could tell it was a man. When I opened the door, I saw it was a gorgeous man. Early twenties, I guessed, dark brown hair gelled straight up in the front, just like his polo-shirt collar. He could well be a rugby boy. He looked me up and down, and smiled.

"Hi," he said, and his smile revealed perfectly straight white teeth. He had stubble all around his jaw; his eyes were bright blue. In his hand was a clipboard with a chart attached.

"Hi," I said, arching my back as I leaned in against the door.

"Sir Ignatius?" he asked.

I smiled. "Not I."

"Is there a Sir Ignatius Power in this house?"

"Not at the moment. He's out foxhunting with Lord Casper."

His eyes narrowed suspiciously. "When will he be back?"

"After he's caught the fox, I assume."

"Hmm . . ." He nodded slowly and looked about him. "Are the foxes fast around here?"

"You're obviously not from around here. Everybody knows about the foxes."

"Hmm. Indeed I'm not."

I bit my lip and tried not to smile.

"So he might be a long time?" He smiled, catching up to my joking.

"He might be a very long time."

"I see."

He leaned against the porch pillar and stared at me.

"What?" I said, feeling like I was melting under his gaze.

"Seriously."

"Seriously, what?"

"Does he live anywhere around here, at all?"

"Definitely not behind these gates."

"What are you then?"

"I'm a Goodwin."

"I'm sure you are, but what's your surname?"

I tried not to laugh but couldn't help it.

"Cheesy, I know, sorry," he apologized good-heartedly, then looked confused as he consulted his chart and scratched his head, making it even more tousled.

I looked over his shoulder and saw a parked white bus with "The Travelling Library" emblazoned across the side.

He finally looked up from his clipboard. "Okay then, I'm definitely lost. There's no Goodwin on this list."

"Oh, it wouldn't be under my name." Byrne was my mother's maiden name, my uncle Arthur's surname, and the name this house would be under. Arthur and Rosaleen Byrne. Jennifer Byrne—it didn't sound right. It felt like my mum should always have been a Goodwin.

"So this must be the Kilsaney residence?" he said hopefully, looking up from his chart.

"Ah, the Kilsaneys," I said, and he looked relieved. "They're the next house on the left, just through the trees." I forced myself to keep a straight face.

"Great, thank you. I've never been around here before. And I'm an hour late. What are they like, the Kilsaneys?" He scrunched up his nose. "Will they give me shit?"

I shrugged. "They don't say much. But don't worry, they love books."

"Good. Do you want me to stop here on the way back out so you can have a look at the books?"

"Sure."

I closed the door and burst out laughing. I waited with excitement for him to return, butterflies fluttering around my heart and stomach as though I was a child playing hide-and-seek. I hadn't felt like this for at least a month. Less than a minute later, I heard the bus returning. It stopped outside the house and I opened the door. He was getting out of the bus, a big smile on his face. When he looked up he caught my eye and shook his head.

"Kilsaneys not home?" I asked.

He laughed, coming toward me, thankfully not angry but amused. "They decided they didn't want any books as it seems, along with the second floor and most of their walls and the actual roof of their home, their bookshelf went missing."

I giggled.

"Very funny, Miss Goodwin."

"It's Ms., thank you very much."

"I'm Marcus." He held out his hand and I shook it.

"Tamara."

"Beautiful name," he said gently. He leaned against the wooden porch pillar. "So seriously, do you know where this Sir Ignatius Power of the Sisters of Mercy lives?"

"Hold on, let me see that." I grabbed the clipboard from him. "That's not 'Sir.' That's 'Sr.,' Sis-ter," I said slowly. "You muppet." I tapped him on the head with the clipboard. "*He's* a nun." Not a transvestite, after all.

"Oh." He started laughing and grabbed the end of his board. I held on tight. He pulled harder and it dragged me out onto the porch. Close up, he was even cuter. "So is that you, Sister?" he asked. "Have you received your calling?"

"The only thing I get called for is dinner."

He laughed. "So, who is she?"

I shrugged.

"You're intent on making me get lost, aren't you?"

"Well, I just got here yesterday so I'm as lost as you are."

I didn't smile when I said that and he didn't smile back either. He got it.

"Well, for your sake, I really hope that's not true." He looked up at the house. "You live here?"

I shrugged.

"You don't even know where you *live*?"

"You're a strange man who travels in a bus filled with books. Do you think I'm going to tell you where I live? I've heard about your kind," I said, walking away from the house and toward the bus.

"Oh yeah?" He followed me.

"There was a guy like you who lured children into his bus tempting them with lollipops, then when they got inside, he locked them in and drove off."

"Oh, I heard about him," he said, his eyes lighting up. "Long greasy black hair, big nose, pale skin, danced around in tight trousers and sang a lot. Also had a penchant for toy boxes?"

"That's the one. Friend of yours?"

"Here." He rooted inside his top pocket and dug out his ID. "You're right, I should have shown you this earlier. The bus is a public library, licensed and everything. All official. So I promise I won't trap you inside."

Unless I asked him to. I studied the ID card. "Marcus Sandhurst."

"That is I. Want to look at the books?" He held his arm out to the bus. "Your chariot awaits."

I looked around, not a soul nearby, including Mum. The bungalow across the way also appeared dead. With nothing to lose, I climbed aboard, and as I did, Marcus sang in the Child Catcher's voice and cackled. I laughed too.

Inside, both walls were lined with hundreds of books, divided into various categories. I ran my finger along them, not really reading the titles, a little on guard at being in the bus with a strange man. I think Marcus sensed this because he took a few steps back from me, gave me plenty of space, and stood by the open door instead.

"So what's your favorite book?" I asked.

"Eh . . . *Scarface*."

"That's a film."

"Based on a book," he said.

"No, it's not. What's your favorite book?"

"Coldplay," he responded. "Pizza . . . I don't know."

"Okay." I laughed. "So you don't read."

"Nope." He sat up on a ledge. "But I'm hoping that this experience will positively change me for the better and that I will be converted to a reader." He spoke lazily, his voice so lackluster and unconvincing it was as though he was repeating something he'd been told himself.

I studied him. "So what happened, Daddy asked his friend to give you a job?"

His jawline hardened and he was silent for a while, and I felt really bad, like I should take back the comment. I don't even know why I said that. I don't even know where it came from. I just had a weird feeling that I must have been close. Maybe I recognized a part of me in him.

"Sorry, that wasn't funny," I apologized. "So what happens here?" I said, trying to break the tension. "You travel around to people's houses and give them books?"

"It's the same as a library," Marcus said, still a little cool from my comment. "People join up and receive membership cards, and that allows them to take out books. I go to the towns where there aren't any libraries."

"Or life forms," I said, and he laughed.

"You're finding it tough here, city girl?"

I ignored that comment and kept studying the books.

"You know what people around here would really appreciate instead of books?"

He smiled suggestively at me.

"Not that." I laughed. "You could actually make some money out of this thing if you got rid of the books."

"Ha! Now that's not very cultured," he said.

"Well, there's no bus service around here. Apparently there's a town fifteen minutes' drive away. How is anybody supposed to get there?"

"Eh . . . the answer would be in your question."

"Yes, but I can't drive because I'm—" I stalled, and he smiled. "Because I'm not *able* to drive," I finished.

"What? You mean Daddy didn't get you a MINI Cooper yet? That's totally uncool," he imitated me.

"Touché."

"Okay." He jumped off the table, filled with energy. "I have to go there now anyway. How about we both go to this wonderful magical town that no human legs can reach."

I giggled. "Okay."

"Don't you need to run it by somebody? I don't want to be done in for kidnapping."

"I may not be a *driver* but I'm not a child." I kept my eye on the bungalow. Rosaleen had been gone a long time.

"You're sure?" he asked, looking around.

He looked anxious, and just because of that I took out my phone and called Mum's mobile, which I know she hadn't touched for a month. I left a message.

"Hi, Mum, it's me. I'm outside the house in a bus full of books and a cute guy is going to drive me to the town. I'll be back in a few hours. In case I don't come back, his name is Marcus Sandhurst, he's five foot ten, has dark hair, blue eyes . . . Any tattoos?" I asked.

He lifted his top. Ooh, he was ripped.

"He's got a Celtic cross on his lower abdomen, no chest hair, and a silly smile. He likes *Scarface*, Coldplay, and pizza, and is hoping to get into books in a big way. See you later."

I hung up and Marcus burst out laughing. "You know me better than most people."

"Let's get out of here," I said.

"Are you always so misbehaved?" he asked.

"Always," I responded, and climbed into the passenger seat in preparation for my adventure out of Kilsaney Demesne.

CHAPTER SEVEN

I Want

There were twelve minutes of a comfortable and not-for-one-second-awkward conversation with Marcus before we reached the town. Only "the town" wasn't at all what I was expecting. Even with my expectations lowered to an all-time low, the reality was so much worse. It was a one-horse town, with not even a horse in sight. A church. A graveyard. Two pubs. A fish-and-chip shop. A gas station with a newsstand. A hardware store. Full stop.

I must have whimpered because Marcus looked at me, worried.

"What's wrong?"

"What's wrong?" My eyes widened as I turned to him. "What's *wrong*? I have a Barbie Village from when I was, like, *five* that's bigger than this."

He tried not to but he laughed. "It's not that bad. Another twenty minutes and you're in Dunshauglin; that's a proper town."

"Another twenty minutes? I can't even get *here*, to this shithole, on my own." I felt my eyes heat up with frustration, my nose starting to itch, my eyes beginning to fill. I felt like kicking the bus down and screaming. "What the hell am I going to do around here on my own? Buy a shovel in there and dig up the dead over there? And have a bag of chips and a pint while I'm doing it?"

Marcus snorted, and had to look away to compose himself. "Tamara, it's really not that bad."

"Yes it is. I want a fucking skinny gingerbread latte and a cinnamon roll, now," I said very calmly, aware that I was beginning to sound like Violet Beauregarde from *Charlie and the Chocolate Factory.* "And while I'm at Starbucks I want to use my laptop and avail myself of their wi-fi service, go online and check my Facebook page. I want to go to Topshop. And then I want to go to the beach with my friends and look at the sea and drink a bottle of white wine and get so drunk that I fall over and vomit. You know, normal things that normal people do. That is what I want."

"Do you always get what you want?" Marcus looked at me.

I couldn't answer. A giant lump of oh-my-God-I'm-in-love kind of feeling had suddenly gathered in my throat. And so I just nodded.

"Okay," he said, perking up, and I swallowed, my Marcus crush sent flying down my esophagus into my stomach. "Let's look on the bright side."

"There is no bright side."

"There's always a bright side." He looked left and he looked right, then he held his hands up and his eyes lit up. "There's no library."

"Oh my God . . ." I head-butted myself on the dashboard.

"Right." He laughed and turned the engine off. "Let's go somewhere else."

"Don't you need the engine *on* to do that?" I asked.

"We're not driving," he said, and climbed around the driver's seat and into the bus. "So, let's see . . . where should we go?" He moved his finger along the spines of the books in the travel section and walked alongside them, reading aloud, "Paris, Chile, Rome, Argentina, Mexico . . ."

"Mexico," I said straightaway, kneeling up on my seat to watch him.

"Mexico." He nodded. "Good choice." He lifted the book from the shelf and looked at me. "Well? Are you coming? Flight's about to leave."

I smiled and climbed over to join him. We sat on the floor, side by side, in the back of the bus, and that day, we went to Mexico.

I don't know if Marcus knows how important that moment was to me. How much he actually saved me from myself, from absolute despair. Maybe he does know and that's exactly what he was doing. He was like an angel who came into my life with his bus of books at exactly the right time, who whisked me away from a terrible place to a faraway land.

We didn't stay in Mexico for as long as we'd hoped. We checked into our hotel, dumped our bags, and headed straight for the water. I bought a bikini from a man selling them on the beach, Marcus ordered a cocktail and was going to go on a Jet Ski alone—I was refusing to get into a wet suit—when someone knocked on the door of the bus and an elderly woman stepped on to look for a book. We got to our feet then and I browsed the shelves while Marcus played librarian. I came across a book about grief; about learning how to deal with personal grief or a loved one suffering from grief. I hovered by that book for a while, my heart pounding as though I'd found a magic vaccine for all worldly diseases. But I couldn't bring myself to lift it from the shelf. I didn't want Marcus to see, I didn't want him to ask me about it, I didn't want to have to tell him about Dad dying. Then I would be the girl whose dad had just killed himself. If I didn't tell him, I didn't have to be that girl. Not to him, anyway. I would just be her on the inside. I'd let her rage inside me, bubble under my skin, but I could go to Mexico and leave her behind in the gatehouse.

Then my eye fell upon a large leather-bound book in the nonfiction section. It was brown, thick, no author's name or title along the spine. I pulled it out. It was heavy. The pages were jagged along the edges as though they'd been ripped.

"So you're like a Robin Hood of the book world," I said to Marcus as soon as the old woman had left the bus, a racy romance under her arm, "bringing books to those who have none."

"Something like that. And what have you got there?"

"Don't know, there's no title on the front."

"Try the spine."

"Not there either."

He picked up a folder from beside him and licked his finger before flicking through some pages. "What's the author's name?"

"There's no author's name."

He frowned and looked up at me. "Not possible. Open it up and see what's on the first page."

"I can't." I laughed. "It's locked."

"Oh, come on," he said with a smile. "Stop messing with me, Goodwin."

"I'm not." I laughed, moving toward him. "Honestly, look."

I passed the book to him and our fingers brushed, causing a tingle of seismic proportions to rush through every single erogenous zone that existed in my body.

The pages of the book were closed with a gold clasp, and attached to that was a small gold padlock.

"What the hell . . ." he said, trying to pull at the lock, making a series of grimaces. "Trust *you* to choose the only book in here that doesn't have an author or a title and is padlocked."

We both started laughing. He gave up on the padlock and our eyes locked.

This was the bit where I was supposed to say, "I'm only sixteen."

But I couldn't. I just couldn't. I told you, I felt older. And everybody always thought I looked older. It wasn't like we were going to have sex on the floor; he wasn't going to prison for staring at me. But still. I should have said it then. If we were in some early nineteenth-century book, back in the good old days when women were men's property and weren't protected at all, then it wouldn't have mattered, we could have rolled around in the hay somewhere and done whatever we wanted and nobody would have been accused of anything. I felt like hunting down that book from the shelves, opening it, and jumping into the pages with him. But it was the twenty-first century. I was sixteen, very nearly seventeen, and he was twenty-two. I'd seen it on his ID card. I had experience in knowing that a guy's horn wouldn't last until my seventeenth birthday.

"Don't look so sad," he said, and reached out and lifted my chin with his finger. I hadn't realized he'd come so close to me and there he was, right before me. Toe to toe. "It's only . . . a book."

I realized I was hugging it close to me, both my arms wrapped around it tightly.

"But I like the book," I said.

"I like the book too, very much. It's a cheeky book, very pretty, but it's obvious we can't read it right now."

My eyes narrowed, wondering if we were talking about the same thing.

"So that means we'll both just have to sit and look at it, until we find the key."

I smiled, and I felt my cheeks pink.

"Tamara!" I heard my name being called. A screeching, desperate call. We stopped gazing at one another and I rushed to the door of the bus. It was Rosaleen. She was running across the road toward me with her face scrunched up, her eyes wild and dangerous. Arthur was standing on the pavement beside his parked car, looking calm. I relaxed a little at the sight of him. What had Rosaleen all riled up?

"Tamara," she said, as she reached the bus, breathless. She looked from Marcus to me, appearing like a meerkat again, on high alert. "Come back to us, child. Come back," she said, her voice shaky.

"I am coming back." I frowned. "I've only been gone an hour." She looked a little confused, then looked at Marcus as if he was going to explain everything.

"What's wrong, Rosaleen? Is Mum okay?"

She was silent. Her mouth opened and closed as if she was trying to find words.

"Is she okay?" I asked again, panic building.

"Yes," she said, "of course she's fine." She still looked confused, but was beginning to calm.

"Then what's wrong with you?"

"I thought you'd . . ." She trailed off, looking around the village, and as though now realizing where she was, she stood up straight, ran a hand across her hair to smooth it down, and fixed her dress, which was crumpled from the drive. "You're coming back to the house?"

"Yes, of course." I frowned. "I told Mum where I was going."

"Yes, but your mother . . ."

"My mother what?" My voice hardened. If everything was so okay with my mother, then what was the problem?

Marcus's hand was on my back, his thumb comfortingly circling the small of my back, reminding me of Mexico, of all the other places I could be.

"You should go with her," Marcus said quietly. "I have to move on now, anyway. He nodded at the book I was hugging in my arms. "You can hold on to that."

"Thanks. See you again?"

"Of course, Goodwin," he said. "Now go."

As I walked across the road and got in the back of Arthur's Land Rover, I noticed three male smokers standing outside the pub, staring. It's not so unusual to be stared at, but it was the way they were staring. Arthur nodded at them. Rosaleen kept her head down, her eyes to the ground. The three men's eyes followed us, and I stared back, hoping to figure out what exactly was their problem. Was it because I was new? But I knew it wasn't just that, because they weren't looking at me. All eyes were on Arthur and Rosaleen.

In the car, nobody said a word the entire way home. Once inside the house, I went to check on Mum despite Rosaleen telling me not to. Mum was still sitting in the rocking chair, not rocking, and looking out at the garden. I sat with her awhile and then left, headed downstairs to the living room, back to the armchair I'd been sitting in before Marcus called. I reached for the photo album but it was gone. Tidied away by Rosaleen. I sighed and searched for it again on the bookshelf. It was gone. I went through every single book on that shelf, but it was nowhere to be found.

I heard a creak at the door and I spun around. Rosaleen was standing there.

"Rosaleen!" I said, hand flying to my heart. "You scared me."

"What were you doing?" she asked, her fingers creasing and then smoothing the apron over her dress.

"I was just looking for a photo album I saw earlier."

"Photo album?" She cocked her head sideways, her forehead wrinkled, her face pinched in confusion.

"Yes, I saw it earlier, before the library bus came by. I hope you don't mind, I took it out to look at it but now it's . . ." I held my hands up in the air and laughed. "It has mysteriously vanished."

She shook her head. "No, child." She looked behind her and then lowered her voice to a whisper. "Now hush about it."

Arthur entered then, with a newspaper in his hand. He glanced from me to her.

Rosaleen looked at Arthur nervously. "I better see to dinner. Rack of lamb tonight," she said quietly.

He nodded and watched her leave the room.

The way he watched her made me not want to ask Arthur about the album. The way he watched her made me think a lot of things about Arthur.

Later that evening, I heard them in their bedroom, muffled sounds that rose and fell. I wasn't sure if it was an argument, but it felt different from the way they usually talked to each other. It sounded like an actual conversation, instead of a series of comments thrown to one another. Whatever they were talking about, they were trying hard for me not to hear them. I had my ear up against the wall, then heard a sudden silence. My bedroom door opened and Arthur was there, staring at me.

"Arthur," I said, moving away from the wall, "you should knock. I need my privacy."

Considering he'd just caught me with my ear to the wall, he did well not to say anything.

"Do you want me to bring you to Dublin in the morning?" he grumbled.

"What?"

"To stay with a friend."

I was so delighted, I punched the air and got straight on the phone to Zoey, forgetting to pursue and not caring as to the sudden reason for my expulsion. And so that was the time I went to stay with Zoey. It had been only two nights in the gatehouse but already I felt different returning to Dublin. Zoey, Laura, and I immediately went back to our usual patch on the beach beside my house. It looked different and I hated it. It felt different and I hated that too.

By the entrance gate a "For Sale" sign had been erected. I couldn't look at it without my blood boiling, my heart rate rising, and my feeling an overwhelming desire to scream like a banshee, so I didn't look. Zoey and Laura were already studying me as though I had landed from another planet, as though they were analyzing everything I said.

We proceeded to get drunk and plotted against Arthur and Rosaleen and their evil country ways. I told them about Marcus and the bus of books and they laughed, thinking him an absolute dork, calling the traveling library the most ridiculously boring thing they had ever heard of. It was bad enough to have a room full of books but to drive around with a bunch of books, well, that was a downright dorkfest.

Their comments hurt me so much, but I tried to hide it. The one source of excitement and escape I'd experienced in the month since Dad died was shredded in an instant. I think that's when I started building up a wall between me and my friends. I think they knew it too. Zoey was looking at me with those dissecting eyes she gives anybody that's in any way different, different being the worst possible offense in the world to her. She and Laura didn't realize that the emotional impact of what I'd gone through was going to change me not just for a few weeks, but the very core of me forever. I'd been trampled on, and like a plant that has been crushed underfoot, I'd no choice but to grow in a different direction than I had before.

CHAPTER EIGHT

Secret Garden

Whenever I left home for a longer length of time than usual, say to go on a school trip abroad, or when I went on shopping trips to London with friends, I always used to bring something with me to remind me of home—just something small. For example, one Christmas we were at a buffet in a hotel and my dad stole a little plastic penguin that was sitting on top of a pudding, and he put it in my dessert. He was trying to be funny but I was having one of those days, which was much like most days, where nothing he said or did could possibly be conceived of as funny. Somehow the penguin ended up in my jacket pocket that day. Then months later, when I put my hand in my pocket and found the little penguin, I finally laughed at Dad's joke, though months way too late. It's since traveled the world with me.

Don't get me wrong: I'm not a sentimental person, I'm not someone who gets that attached to anything or anyone. Not like some others who just have to look at something, like a piece of fluff, and it sends tears to their eyes because it vaguely reminds them of something somebody once said once upon a time. No, bringing something with me was just a little ammunition really, to make me feel like I wasn't totally and utterly alone, that I had a little piece of home with me. Not sentimentality, just plain old insecurity.

Even though I certainly wasn't getting attached to the gatehouse in any way, I brought the book I'd found in the traveling library with me to Zoey's house. I still hadn't managed to unlock it and I certainly had no intentions of reading it while I was there, not when my friends were so busy telling me about their new source of entertainment—wait for it—going out without underwear on. Honestly, I had to laugh. Their inspiration was a photo of Cindy Monroe, a hundred-pound, five-foot-tall American reality TV star, getting out of a car to go into a club, and she wasn't wearing any knickers. Zoey and Laura seemed to think this was a great new leap forward for women. I think that when the women's libbers took off their bras and burned them, this wasn't exactly what they were hoping for. I said this to Zoey and she studied me thoughtfully, her eyes squinting almost closed, and she opened her eyes wide and said, "No, it's fine, my top was totally backless so I couldn't wear a bra either."

Totally backless. Very dead. Another one of those phrases. It was either backless or it wasn't. I've no doubt that it was.

Anyway, when I was sent away to Zoey's house—"sent away" being the operative words—I felt like I'd been told to go sit on the naughty step to think about what I'd done. Despite the fact that I should have felt that I was heading home, that I was heading toward feeling more me again, I didn't feel like it at all. And so I brought a piece of my new world with me. I brought the book. I knew it was there in my bag in Zoey's room, and as we stayed up all night talking about everything, I knew that it was listening to me, this foreign thing from my detested new life, gaining an insight into the life I once had. The book felt like my little secret from Laura and Zoey, a pointless and boring one but a secret all the same, lying beside me in my overnight bag.

And so the next day when Arthur's Land Rover turned back into the side entrance to Kilsaney Demesne, and I was once again gobbled up by my new desperate nonlife, I decided to take the book and go for a walk with it. The book; my secret that nobody else knew about. The first thing that was mine since I'd arrived here.

I hadn't yet walked *around* the grounds. To and from the castle, yes, but around the one hundred acres, no. All my previous visits throughout my childhood had been made up of tea and ham sandwiches in a quiet kitchen while Mum talked about things I didn't care about with my strange aunt and uncle. I'd do anything—eat twenty sloppy egg sandwiches and two slices of whatever cake was going—to get out of that kitchen and wander in the front garden that wrapped its way around to the back. Nowhere else interested me. I wasn't much of an explorer; anything that involved movement or physical effort bored me. And I was never intrigued enough by this place. On that day I still wasn't, but I was bored and so I dumped my overnight bag, which Arthur snot-snorted at and brought into the house for me, and I was gone.

I walked away from the house, away from the castle, along a narrow roadway. The route was heavily shaded by the hundred-foot-tall native oaks, the ash and yew which lined it. It smelled sweet. The ground was soft, thousands of years of falling foliage and bark laid on the earth, giving me a spring in my step as if I could run from corner to corner in Lycra doing somersaults. It was a hot day, but I was cool under the elderly trees. The birds were like hyperactive monkeys, with their constant chirpy calls and Tarzan-like swoops from one tree to another. Tired from my all-nighter with my friends, I just kept walking, my head bursting with their conversations, the things I had learned—Laura had had to take the morning-after pill—but none was as loud as the conversations I was having with myself. Those I could never switch off. I don't think I'd ever thought so much, and talked so little, in my life since coming here.

Every now and then, when the trees broke their security barrier, I could see the castle in the distance, looking out over its lawn, at the small lakes that dotted the grounds, at the majestic trees that stood alone punctuating the landscape. Tall and elegant poplars rose up like feathers to tickle the sky, wide oaks with heavy caps spread out like wild mushrooms. Then the castle disappeared again, playing peekaboo with me, and the pathway began to curve to the left so that I would soon be able to turn and face the keep head on. Another twenty minutes' walk and I could see the main gateway farther up ahead on my right. I immediately slowed. The darkened gothic entrance did not appeal to me, all chained up like some prisoner of war left to rot along the side of the road. Long grasses and decrepit weeds climbed the gate and poked out through the rusted bars like long, gangly, starved arms waving at passersby to be fed or released. The once grand roadway that led directly to the castle had been ignored, unused and unmaintained. It was overgrown and hidden by grasses, like the yellow brick road in the *Return to Oz*. I shuddered. I didn't take to the gate as I had to the castle behind it. Its scars were grotesque. Unlike the castle's, which made me want to raise a hand and trace them with my finger, these scars were ugly and made me want to look the other way.

I decided to find another route to take, anything to prevent me from passing that ghastly gothic gate, and so I broke through the trees and walked across the grounds instead. I felt safer then, cocooned in the bosom of the trees rather than on that well-worn path on which Normans and their horses had pounded, wildly waving peasants' severed heads on the tips of their swords.

The tree trunks were fascinating, aged and wrinkled like elephants' legs. They twisted around one another like lovers. Some rose from the ground, arched as though in agony and reaching out, then growing on, turning and shifting to a new position. The roots snaked their way from under the surface, rising above the ground and back down again, as though they were slippery eels in the waters. I occasionally tripped on a raised root, and was caught each time by a helpfully placed tree trunk. The trees did that, tripped me and caught me, tickled me with their leaves and webs, and smacked me in the face with their branches.

From one city of trees I made my way to another. The air smelled sweet with bees filling the flowering trees, greedily hopping from one cluster of petals to another, wanting it all, too impatient to choose just one. Around me on the wood floor was fruit of some kind, there from seasons ago, some decayed and rotten, some dried out like prunes. I stopped to pick one up and tried to decipher what it once was. I smelled it. Vile. As I dropped it and wiped my hands, I realized the trunk beside me was covered in engravings. The poor tree had been carved into over and over again, like a pumpkin emptied of its flesh to bear its fangs. It clearly hadn't been inscribed all on the same day, nor the same year, perhaps not even the same century. From seven feet up all the way down it was covered in various names etched into the bark, some framed by hearts, others in boxes, but all declaring eternal friendships and loves.

I ran my finger over the names "Frank and Ellie," "Fiona and Stephen," "Siobhan and Michael," "Laurie and Rose," "Michelle and Tommy," "2gether, 4ever." I wondered if any of them still were. None of the other trees bore the same scars. I stepped back to examine the area and discovered why. There was more of a clearing around this particular tree. I could imagine blankets laid down, picnics and parties, friends gathering and lovers sneaking out to be together under the fruit tree.

I left the orchard and searched for the next tree town. Then a wall came into view just ahead of me and suddenly my game with the trees was over.

I tried to tread carefully without making a sound, but the woods gave me away. Leaves rustling and echoes of twigs snapping and crunching beneath my feet alerted the walls to my arrival. I didn't know what building was ahead of me but it wasn't the castle, for I had passed that a while ago. I didn't know of any other buildings on the grounds apart from the dilapidated cottages at the other three gate entrances, long closed up after everybody upped and left. The stone of the wall wasn't the same as the castle's but to my inexperienced eye it wasn't far off. It was old and crumbling. The top of the wall was uneven, and it no longer touched what it once reached for. There was no roof, just a wall. I couldn't see a door or a window for the wall's entire length. I stepped to the edge of the woods, feeling like a hedgehog that had just left its natural habitat. I left my tall tree friends behind, and under their watchful eyes I walked the length of the wall.

When the wall ended, I turned the corner and saw it continue down another way. Suddenly I heard a woman humming from behind the wall. I got a jolt. Apart from my uncle Arthur, I wasn't expecting to come across any other human here. I hugged the book close to my chest and listened to the humming. It was soft, sweet, and happy, far too liberated to be Rosaleen, too joyous to be my mother. It was passing-the-time kind of humming, a distracted sound, a tune that wasn't familiar to me, if it was a real one at all. The summer breeze blew and brought a sweet smell and her song along with it. I closed my eyes and leaned my head against the wall, directly on the other side from the woman, and I listened.

As my head touched the brick, she stopped humming and my eyes opened quickly and I straightened up.

I looked around. She wasn't in sight, and so she couldn't have spotted me. When my heart slowed to its normal rhythm she began humming again. I continued along the wall, my fingers trailing over the gray stone, cobwebs, crumbling rock, and rough edges passing beneath my hot fingers. The sun beat down on me, the trees no longer my personal parasol. Then the wall came to an abrupt stop and I looked up to see a large ornamental stone archway marking an entrance.

I peeked my head inside so that I wouldn't be revealed to the mystery hummer and discovered a walled garden, immaculately kept. From my position outside the arch I could see large formal beds set against the backdrop of climbing roses, fully bloomed, which lined both sides of the footpath leading to another entrance on the other side. I dared to move a little more to see the rest of the garden. In the center were more flowers—geraniums, chrysanthemums, carnations, others I couldn't name. Flowers tumbled out from hanging baskets and oversized ornamental stone pots that lined the central walkway through the garden. I couldn't quite believe this little oasis amid all the green, as though somebody had taken a fizzy drink, shaken it, and opened it here in the middle of these crumbling walls, spraying color over every inch of the place. Bees were flying from one flower to the other, vines climbed up the walls twined around beautiful flowers. I could smell the rosemary, lavender, and mint from a nearby herb garden. There was also a small greenhouse in the corner of the garden, beside that a dozen or so wooden boxes on stands, and then I realized that, swept up by my curiosity, I had unknowingly wandered into the garden and the humming had stopped.

I wasn't sure what to expect but I definitely wasn't expecting what I saw. At the end of the garden the source of the humming, the person that was currently staring at me, was dressed in what appeared to be a white spacesuit, her head covered in a black veil, her hands in a pair of rubber gloves, and on her feet a pair of calf-length rubber boots. She looked like she'd just stepped off a spaceship and into a nuclear disaster.

I smiled nervously and waved my free hand. "Hi. I come in peace."

She stared at me for a little longer, frozen still like a statue. I felt a bit nervous, a bit awkward, and so I did what I usually do when that happens.

"What the fuck are you staring at?"

I don't know how she took that, seeing as she had a Darth Vader helmet on. She stared at me a little longer and I waited for her to tell me that I was Luke and she was my father.

"Well now," she said brightly, as if snapping out of a trance, "I knew I had a little visitor." She took her entire head attire off, revealing herself to be far older than I expected. She must have been in her seventies.

She came toward me and I half expected her to jump from one foot to the other as though there was no gravity. She was wrinkled, very wrinkled, her skin falling downward as though time had melted her. Her blue eyes sparkled like the Aegean Sea, reminding me of a day out on Dad's yacht—when you looked down, the sea was so clear you could see the sand and hundreds of multicolored fish beneath. But there was nothing beneath her eyes, so translucent they practically reflected back all of the light coming into them. Then she took off her gauntlets and held her hands out.

"I'm Sister Ignatius," she said with a smile, not shaking my hand, but holding it in both of hers. Despite the hot day and the heavy glove, it was as smooth and as cool as marble.

"You're a nun," I blurted out.

"Yes." She laughed. "I am a nun. I was there when it happened."

It was my turn to laugh; everything making sense then. The cabinet of honey jars, the dozens of wooden boxes around the walled garden, the ridiculous spacesuit on this old woman.

"You know my aunt."

"Ah."

I didn't know quite how to take that response. She didn't register surprise, nor did she question me. She was still holding my hand. I didn't want to move my hand, seeing as she was a nun, but it was freaking me out. I kept talking.

"My aunt is Rosaleen, and my uncle is Arthur. He's the grounds-keeper here. They live in the gatehouse. We're staying with them for . . . a little while."

"We?"

"Me and my mum."

"Oh." Her eyebrows lifted so high they looked like caterpillars about to become butterflies and flutter away.

"Didn't Rosaleen tell you?" I was a little insulted, though quite thankful for Rosaleen's respect for our privacy. At least the whole one-horse town with no horse wasn't talking about the new folk.

"No," she replied. And then without a smile and with an air of finality she repeated, "No."

She seemed a little cross and so I jumped in to defend Rosaleen and save whatever friendship they did or didn't have. "I'm sure she was just protecting our privacy, giving us a little time to deal with . . . it."

"Deal with . . ."

"The move here," I said slowly. Was it bad to lie to a nun? Well, I wasn't exactly lying . . . I kind of panicked then. I felt my body heat up and go clammy. Sister Ignatius was saying something, her mouth was opening and closing, but I couldn't hear a word of it. I just kept thinking about lying to her and of those Ten Commandments and hell and everything, but not just that, I thought about how nice it would be to say the words aloud to her. She was a nun, I could probably trust her.

"My dad died," I blurted out quickly, interrupting whatever nice thing she'd been saying. I heard the terrible tremble in my voice and then all of a sudden, from absolutely nowhere, tears were gushing down my cheeks.

"Oh, child," she said, immediately opening her arms and embracing me. The book separated us as I still clung to it. Even though she was a total stranger, she was a nun, and so I rested my head on her shoulder and didn't hold back, making snotty and throaty noises and all, while she rocked me and rubbed my back. I was in the middle of a really embarrassing wail of "Why did he do it? *Whyyyyy . . . ?*" when a bee flew directly into my face and bounced off my lip. I screamed and pushed myself out of Sister Ignatius's arms.

"Bee!" I shrieked, hopping about and trying to dodge it as it followed me. "Oh my God, get it off me."

She watched me, her eyes lighting up.

"Oh my God, Sister, please, get it off me. Shoo, shoo!" I waved my arms around. "They must listen to you. They're your bloody bees."

Sister Ignatius pointed her finger and shouted in a deep voice, "Sebastian, no!"

I stopped jerking around to stare at her, my tears now stopped. "You are not serious. You do not name your bees."

"Ah, there's Jemima on the rose, and Benjamin on the geranium," she said perkily, eyes bright.

"No way," I said, wiping my face, embarrassed by my breakdown. "I thought *I* had mental problems."

"Of course I'm not serious," she said, and then she started laughing, a wonderful throaty laugh that instantly made me smile. I think that's when I knew I loved Sister Ignatius.

"My name is Tamara."

"Yes," she said, studying me as if she already knew.

I smiled again. She had a face that made me do that.

"Are you allowed to, like, talk? Shouldn't you be quiet?" I looked around. "Don't worry, I won't tell."

"Many of the sisters would agree with you." She chuckled. "But yes, I'm allowed to talk. I haven't taken a vow of silence."

"Oh. Do other nuns look down on you for that?"

She didn't answer and just laughed again, this time a sweet, clear, singsong laugh.

"So have you not seen people for ages? Is talking to me against the rules? Did you know Obama's the U.S. president now?" I joked. When she didn't respond, my smile faded. "Shit. Are you not supposed to know stuff like that? Stuff from the 'outside world'? It must be a bit like being in *Big Brother*, being a nun."

"Aren't you a peculiar thing?" She'd said it sweetly and so I tried hard not to be insulted.

"What's that you've got there?" she asked, looking at the book that I was still hugging.

"Oh, this." I finally stopped squeezing it. "I found it yesterday on the . . . oh, actually, I owe you a book."

"Don't be silly."

"No, really I do. Marcus, I mean, the traveling library came by the day before yesterday looking for you and I didn't know who you were."

"Then you do owe me a book," she said, a twinkle in her eye. "Let me see, who's it by?"

"I don't know who or what it is. It's not the Bible or anything, so you might not like it," I said, reluctant to hand it over. "There could be sex scenes in it, swear words, gay people, divorced people, things like that."

She looked at me and pursed her lips, trying not to smile.

"I can't open it," I said finally, handing it to her. "It's locked."

"Well, I'll see to that. Follow me."

She immediately set off out the other entrance of the walled garden with the book in her hand.

"Where are you going?" I called after her.

"Where are *we* going," she corrected me. "Come and see the sisters. They'll be delighted to meet you. And I'll open the book while you do so."

"Uh. No, it's okay." I ran to catch up with her and take the book back.

"There's just the four of us. We don't bite. Particularly when eating Sister Mary's apple pie, but don't tell her I said that," she added under her breath and chuckled again.

"But, Sister, I'm not very good with holy people. I don't really know what to say."

She laughed that throaty laugh again and waddled in her funny-looking suit toward the orchard.

"What's the deal with the tree with all the engravings on it?" I asked, skipping alongside her to keep up.

"Ah, you've seen our apple orchard? You know, some people say the apple tree is the tree of love," she said, her eyes widening. "Many of the young ones around here have declared their love to one another on that tree." She power-walked on, snapping out of her magical love story. "Plus, it's great for the bees. And the bees are great for the trees. Oh, that rhymes." She chuckled. "Arthur does a wonderful job of keeping it. We get the most delicious Granny Smith apples."

"Oh, so that's why Rosaleen makes three thousand apple tarts a day. I've eaten so many apples they're literally coming out of my—"

She looked at me.

"Ears."

She laughed and it sounded like a song.

"So," I panted, trying to keep up with her pacy strides, "how come there's only four of you?"

"Not so many people want to be nuns these days. It's not, what you'd say, cool?"

"Well, it's not just that it's not cool, which it totally isn't, no offense to God or anything, it's probably just a sex thing. If you were allowed to have sex I'd say loads of girls would want to be nuns. Though at the rate I'm going, I'll be joining you." I rolled my eyes.

Sister Ignatius laughed. "All in good time, my child, all in good time. You're only seventeen. Almost eighteen, my word."

"I'm sixteen."

She stopped walking then and examined me, a curious expression on her face. "Seventeen."

"Seventeen in a few weeks." I caught my breath.

"Eighteen in a few weeks," she said with a frown.

"I wish, but seriously I'm sixteen, though people always think I'm older."

She stared at me as though I were a foreign object, thinking so hard I could almost smell her brain frying. Then she took off on her heel again. Five minutes of power-walking later, I was panting but Sister Ignatius had barely broken a sweat, and we came across some more buildings, more like outhouses, and some old stables. In front, there was a church.

"There's the chapel there," Sister Ignatius explained. "It was built by the Kilsaneys in the late eighteenth century."

Remembering that part from my school project I couldn't take my eyes off it, unable to believe that what I'd stolen from the Internet essay was actually real. It was a small chapel, gray stone, two pillars in the front as cracked as a desert earth that hasn't seen water for decades. On the top was a bell tower. Beside it was an old graveyard protected by three thin rusty iron railings. Whether it was to keep the buried in or the wanderers out, it wasn't clear, but it made me shudder just looking at it. I realized I'd stopped walking and was staring at it—and Sister Ignatius was staring at me.

"Great. I live on the grounds of a graveyard. Just swell."

"All generations of the Kilsaneys are buried there," she said softly. "Or as many as possible. For the bodies they couldn't find they planted headstones."

"What do you mean, 'for the bodies they couldn't find'?" I asked, horrified.

"Generations of war, Tamara. Some of the Kilsaneys were sent off to Dublin Castle to be imprisoned, others left through travel or revolution."

There was a silence while I took in the old headstones, some green and covered in moss, others black and lopsided, the inscriptions so faded you couldn't read the letters.

"That's just creepy. You have to live beside that?"

"I still pray in there."

"Pray for what? For the walls not to cave in on your head? It looks like it's about to fall apart any second."

She laughed. "It's still a consecrated church."

"No way. Are there weekly Masses in there?"

"No," she said. "The last time it was used was . . ." She pinched her eyes shut and her lips moved open and closed as though she was doing decades of the rosary. Then her eyes popped open wide. "Do you know what, Tamara, you should check the records to get the exact date. The names of everybody are included too. We have them in the house. Come in and have a look, why don't you."

"Eh. No. You're grand, but no thanks."

"You will when you're ready, I suppose," she said, and moved along again. And again I rushed to keep up with her.

"So how long have you lived here?" I asked, following her into an outhouse, which was used as a toolshed.

"Thirty years."

"Thirty years here? Must have been so lonely all that time."

"Oh no, it was far busier back then when I arrived, believe it or not. The three sisters were a lot more mobile then. I'm the youngest, the baby," she said, and laughed that little-girl laugh again. "There was the castle, and the gatehouse . . . they were indeed busier times. But I like the quiet now too. The peace. The nature. The simplicity. The time to be still."

"But I thought the castle was burned down in the twenties."

"Oh, it was burned out many times in its history. But it was only partly burned on that occasion. The family worked hard to refurbish it. And they did a wonderful job. It was truly beautiful."

"You've been inside it?"

"Oh, indeed." She looked surprised by my question. "Lots of times."

"So what happened to it?"

"A fire," she said, then looked away. She located her toolbox on the cluttered worktable and opened it. Five drawers slid out, each filled with nuts and bolts. She was like a little DIY magpie.

"Another fire?" I rolled my eyes. "Honestly, that's ridiculous. Our smoke alarms were connected to the local fire station. Want to know how I found out? I was smoking in my room and I didn't open the window because it was absolutely freezing out and whenever I opened my doors they used to just slam shut, which was a total head wreck. So I'd up my music really loud and next minute my bedroom door was being bashed down by this hot fireman, pardon the pun, who thought my room was totally on fire."

Sister Ignatius stayed silent as she listened to me and looked through the toolbox.

"By the way, he thought I was seventeen too." I laughed. "He called the house afterward looking for me but Dad answered the phone and threatened to have him arrested. Talk about dramatic."

Silence.

"Anyway, was everybody okay?" I asked.

"No," she said, and when she looked at me briefly I realized that her eyes were filled with tears. "Unfortunately not." She blinked them away furiously while she continued noisily rooting through the drawers, her wrinkled but sturdy-looking hands pushing through nails and screwdrivers. On her right hand was a gold ring that looked like a wedding ring, so firmly on her finger, her flesh growing around it, I doubt she could ever take it off even if she wanted to. I would have liked to ask more questions about the castle but I didn't want to upset her further, and she was making such a racket with her toolbox I couldn't possibly be heard anyway.

She tried and tested a few screwdrivers on the book lock and I grew bored and shuffled lazily around the shed. Shelf upon shelf of junk filled the walls. A table spanning the three walls was also filled with all sorts of knickknacks and contraptions that I didn't know the use for. It was Aladdin's cave for the DIY obsessed.

I looked around but my head hopped with new questions about the castle. So it had been lived in after the fire in the 1920s. Sister Ignatius had said she'd been here thirty years and had been in the house after the refurbishment. That would take us back to the late seventies. I was under the impression the castle had been lying idle for so much longer than that.

"So where is everybody?" I asked.

"Inside. It's recreation hour. *Murder, She Wrote* is on now. The sisters love that."

"No, I mean from the Kilsaney family. Where are they all?"

She sighed. "The parents moved away to stay with cousins in Bath. They couldn't take looking at the castle like that. They hadn't the time nor the energy, nor the money, mind you, to rebuild it."

"Do they ever come back?"

She looked at me sadly. "They passed away, Tamara, I'm sorry to say."

I shrugged. "That's okay. I'm not bothered." My voice was too perky, sounded defensive somehow. Why? I shouldn't have been bothered by this. I didn't know them from Adam—so why should I care? But oddly I did care. Maybe it was because since Dad had died I felt every sad story was my story. I don't know. Mae, my nanny, used to love watching programs about real-life cases being solved. When Mum and Dad were out she used to take over the television in the living room and watch *The FBI Files*, which used to freak me out. Not for the gory details—I'd seen worse—but by the fact she was so fascinated by how to cover up crimes. I used to think she was going to kill us all in our sleep. But she also made the best lattes and so I didn't probe her too much in case she got insulted and stopped making them. I learned from watching one of these shows that the word "clue" actually came from "clew," meaning a ball or thread of yarn, because in a Greek myth, a Greek guy uses a ball of yarn to find his way out of the Minotaur's labyrinth. It's something that helps you get to the end of something, or perhaps to the beginning. It's the same as Bar-

bara's GPS and my line of bread crumbs from the gatehouse back
to Killiney: Sometimes we have absolutely no idea where we are,
so we need the smallest clue to show us where to begin.

Finally the lock Sister Ignatius had been working on gave way
and unlatched.

"You are a dark horse," I teased her.

She laughed heartily. As she lifted open the heavy front cover
my heart fluttered. The voice of Zoey and Laura told me to be embarrassed about this and I was momentarily until the Tamara of
this new world beat them away with a stick. But when Sister Ignatius fully opened the book the embarrassment came back, bringing
anger with it, for there was nothing in the book. Nothing at all on
the pages.

"Hmm . . . well, look at that," Sister Ignatius said, flicking
through the thick, cream, woven, deckle-edged pages, which looked
as though they'd come straight from another time. "Blank pages
waiting to be filled," she continued with her voice of wonder.

"How exciting." I rolled my eyes.

"More exciting than an already filled one. Then you definitely
wouldn't be able to use it."

"Then I could read it. Hence it being called a book," I snapped,
once again feeling this place had let me down.

"Would you prefer to be given a life already lived too, Tamara?
That way you can sit back and observe it. Or would you rather live
one yourself?" she asked, her eyes smiling.

"Eh, you keep it," I said, stepping away, no longer interested in
the thing I'd been lugging around.

"No, dear. That's yours. You use it."

"I don't write. I hate it. Writing gives me bumps on my fingers.
And headaches. I'd rather e-mail. Anyway, I can't. It's the traveling library's. Marcus will want it back. I'll have to give it back the

next time I see him." I noticed my voice had softened on the last sentence. Quite immaturely, I fought back a smile.

It seemed Sister Ignatius noticed everything, and she smiled then and raised her eyebrows. "Well, you can still meet up with Marcus *to discuss the book*," she teased. "He'll understand, as I do, that somebody must have donated the diary to the library, mistaking it for a book."

"If I take it don't I break a commandment or something?"

Sister Ignatius rolled her eyes as I had been doing, and despite my bad mood, I had to grin.

"But I've nothing to write," I said, a little softer this time.

"There's always something to write. Write some thoughts. I'm sure you've plenty of those."

I took the book back, ranting on about how writing diaries was for dorks. But for all my talk, I was surprisingly relieved to have it back in my arms again. It felt right sitting there.

"Write what's up there." Sister Ignatius pointed at her temple. "As a great man once said, this is a secret garden. We've all got one of those."

"Jesus?"

"No, Bruce Springsteen."

"I found yours today." I smiled. "So yours isn't a secret anymore, Sister."

"Ah, there you have it. It's always good to share it with someone." She pointed at the book. "Or something. You should write a few of your thoughts down, Tamara, I think you'll find it helpful."

"How is writing them down helpful?" I ruffled my nose. "Isn't thinking your thoughts enough? Why would I want to go over them all over again?"

Sister Ignatius smiled patiently. "Lots of people do it, Tamara, there's nothing to be afraid of."

"I'm not afraid. I just don't see the point."

"It will help release your worries and clear your mind. Ease all the tension from up there." She touched my forehead gently with her forefinger. "Imagine, you can tell those pages things you don't want to tell anybody else and it will never tell a soul. The best friend a girl could have." She winked.

I doubted her words but allowed them to sink in as I flicked through the hundreds of empty pages in front of me. Despite previously thinking I'd never want to keep a diary in my life, I suddenly felt there could never be enough pages in the world for me to share all the thoughts I'd been having since Dad died. I closed the book and hugged it close to me.

Sister Ignatius was looking at me expectantly.

"Well . . . if you think it will help . . ."

"It will, my dear." Her blue eyes sparkled and despite myself, I felt a burst of hope somewhere inside of me. "I promise you that."

CHAPTER NINE

A Long Good-bye

The evening was closing in by the time I made my way back to the gatehouse with my stomach grumbling, not having eaten since Zoey's mum had made pancakes and blueberries for lunch. As before, Rosaleen was standing at her open door looking out, her face furrowed with worry, frantically searching from left to right. How long had she been doing that?

She jumped to attention when she saw me coming, pushed her hands down the front of her dress to smooth it out. The dress was chocolate brown with a stitched green vine climbing from hem to collar. A hummingbird flitted near her boob, and later I noticed another by her left bum cheek. I don't think that was the designer's intention, but her height dictated their ironic placement.

"Well, there you are, child."

I felt like snapping at her that I wasn't a child but I gritted my teeth and smiled. I needed to exercise more tolerance with Rosaleen. Tonight I'd be Tamara Good.

"Your dinner's keeping warm in the oven. We couldn't wait any longer, I could hear himself's belly talking to me."

Tamara Good smiled again and said sweetly, "Thank you, Rosaleen. I look forward to it in just a few moments."

I turned to make my way to the stairs but her sudden movement, a jerk like an athlete at a starting line anticipating the gun, kept me rooted to the spot. I didn't look at her and just waited for her to speak.

"Your mother's sleeping so you'll not bother her now." She'd lost that stammering eager-to-please tone. Tamara Not-So-Good ignored her and I continued to make my way upstairs. I knocked gently on Mum's door while Rosaleen's searing eyes branded me from behind, and, not expecting a response from Mum anyway, I entered.

The room was darker than before and Mum was in bed. The curtains had been drawn but it was the sun that had slipped into something more comfortable for the evening that made the place cooler and dimmer. The yellow blankets were pulled up to her chest, her arms were constricted down by her side under the covers as though a giant spider had rolled her into its web to eat her. I can only imagine Rosaleen had tucked her in this way; it was physically impossible for Mum to have trapped herself under the blankets so tightly. I loosened the blankets, lifted her arms out by her side, and knelt down beside her. Her face was peaceful, as though she was merely having one of her favorite crème-fraîche-and-yogurt-wrap spa treatments. She was so still I had to move my ear to her face to make sure she was breathing.

I watched her then, her blond hair around her on the pillow, her long eyelashes closed over her perfect blemish-free skin. Her lips were ever so slightly parted and were breathing soft, sweet, warm breaths.

Perhaps as I've been telling this story, I've been giving the wrong impression of my mother. The grieving widow mindlessly looking out of a window while sitting in a rocking chair in a bell-sleeved nightgown makes her sound so old. She's really not old at all.

She's only thirty-five, much younger than all my friends' mums. Mum had me when she was eighteen. Dad was older than her, at twenty-eight. Dad loved telling me the story about how they met, though it always differed slightly each time. I think he enjoyed telling different versions, leaving the truth as something the two of them would only ever know. I never minded that. Perhaps the true story wouldn't have lived up to all the other stories I'd heard and imagined. The common denominator in all of his stories is that they met at a posh banquet dinner somewhere, and when their eyes met he knew he just had to have her. One time I heard this and started laughing and told him it was exactly what he'd said about the filly he'd seen when he came back from the Goffs sale.

He shut up then, lost the smile and the distant look, while Mum seemed to ponder my words in a long silence. I wanted to tell them that I didn't really mean it, that it was just the way I was, bitchy remarks dropping from my mouth without intention or planning. But I couldn't say that to my parents. I was too proud. I wasn't used to saying sorry. But refusing to take it back wasn't just because of all that. I was too proud. It *was* exactly what Dad had said when he came home from Goffs. It was also exactly what he said when he saw a new watch, or a new boat, or a new suit: "You should see it, Jennifer. I have to have it." And when Dad had to have something, he got it. I wondered if Mum was as powerless as the filly in Goffs, as the yacht in Monaco, and everything else in the world that Dad had to have. And if so, I don't pity her at all for her weak-mindedness then.

I don't doubt that Dad loved Mum. He adored her. He was always looking at her, touching her, opening doors for her, bringing her flowers, shoes, handbags, constant surprises to show her he was thinking of her. He was always complimenting her on the most ridiculous things, which annoyed me to no end. He never complimented me on any of those things. And don't go all Sigmund Freud on me, I wasn't jealous—he was my dad, not my husband, and I know the same rules do not apply, nor would I want them to. But you can't lose a daughter, can you? A child of yours will always be your child, whether you see them or care for them or not. A wife, now, she can easily be lost. She can grow bored and wander off. Mum was so beautiful she could have had most men she met, and Dad knew this.

"Sweetheart, tell them, tell them what you said yesterday when the waiter asked if you'd like dessert. Go on, tell them, sweetheart."

"Oh, it's not a big deal, George, really."

"Oh, tell them, Jennifer, sweetheart. It was so funny, really it was."

And then Mum would say, "I simply said that I'd put on the calories just looking at the dessert menu," and people would smile and laugh lightly while Dad's face beamed with pride at the hilarity of his wife. I would want to stand up and shout, "But that's fucking ridiculous! That joke is three thousand years old! And it's not even funny!"

I don't know if Mum ever saw Dad's doting the way I did. She always just smiled that smile that hid a million responses. Maybe that's what made Dad nervous: how much she kept inside. Maybe he never knew how she really felt. They weren't like other couples that sometimes rolled their eyes at each other, or picked up on earlier comments they'd made to discuss or debate them further. They were just both sickeningly agreeable with each other. Mum pan-faced, Dad always complimentary. Or maybe I simply don't understand what was going on between them because I've never been in love. Maybe love is thinking that every time your partner does or says something mundane that you want to start a crowd wave from here to Uzbekistan in utter delight. I've never had that with anyone.

I always felt Dad and I were total opposites. When he was afraid of someone leaving, he complimented them on everything. For example, if Mum's friends visited, they usually annoyed him and he'd ignore them the entire time they were over, but then when they were leaving he'd make sure he gave them the warmest hug and sendoff possible. Dad was a stand-at-the-front-door-and-wave-until-you-can't-see-the-car-anymore kind of person.

Dad was more into last impressions than first ones, which makes his death all the more symbolic. I was the opposite. Just as I'd given Barbara an easy way to leave me by making bitchy remarks to her, I'd done the same to my mum and dad all my life. I make it easier for people to leave by making them hate me a little. What I didn't realize, though, until later, was that other people kept tabs on my spoiled behavior, stored away my sarcastic throwaway comments.

Dad had been acting oddly in the weeks leading up to his death, maybe even longer, but I'm not too sure. And for some reason, I thought that he was going to leave us. I felt there was something peculiar about his behavior, but I couldn't put my finger on it. He was unusually nice. Like I said, he was always nice to Mum, usually nice to me if I was nice back, but this kind of nice was like a long and drawn-out wave good-bye from the door. A very long and very nice last impression. Long good-bye, very dead. I felt something was coming. Either we were leaving or he was.

So I did what I always did: I started to push him away. I was bitchier than usual, more badly behaved than usual; smoked in the house, came home drunk, that kind of thing. I challenged him a lot more. Our fights were more vicious, my retorts more personal. Horrible stuff. I did what I'd done ever since I was a kid when I didn't want them to go out for the night. I basically told him to leave. On the night he actually did it. Any other night and I could have just mourned him. Now I'm mourning him *and* hating myself and it's almost too much for me to bear. I gave him the worst good-bye and he did the worst thing in response. I know it wasn't entirely because of me, but I couldn't have helped.

I don't know if Mum felt something was wrong with him too. Maybe she did but she has never said. If she didn't sense it, then I was the only one. I should have said something to her. Better yet, I should have done something to stop him.

I'm sorry, Dad.

What if, what if, what if . . . What if we knew what tomorrow would bring? Would we fix it? Could we?

CHAPTER TEN

Stairway to Heaven

I chose to eat breakfast with Mum in her bedroom the next morning. This seemed to concern Rosaleen, who hung around Mum's bedroom a little too long moving furniture, setting up a table for both of us in front of the window, adjusting the curtains, opening a window, closing it a little, opening it a little more, questioning me on whether it was too breezy.

"Rosaleen, please," I said gently.

"Yes, child," she said as she continued to make the bed, furiously thumping pillows, tucking in the blankets so tightly, I wouldn't have been surprised if she'd licked the flat sheets before turning them over the blanket and sealing them like an envelope.

"You don't have to do that. I'll make the bed after breakfast," I said. "You go downstairs to Arthur. I'm sure he'll want to see you before he goes to work."

"His lunch is on the counter all ready to go—he knows where it is." She kept plumping, smoothing, and as if it wasn't right she started again.

"Rosaleen," I repeated gently.

Even though I knew she didn't want to, she quickly glanced at me. When our eyes clicked, she knew her game was up, but she just stared at me and in those eyes she dared me to say it. She didn't think I would. I swallowed.

"If you wouldn't mind, I'd just like to spend a little time with Mum. On our own, please." There, I'd said it. Tamara Grown-Up had spoken up for herself. But my request was inevitably followed by the wounded look, the slow release of the pillows falling to the bed, followed by a whispery "Well."

I didn't feel bad.

Finally she left the room and I remained quiet for a while. Not hearing the creak of the landing, I knew she was still outside the door. Listening, guarding, protecting or locking us in—I wasn't sure. What was she so afraid of?

Instead of trying to drag conversation out of Mum as I'd been trying to do for the past month, I decided to instead sit with her patiently in the silence that seemed to comfort her. Occasionally I lifted a slice of fruit to her and she took it and nibbled on it. I watched her face. She looked totally enchanted, as though she was watching a great big screen outside in the back garden which I couldn't see. Her eyebrows rose and fell as she reacted to something somebody said, her lips smiled coyly as she remembered a secret. Her face hid a million secrets.

Having spent enough time with her, I kissed her on the forehead and left the room. The diary was now hidden under my bed. I felt as if I was running off to tend to my big secret. I was also kind of embarrassed, I must admit. My friends and I didn't keep diaries. We didn't even write to each other. We kept in touch through Twitter and Facebook, posting photos of ourselves while on holiday, of our nights out, trying on dresses in department-store changing rooms and looking for second opinions. We texted one another continuously, we e-mailed gossip and jokes, but it was all on-the-surface stuff. We talked about things you can see, things you can touch, nothing deeper. Nothing emotional.

This diary is the kind of thing Fiona would do—the girl in our class who nobody spoke to apart from Sabrina, the other dork, but she was out of school more than in because of some kind of migraine problem. But this is what Fiona used to do: find a quiet place to go to on her own, a corner of a classroom when the teacher wasn't in or beneath a tree in the school grounds at lunchtime, and bury her nose deep in a book or furiously scribble something in a notebook. I used to laugh at her. But the joke was clearly on me. Who knew what she was writing.

There was only one place I could possibly go to write in the diary. I reached for it under my bed and ran down the stairs shouting, "Rosaleen, I'm going out . . ." My flip-flops banged down the creaky stairs, and as I leaped off the final step and landed on the ground with all the grace of an elephant, Rosaleen appeared before me.

"Jesus, Rosaleen!" My hand flew to my heart.

Her eyes moved over me quickly, registered my diary, then went to my face. I wrapped my arms around it protectively, making sure one side of my cardigan covered half the book.

"Where are you going?" she asked quietly.

"Just out . . . and about."

Her eyes flicked down to the diary again. She just couldn't help herself.

"Can I fix you some food to have with you? You'll be starving hungry."

Starving hungry. Hot sun. Long good-bye. Very dead.

"There's some fresh brown bread and chicken, some potato salad and baby tomatoes . . ."

"No, thanks, I'm still full from breakfast." I made a move to the door again.

"Some sliced fruit maybe?" She raised her voice slightly. "A ham and cheese sandwich? There's leftover coleslaw from—"

"Rosaleen. No. Thank you."

"Okay." Another wounded look. "Well, be safe now, won't you? Don't go wandering too far. Stay within the grounds. Within eye-shot of the house."

Within eyeshot of her, more like.

"I'm not going off to war." I laughed. "Just . . . around."

In the closed space of the house, where everyone always knew where everyone else was at any given time, I wanted a few hours of my own place, my own time.

"All right," she said.

"Don't look so worried."

"I'm just not sure . . ." She looked down at the floor, unclasped her hands to smooth down her tea dress. "Would your mother let you go?"

"Mum? Mum would let me go to the moon, if it kept me from whining all day."

I'm not sure if relief was what passed over Rosaleen's face. Just more worry. Suddenly a few chips fell into place for me, and I re-laxed a little. Rosaleen wasn't a mother, but all of a sudden, in her quiet house, as my mum had switched to sleep mode, Rosaleen had to do the mothering of both of us.

"Oh, I understand," I said softly. I reached out a hand and I touched her. Her body tensed so much that I quickly let go. "You don't have to worry about me. Mum and Dad pretty much let me go wherever I wanted. I used to spend the entire day in town with my friends. I even went to London one day with my friend. We were over and back in a day. Her dad has his own jet. It was totally cool. There were only like six seats and it went to London just for me and Emily. Then for her seventeenth birthday her parents let us all fly to Paris. Her older sister came with us to keep an eye on us, though. She was nineteen, in college and everything."

Rosaleen listened intently; far too eagerly, too anxiously, too desperately.

"Oh, isn't that lovely," she said brightly, her green eyes hungry for all the words that came from my mouth. I could see her gobbling them up as soon as I'd said them. "Your birthday isn't far off. Is that the kind of thing you'd get for your birthday?" She looked around the hallway of the gatehouse as if she might find a plane in there somewhere. "Well, we wouldn't be able for the likes of that . . ."

"No, no, that's not what I meant. That's not why I told you the story. It was just . . . It doesn't matter, Rosaleen," I said quickly. "I'd better go." I pushed past her to get to the door. "Thanks, though," I said. The last thing I saw before I closed the door was her concerned look, as though she'd said something wrong. Worrying about what their life could and couldn't offer me. Turns out my old life was offering me more than it could deliver anyway, the moon and stars, and I had stupidly believed it. I used to think that it was better to have too much than too little, but now I think if the too much was never supposed to be yours, you should just take what you need and give the rest back. That way, you never have to give back the things you love.

As I was walking down the garden path the postman came toward me. Excited to see another person, I greeted him with a big smile.

"Hi." I stopped and blocked him in his path.

"Hello, miss." He tipped his hat, which I thought was very old-fashioned and kind.

"I'm Tamara." I held out my hand.

"Nice to meet you, Tamara." He thought I was holding my hand out for the post and he plonked some envelopes into my palm.

Behind me I heard the door open and Rosaleen came rushing out.

"Morning, Jack," she called, power-walking down the path. "I'll take those." She practically tore the mail from my grasp. "Thank you, Jack." She looked at him sternly while stuffing the envelopes into her apron pouch like a mother kangaroo.

"Right so." He bent his head as though he'd just been told off. "And for over the road." He handed her more envelopes, then he turned on his heel, hopped on his bike, and cycled off around the corner.

"I wasn't going to eat them," I said to Rosaleen's back, slightly stunned.

She laughed and went inside the house. Curiouser and curiouser.

Back to the one place that I could go to write this diary. Feeling the heat of the road beneath my rubber flip-flops, I made my way toward the castle. I smiled when the trees gave way like a curtain parting for the main act.

"Hello again," I said.

With great respect I wandered through the castle's rooms. I couldn't believe that a fire had done all of this damage. There was nothing, absolutely nothing to suggest that anybody had lived here for at least a century. No fireplaces left on the walls, no tiles, no wallpaper. Absolutely nothing but bricks, weeds, and a staircase that climbed to a second floor that didn't exist, leading up to the skies, as though with one giant leap you could reach a cloud. A stairway to heaven.

I took my place on the bottom steps and set the diary on my lap. I twirled in my hand the heavy pen that I'd stolen from Arthur's writing desk and stared at the closed book, trying to think of what to write. I wanted my first words to mean something, I didn't want to make a mistake. Finally I thought of a beginning and opened the book.

My jaw dropped. The first page had already been written, each line neatly filled . . . in *my* handwriting.

I stood up, alert, rigid, and the diary fell from my lap and down to the floor. I looked around quickly, my heart racing, trying to see if this was somebody's idea of a cruel joke. The crumbling walls stared back at me and suddenly there were movements and noises all around me that I hadn't noticed before. Shrubs and weeds rustled, rocks moved, I heard footsteps from behind and inside the walls, but nothing surfaced or showed itself. It was all my imagination. Perhaps the filled pages of the diary were too.

I took a few deep breaths and retrieved the diary from the ground. The leather, scraped by the stones and rocks, was dusty, and I wiped it against my shorts. The first page had been ripped by the fall but the writing hadn't been just my mind playing tricks. It was still there— the first page, second page—and as I furiously flicked through, I could see my handwriting throughout the first five pages.

It was impossible. I compared the date on the top of the first page to the date on my watch. It was dated tomorrow, Saturday. Today was Friday. My watch must have been wrong. I immediately thought about Rosaleen, how her eyes had run over the diary that morning. Was it she who had written in it? She couldn't have. The diary had been safely stored under my bed. Feeling dizzy, I sat back down on the staircase and read the entry. My eyes kept jumping over the words manically, so I had to go back a few times and start again.

Saturday, 4 July
Dear Diary,

Is that what I'm supposed to write? I've never written in one of these before, and I feel like an absolute dork, beyond words. Okay so, Dear Diary, I hate my life. Here it is in a nutshell. My dad killed himself, we lost our house and absolutely everything. I lost my life, Mum lost her mind, and now we're living in hicksville with two sociopaths. A few days ago I spent the afternoon with a really cute guy called Marcus who is Vice President of Dork Central, a traveling library. Two days ago I met a nun who keeps bees and breaks locks and yesterday I spent most of the morning sitting in a ruin—

"Ruin" had been crossed out and beside it was:

castle on a stairway to heaven that looked very tempting to climb and leap for a cloud that would carry me away from here. Now it's nighttime and I'm back in my bedroom writing in this dorky diary that Sister Ignatius talked me into doing. Yes, she's a nun and not a transvestite, as I'd previously thought.

I sighed and looked up from the page. How could this be? I searched around me for answers. I thought about running back to the house to tell Mum, to tell Rosaleen, to phone Zoey and Laura. Who on earth would believe me? And even if they did, what could they do anyway?

The castle was so still, it seemed like the clouds above, so perfectly round and white like cherubs, were moving at a hundred miles an hour. There was the occasional rustle under a weed, dandelion seeds drifted through the air, drifting close and then darting away suddenly as the breeze took them. I took a deep breath, lifted my face to the hot sun—hot sun. Very dead. I closed my eyes and exhaled slowly. I opened my eyes and continued reading, the hairs on the back of my neck continuing to stand up.

Mum still hasn't come out of her room. I decided to eat breakfast in the back garden beside the tree this morning because I knew that she'd see me. I rolled out the blue cashmere blanket from my room and laid out some sliced fruit. It felt and tasted like cardboard. I wasn't hungry, all of my energy was going into trying to will Mum to come outside. I just thought that if she got some air, if she took a look around this place, came to this castle, maybe she'd see what I see, that she'd snap out of the trance she's caught in. Of course she doesn't want life to go on while she's sitting up there in that bedroom. It's only when you come outside and realize life is moving on, that you just have to go with the flow.

I don't know why Rosaleen and Arthur aren't doing more to help her. Breakfast, lunch, and dinner big enough to feed an army aren't going to cure her. Nor is silence. Apart from the bizarre forehead-touching greeting Arthur and Mum had when we arrived, he hasn't said one word to her. How weird is that?

After the rain of yesterday, I feel smothered with a cold. All I want to do is curl up in a ball and die but . . .

Okay, so that's when I knew this whole thing was ridiculous because it was the most beautiful hot day today. No rain whatsoever. I continued reading with a cocked eyebrow, armed with the knowledge that I was being punked or something, and I waited for Zoey and Ashton Kutcher to jump out from behind the crumbling pillars.

. . . Rosaleen practically wrapped me up in cotton wool, stuck me in front of the fire, and force-fed me chicken soup. I lost half the day sweating profusely next to that ghastly fire and trying to convince her I wasn't dying. She made me cover my head with a towel and stick my face over a bowl of boiling hot water filled with Vicks to

clear my nose, and while under there snotting myself, I was almost
sure I heard the doorbell ring. Rosaleen assured me it didn't and I
can't figure out why she'd lie about that. Was it somebody I wasn't
supposed to see? Or who wasn't supposed to see me? Anyway, I
should have taken Sister Ignatius up on her offer to dry off in her
house. How scary can a house of nuns be?

Rosaleen reacted so unusually at dinner today—shepherd's pie,
yum—when I told her I'd spent time with Sister Ignatius. She
kept interrogating me on what kinds of things Sister and I talked
about. Honestly, it was so weird even Arthur seemed uncomfort-
able. I mean, did she think I was lying about it? I wish I hadn't
told her what I'd learned from Sister Ignatius about the castle. She
seemed angry at me for even asking. Now I know that whatever
information I need to learn, it most certainly can't be from Rosa-
leen.

In case I die of dehydration and somebody finds this diary, I
should mention that I cry every night. I go through the entire day,
save for bluebottle and ruined-castle breakdowns, as strong as can
be and then as soon as I crawl into bed and lie in the darkness, then
I cry. Sometimes for such long periods of time my pillow becomes
soaked. Rolling down the edges of my eyes, along my ears and tick-
ling down my neck, sometimes down to my vest, I just let the tears
go wherever. I'm so used to crying now, I don't notice it sometimes.
Does that make sense? Before, if I cried it was because I'd fallen
and hurt myself, or because I'd had a fight with Dad, or I was
totally drunk and the slightest thing made me upset. But now it's,
like, whatever . . . I'm sad so I'll cry. Sometimes I start and then
stop as I convince myself that everything will be fine. Sometimes I
don't believe myself and I start again.

Who else apart from me could know that?

I have lots of dreams about Dad. Rarely is he really Dad, but instead a mixture of different people's faces. He started off as him, then he became a school teacher, then Zac Efron, and then some random person without a recognizable face. It had something to do with us living in a hive, crammed together like bees, and smoke was filling the room and Dad kept telling me to get out. I woke up when Rosaleen dropped a pot or something on the kitchen floor. I've heard people say that when they dream about a loved one that has died, they feel that it's real, that the person is really there, sending them a message, giving them a hug. That somehow dreams are a blurred line between here and there, like a meeting room in a prison. You're both in the same room, yet on different sides and in different worlds. I used to think that people who talked like that were quacks, but now I know that that is just one of the many things I was wrong about. It's got nothing to do with religion, or mental stability, but it has every-thing to do with the human mind's natural instinct, which is to hope beyond all hope that someday you'll see them again, that you can still feel them near you. Hope like that, as I thought before, doesn't make you a weak person. It's hopelessness that makes you weak. That said, I know that Dad isn't in my dreams. There is no secret message or secret hug. I don't feel him with me here in Kilsaney. They are merely obscure dreams with no meaning or words of advice. Mirrored seg-ments of my day broken up as though a jigsaw puzzle.

Maybe Sister Ignatius was right. Maybe this diary will help me. Sister Ignatius is a funny woman. I haven't been able to stop thinking about her since I met her a few days ago.

Yesterday. I'd only met her yesterday.

I like her. It started lashing rain while I was in the castle yester-day and I could see Rosaleen coming down the road toward me with a coat in her hand, so I felt bad, but I just had to run in the opposite direction. I didn't want her knowing that I spent time here; I didn't want her to think that her guess was right. I didn't want her knowing anything about me. I had no idea where I was running to. The rain came down really, really hard—less of a sun shower and more of a power shower, and I was soaked right through to the skin, but it was like I was on autopilot, my body just switched off and I ran, and without really concentrating I ended up at the walled garden. Sister Ignatius was standing in the greenhouse, waiting for the rain to stop. She had a spare beekeeping suit for me. She said she had a feeling I'd be back.

Because I'd interrupted her the day before she hadn't been able to get back to checking the hives. She'd other duties to attend to. Praying and stuff. So she showed me the inside of the hives yesterday. She drew on the queen bee with a marker so that I could see which one it was, she pointed out the drones, the worker bees too, and then showed me how to use the smoker. Looking at it made me feel dizzy. Something weird was happening to me. She didn't notice. I had to put my hand out and hold on to the wall so I wouldn't crumple to the ground. While I was feeling like that, she invited me back next week to help her extract the honey, which she then sells at the market. I was so busy trying to breathe that I just said no. I just wanted to get away. I wish I'd just told her that I didn't feel well. She seemed so disappointed and now I feel really bad.

I'm sitting with my back against the bedroom door writing this because I don't want Rosaleen to walk in. The less she knows about this diary, the better. Already she is trying to climb inside my head; so I'll have to hide it. There's an interesting-looking loose floorboard over by the corner chair that I might investigate tonight.

While I'm in the safety of the house, I just want to say that I had a funny feeling while in the castle yesterday morning. I felt like somebody was there. Like somebody was watching me. It was such a sunny morning, right up until that freak cloud squeezed itself right on top of my head, and I was just sitting on the step with this diary on my lap, and I couldn't think of what to write and how to begin the first page and so I sunbathed instead. I don't know how long I had my eyes closed for but I wish I'd kept them open. Someone was definitely there.

I'll write again tomorrow.

I finished reading and looked around, my heart so loud in my ears that my breathing was rapid and sharp. That was now. I'd been writing about me *now*.

I suddenly felt a thousand eyes on me. As I stood up and ran down the steps, I tripped on the last one and slammed into the wall. I grazed my hands and my right shoulder, dropped the book on the floor again. I felt around on the ground for it, and as I grabbed it my hand brushed against something furry and soft. I yelped and jumped away, ran into the room next door. There seemed to be no doorways out of there, just all four walls. I felt a few raindrops on my skin and soon moved as they quickly fell faster. I went to a hole in the wall where a window used to be and tried to climb out. Once up on the ledge, I saw Rosaleen charging her way up the road with what looked like a raincoat in her hands. She was power-walking forward, a stormy look on her face, her hand held above her head as though that alone could stop her from getting wet.

I rushed to the other window, looking out to the back of the castle and I climbed out, my knees scraping against the wall as I leaped up to catch the windowsill. I landed on concrete on the other side, feeling the sting in my feet as the lack of support in my flip-flops sent pain shooting up my legs. I spied Rosaleen coming closer to the castle. I turned away, and ran.

I was so confused after reading what I'd read that I couldn't think straight. I didn't know where to go, who to turn to, who to trust. Despite my mind feeling completely out of control, my body ran as though it was on autopilot, as though it knew exactly where it was going. It was only when I reached the walled garden, completely soaked to the skin, that I made the connection to the diary and a shudder went through my entire body, summoning goose pimples from head to toe.

As I stood at the garden entrance, frozen with fear and trembling, a white shadow through the frosted glass of the greenhouse caught my attention. Then the door opened and Sister Ignatius appeared with a spare bee suit in her hand. Just as the diary had said.

"I knew you'd come back," she called, and her blue eyes sparkled mischievously against her pale skin.

CHAPTER ELEVEN

Where There's Smoke

I joined Sister Ignatius in the greenhouse. I stood beside her, my body rigid and tight. My shoulders were hunched up past my ears as though I was trying to disappear into my body like a tortoise. I clung to the diary so tightly my knuckles were white.

"Oh, look at you," she said in her joyful, carefree voice. "You're like a drowned rat. Let me dry you off—"

"Don't touch me," I said quickly, taking a step back. I angled my body away from her but sneaked a look at her now and then over my shoulder.

"What's happened, Tamara?"

"Don't pretend you don't already know."

I saw her eyes narrow momentarily, then open wide. She registered something. She knew something in my face. She looked like someone who had been caught.

"Admit it," I said.

"Tamara," she began, then paused, searching to find the right words. "Tamara, look at me. I'm . . . Let me explain . . . We should go somewhere else to talk. Not here. Not in this greenhouse. Not with you like this."

"No. First I want to hear you admit it."

"Tamara, I really think that we should go inside and—"

"Admit that you wrote it," I snapped.

Her face instantly changed to utter confusion. "Tamara, I don't understand. Admit that I wrote what?"

"The diary," I exploded, and pushed it in her face. I flicked ferociously through the pages. "Look, it's been written in. I hid it in my bedroom, and this morning I brought it to the castle to write in it, just like you told me to, and look. How did you do it?" I shoved it under her nose and flicked through the pages, my wet hands blurring the ink. She blinked furiously to try to focus on the pages as they raced by.

"Tamara, calm down, I can't see anything, you're going too fast."

I went even faster. She reached out and with those thick hands, she grabbed my wrists tightly and said firmly, "Tamara. Stop."

It worked. She took the diary from my hands and opened the first page. Her eyes raced across the first few lines.

"This isn't for me to read. These are your private thoughts."

"I didn't write them." I knew by then, by the confusion on her face, that she hadn't either.

"Well . . . who did?"

"I don't know. Look at the date on the first page."

"Tomorrow."

"Some of the things written are about what happens tomorrow."

The rain pelted against the glass of the greenhouse, so loud it felt like it was going to break through.

"How do you know that, if tomorrow hasn't happened yet?" Her voice had softened, as though she was trying to coax a mental patient to put down a knife. She may very well have been, only I didn't pick up the knife, somebody had put it in my hands. This was not of my own doing.

"Perhaps you got up in the middle of the night and wrote it, Tamara." She continued, "Maybe you were so sleepy you don't remember doing it. I've often done funny things half asleep or half awake. I've wandered around the house looking for things when I don't know what I'm looking for, moving things, and when I wake up in the morning and go to find something, I'm in a right muddle." She chuckled.

"This isn't the same thing," I said quietly. "I've written about things that have happened today that I couldn't have known about. The rain, Rosaleen and the coat, you . . ."

"What about me?"

"I wrote that you'd be here."

"But I'm always here, Tamara, you know that."

Sister Ignatius kept talking then, trying to rationalize the situation, telling me a story about a time she'd wandered into Sister Mary's room during the night, apparently looking for gardening gloves because she'd been dreaming of planting turnips. I tuned her out. How could I have written five pages and not remembered? How could I have predicted the rain, Rosaleen's arrival with the raincoat, Sister Ignatius waiting right here in the greenhouse with the spare beekeeping suit?

"Our minds do unusual things sometimes, Tamara. When we're looking for things it takes it upon itself to go down its own route. All we can do is follow."

"But I'm not looking for anything."

"Aren't you? Ah, now the rain's stopped. I told you it would. Why don't we get you to the house to dry you off and get something hot inside you? I made a soup yesterday with my own grown veg. It will be just right now, I'd say, if Sister Mary hasn't sucked it up with a straw. She dropped her dentures yesterday and Sister Peter Regina accidentally stomped on them. She's had to eat everything through a straw since." She covered her mouth. "Oh, forgive me for laughing."

I was about to protest when I remembered my comments in the diary about being smothered with a cold. Perhaps I could change what was going to happen. It seemed crazy, but what did I have to lose at this point? I followed her out of the garden and through the trees to her home.

The house was just like Sister Ignatius. It lacked a deceptive brick in its making, as it was as old on the inside as it was on the outside. We entered through the back door, a small hallway filled with Wellington boots, raincoats, umbrellas, and sunhats, every necessity for every kind of weather. Uneven, cracked stone flagging floored the walkway to the kitchen. The kitchen was something from the 1970s. Shaker-style cabinets, linoleum flooring, plastic countertops, avocado and burnt orange in every possible place from an era obsessed with bringing the outside in. There was a long pine table with a bench on either side, long enough to feed the Waltons. From a room off the kitchen a radio blared. Brown swirly carpet led my eyeline to a big television set with a booty that came out thirty inches from the wall. On top, cream lace dangled over the front of the screen and upon that a statue of Mary. On the wall above it was a simple wooden cross.

The house smelled old. Musty damp mixed with generations of cooked dinners and greasy cooking oil. Somewhere in there was the scent of Sister Ignatius, a clean talcum powder soapy smell, like a freshly bathed baby. Like Rosaleen and Arthur's house, this had the feel of the generations of people who had lived there before, families that had grown up, run and shouted through the hallways, broken things, grown things, fallen in love. Instead of the occupants owning the house, the house owned a part of each of them. We never had that feeling in our house. I loved our house but every bit of life was cleaned away by our maid, who rid the rooms of our scents and replaced them with bleach. Every three years a room was done up in a new style, old furniture thrown out, new furniture moved in, a new painting to match the new sofa. There was no eclectic collection of items gathered through the years. No sentimental clutter crammed together oozing secrets. It was all new and expensive, it all lacked anything of sentiment.

Sister Ignatius hurried off in her beekeeping suit, walking like a toddler with a bulging diaper. I took off my cardigan, laid it across the radiator. My wet vest was now see-through and my flip-flops squelched, but I daren't take them off in case dirt from all these previous families stuck to my soles.

Sister Ignatius returned with a towel in one hand and a T-shirt in the other.

"I'm sorry, this is all I could find. We're not in the habit of dressing seventeen-year-olds."

"Sixteen," I corrected her, checking out the woman's pink marathon T-shirt she handed me.

"I ran it every year from '61 to '71," she explained, turning to the Aga to prepare the soup. "Not anymore, I'm afraid."

"Wow, you must have been fit."

"What do you mean?" She struck a pose in her beekeeping suit and kissed a padded biceps. "I haven't lost it yet."

I laughed and lifted my vest over my head and laid it on the radiator too, then put the T-shirt on. It went to mid-thigh. I took off my shorts and used my belt to turn the T-shirt into a dress.

"What do you think?" I walked an imaginary runway for Sister Ignatius and posed at the end.

She laughed and wolf-whistled. "My word, to have a pair of legs like that again." She tutted and shook her head as she brought two bowls of soup to the table. I devoured mine.

Outside the sun shone and the birds sang again as though the rain had never fallen, as though it had all been a figment of our imagination.

"How's your mother?"

"She's fine, thank you."

Silence. Never lie to a nun.

"Okay, she's not fine. She sits in her bedroom all day looking out the window, smiling."

"She sounds happy."

"She sounds crazy."

"What does Rosaleen think?"

"Rosaleen thinks that a lifetime's supply of food in one day will keep anyone going."

Sister Ignatius's lips twitched at that.

"Rosaleen says it's just the grief."

"Perhaps Rosaleen is right."

"What if Mum whipped off her clothes and rolled around in the mud singing Enya songs? What then? Would that be the grief?"

Sister Ignatius smiled and her skin folded over like origami. "Has your mum done that?"

"No. But it doesn't seem far off."

"What does Arthur think?"

"Does Arthur think?" I responded, slurping the hot soup. "No, I take that back, Arthur thinks, all right. Arthur thinks but Arthur does not say. I mean, some brother he is. And he either loves Rosaleen so much, nothing she says bothers him, or he can't stand her so much, he can't stand talking to her. I really can't figure them out."

Sister Ignatius looked away, clearly uncomfortable by what I was saying.

"Sorry."

"I think you're doing Arthur an injustice. He adores Rosaleen. I think he'd do absolutely anything for her."

"Even marry her?"

She glared at me then and I felt the slap from her stare.

"Okay, okay. I'm sorry. It's just that she's so . . . I don't know . . ." I searched for the word, searched for how she made me feel. "*Possessive*."

"Possessive." Sister Ignatius pondered that. "That's an interesting choice of word."

I couldn't help but feel pleased she thought so.

"You know what it means, don't you?"

"Of course. It's as if she owns everything."

"Hmm."

"I mean, she's looking after us so well and everything. She feeds us three hundred times a day, in keeping with the dietary requirements of a dinosaur, but I wish she'd just chill out, back off from me a little and let me breathe."

"Would you like me to have a little word with her, Tamara?"

I panicked. "No, she'll know I talked to you about her. I haven't even mentioned I've met you. You're my dirty little secret," I joked.

"Well." She laughed, her cheeks pinking. "I've never been *that*." Once she'd recovered from her embarrassment she assured me she wouldn't let Rosaleen know that I'd spoken about her. We talked more about the diary, about how and why it was happening, and she assured me that I shouldn't worry, my mind was under a lot of pressure and she was sure I must have written the pages sleepily and just forgotten. I instantly felt better after our chat, though I was now concerned about my sleeping habits. If I could write a diary in my sleep, what else was I capable of? Sister Ignatius had the power to make me feel that everything obscure was normal, that everything was divine and wondrous and nothing worth stressing myself about, that answers would come and the clouds would clear and the complicated would become simple and the bizarre would become ordinary. I couldn't help but believe her.

"My, look at that weather now." She turned to gaze out the window. "The sun is back. We should go quickly and see to the bees."

Back outside in the walled garden I was suited up and feeling like the Michelin Man.

"Do you keep bees for extra time off?" I asked as we made our way with the equipment to one of the hives. "I do that at school. If you sing in the choir you sometimes get classes off to take part in competitions or perform at church, like when one of the teachers get married. If I was a teacher and I got married, I wouldn't want the snotty little bitches who give me hell all day to sing on the happiest day of my life. I'd go to St. Kitts or Mauritius. Or Amsterdam. It's legal for a sixteen-year-old to drink there. But only beer. I hate beer. But if it's legal I wouldn't say no. Not that I'd be getting married at sixteen. Is that even legal? You should know, you know your man." I jerked my head toward the sky.

"So you sing in a choir?" she asked as though she hadn't heard a word of anything else I'd said.

"Yeah, but never outside school. I've never been to compete. The first time one of those came up we were skiing in Verbier, and the second time I had laryngitis." I winked. "My mum's friend's husband is a doctor so he used to give notes whenever. I think he fancied my mum. You wouldn't catch me dead at one of those competitions, though apparently our school is actually really good. We won the All-Ireland twice."

"Oh, what kinds of things do you sing? 'Nessun Dorma' was always my favorite."

"Who's that by?"

"'Nessun Dorma.'" She looked at me, shocked. "It's one of the finest tenor arias from the final act of Puccini's opera *Turandot.*" She closed her eyes and hummed a bit of it. "Oh, I love it. Famously sung by Pavarotti, of course."

"Oh yeah, he's the big dude who sang with Bono. I always thought he was a celebrity chef, for some reason, until I saw his funeral on the news. I must have been confusing him with someone else—you know, the guy who makes pizzas with weird toppings on the Food Network. Chocolate and stuff? No, we didn't sing anything like his songs. We sang 'Shut Up and Let Me Go' by the Ting Tings. But it sounded completely different with all the harmonies, really serious, like one of those operas."

"The Food Network, now I don't have that one at all."

"Neither do Rosaleen and Arthur. You probably wouldn't like it, but there is the God Channel. There's probably stuff on that you'd like. They just talk about God all day."

Sister Ignatius smiled at me again, wrapped her arm around my shoulders, and squeezed me close to her, and we walked like that toward the garden.

"Now let's get down to bizzz-ness," she said as we reached the hives. "So, a very important first question, and I probably should have asked you this earlier: Are you allergic to bees?"

"I have no idea."

"Have you ever been stung by a bee?"

"No."

"Hmm. Okay. Well, irrespective of all the protective measures, you may receive the occasional sting."

I stared at her blankly.

"Oh, don't look at me like that, Tamara. Okay then, off you go to Rosaleen. I'm sure she's got the lovely hind legs of a cow for you to snack on while you wait for your dinner."

I was silent.

"You will not die from this sting," she continued. "Unless you're allergic, of course, but that's a risk I'm willing to take. I'm brave like that." Her eyes twinkled mischievously. "There'll be a slight swelling in the affected area, later followed by some itching."

"Like a mosquito bite."

"Exactly. Now this here is a smoker. I'm going to blow some smoke into the hive before inspecting it."

Smoke began to exit through the nozzle of the smoker. I was already feeling a little funny as everything I read from the diary early that morning was coming true, playing out before me like a script. Sister Ignatius held the nozzle under the hive.

"If a beehive is threatened, guard bees will release a volatile pheromone substance called isopentyl acetate, known as an alarm odor. This alerts the middle-aged bees in the hive, which are the ones with the most venom, to defend the hive by attacking the intruder. However, when smoke is blown in first, the guard bees instinctively gorge themselves on honey, a survival instinct in case they must vacate the hive and recreate it elsewhere. This gorging pacifies the bees."

I watched the smoke drift into the bees' home. Then suddenly I thought about the panic they must be feeling. A wave of dizziness came over me. I reached out to hold on to the wall.

"I'm going to extract the honey next week. That suit is yours if you want to join me. It'll be nice to have a bit of company. The sisters aren't interested in beekeeping. I like to be alone sometimes, but you know, it's nice to have company once in a while."

My head swirled as I imagined the smoke in the hive, the bees gorging themselves on food, the sheer and utter panic of it all. I wanted to snap at her and tell her to stop talking, that I had no interest in extracting honey with her, but I heard the tone in her voice, the excitement, the delight over company, and I remembered the wish I'd made in my diary about wanting to take back my response. I held my tongue and nodded, feeling faint. All that smoke.

"Or at least it's nice to have somebody with me who pretends they're enjoying it. I'm old. I don't care much anymore. But that's great that you've volunteered. I think Wednesday will be a good day to do it. I'll have to check the weather forecast and make sure it's a nice day. Don't want us getting soaked again like today . . ." On and on she went until I felt her staring at me. She couldn't see my face nor I hers underneath the netting of our headgear.

"What's wrong, dear?"

"Nothing."

"Nothing is never nothing. It's always something." She paused. "Is the diary still worrying you?"

"Well, yeah, of course . . . But it's not that . . . It's nothing."

We were silent for a while and then I asked, "Was there anyone in the castle when it caught on fire?"

She paused before answering. "Yes, unfortunately there was."

"Just watching that . . . that smoke going in the hive just now. I can imagine the panic and the people being so afraid." I held on to the wall again.

Sister Ignatius looked at me with concern.

"Did anyone die?" I asked.

"Yes. Yes, indeed. When the fire ravaged that home, it ravaged so many people's lives. You have no idea."

That home. Home. It made it all the more mysterious that the castle could be called such a thing. It had meant something to people once upon a time, whoever they were.

"Where do they live now? The people who survived."

"You know, Tamara, Rosaleen and Arthur have been here for so much longer than I—you should really ask them that. Ask me a question and I'll never lie, you understand? But this one you should ask them."

I shrugged, a little puzzled by her response.

"Do you understand me?" She reached out and gripped my forearm. I felt her strength through my gauntlet. "I'll never lie."

"Yes, yes, I understand."

"You'll ask them, won't you?"

I shrugged again. "Whatever."

"Whatever, whatever, the language of sloths. Now, I'm going to lift this lid off and show you the inhabitants of the honeycomb empire."

"Whoa. How did you get them all in there?"

"Ah, that was the easy part. Like all of us, Tamara, a swarm is always actively looking for a home. Now, do you know how I'm going to show you which one is the queen bee?"

"You're going to draw on it with a marker."

"However did you know that?"

"Apparently I wrote it in my diary when I was sleepwalking. Lucky guess, huh?"

"Hmm."

When I got back to the house later, it was late. I'd spent the entire day out. Arthur was returning from work too, walking down the road in his lumberjack shirt. I stopped on the path and waited for him.

"Hi, Arthur."

He threw his head back at me.

"Good day?"

"Ah."

"Good. Um, could I have a word with you before we go inside, please?"

He stopped. "Is everything all right?" Concern that I hadn't seen before crossed his face.

"Yes. Well, no. It's about Mum—"

"Well, there you are," Rosaleen called from the front door. "You both must be starved. I've the dinner just out of the oven, piping hot and ready to go."

I looked at Arthur, and he looked back at Rosaleen. There was an awkward moment as Rosaleen refused to leave us to our conversation. Arthur gave in and walked up the garden path and into the house. Rosaleen stepped aside for him to enter and then back to where she was standing to look at me, then went inside to see to the dinner. A few minutes later, once we were all seated at the table, Rosaleen prepared Mum's food on a tray to bring upstairs. I took a deep breath.

"Shouldn't we try and get Mum to eat downstairs with us?"

There was a silence. Arthur looked at Rosaleen.

"No, child. She needs her peace."

I'm not a child. I'm not a child. I'm not a child.

"She has plenty of peace all day," I said. "It would be a good idea for her to see people."

"I'm sure she'd rather have her own space."

"What makes you think that?"

Rosaleen ignored me and carried the tray upstairs. For one minute Arthur and I would be alone. As if reading my thoughts Rosaleen immediately came back to the kitchen. She looked at Arthur.

"Arthur, would you mind getting a bottle of water from the garage? Tamara doesn't like the tap."

"Oh no, I don't mind. I'd rather drink from the tap," I said quickly, stopping Arthur from getting to his feet.

"No, it's no bother. Go on, Arthur."

He stood.

"I don't want it," I said firmly.

"If she doesn't want it, Rosaleen . . ." Arthur said so quietly I could barely make out his words.

She looked from him to me and then legged it up the stairs. I had a feeling it would be her fastest trip ever.

Arthur and I sat in an initial silence. Then I spoke quickly.

"Arthur, we have to do something about Mum. It's not normal."

"None of what she's been through is normal. I'm sure she'd rather eat alone."

"What?" I threw my hands up. "What is it with you two? Why are you so obsessed with locking her away on her own?"

"Nobody wants to lock her away."

"Why don't you go talk to her?"

"Me?"

"Yes, you. You're her brother, I'm sure there's stuff that you can talk about that will bring her back to us."

He covered his mouth with his hand, looked away from me.

"Arthur, you have to talk to her. She needs her family."

"Tamara, stop it," he hissed, and I was taken aback.

He looked hurt for a moment. A deep sadness flicked through his eyes. Then, as though he'd summed up some sort of courage, he quickly looked to the door of the kitchen and then back to me. He leaned in toward me and opened his mouth, his voice hushed. "Tamara, listen—"

"Now, there we are. She's in great form." Rosaleen said, rushing back into the kitchen, out of breath.

"What?" I asked Arthur, leaning on the edge of my seat. What was he about to tell me?

Rosaleen's head turned like an antenna finding a signal.

"What's that you're talking about?"

For once it seemed Arthur's snot-snort came in handy. It was enough of a response for Rosaleen.

"Well, dig in," she said perkily, fussing about with serving spoons and bowls of vegetables.

It took Arthur a while to begin. And he didn't eat much at this meal.

That night I sat staring at the diary for hours. I kept it open on my lap, waiting for the moment the words would arrive. I couldn't even last until midnight because when I woke up at one A.M., the diary was still open on my lap, every single line filled in my hand-writing. Gone was yesterday's forecast and in its place was another entry, a different entry for tomorrow.

Sunday, 5 July
 I shouldn't have told Weseley about Dad.

I read that sentence a few more times. Who on earth was Weseley?

CHAPTER TWELVE

The Writing on the Wall

I suppose it was inevitable I would dream the dream I was supposed to dream that night.

As I lay in bed, caught in the irony of forcing myself to drift away, my mind went over and over the first diary entry I had read in the castle before it had cleared and made way for the next one. Thankfully, I had read it so many times before the words disappeared that I knew almost every line by heart. Everything that I'd read had come true that day. I wondered if tomorrow would yield the same supernatural results, if it would all somehow be revealed as somebody's cruel idea of a joke, or if Sister Ignatius was right and the late-night scribbles of a sleepwalker would reveal themselves to be mere inconsequential babble.

I had heard about things people did when they were asleep. Sleep epilepsy, weird sexual acts, eating, cleaning—even sleepwalking murder. Anyway, if all of those things were possible, then I supposed it was also possible that I could have written in my diary in my sleep and somehow predicted the future.

I believed more in the homicidal somnambulism defense.

Knowing the dream that I was going to have—well, according to the Tamara of Tomorrow—my mind tried to think of ways to change the dream, of ways to stop Dad from becoming my English teacher and to keep him around so that we could actually talk. I tried to think of a special code that he only would understand, which would somehow summon him from the dead to communicate with me. I obsessed about it all so much, I inevitably fell asleep and dreamed exactly what was written in the diary: my dad shouting at me to leave the hive we lived in as smoke entered the rooms.

You could say that the diary was right, or a more cynical mind would suggest that because I'd allowed my mind to obsess over the details of the already documented dream, I forced myself to dream the dream. But I did, as forecast, wake the next morning to the sound of Rosaleen dropping a pot on the floor with a yelp.

I threw the covers off and fell to the floor on my knees. Last night I had taken my own forecasting voice's advice by hiding the diary under the floorboard. If Tamara of Tomorrow felt it was important to do this, then I was going to follow her advice. Who knew why she—or I—was going to such great lengths to hide the diary? Maybe Rosaleen had gone snooping. The last few nights I'd taken to blocking the bedroom door with the wooden chair. She hadn't watched me sleep since the first night. As far as I knew.

I was sitting on the floor beside the bedroom door rereading last night's entry when I heard steps on the stairs. I looked through the keyhole and saw Rosaleen leading Mum back up the stairs. I almost jumped up and did a song and a dance when, after Mum's door closed, Rosaleen knocked on mine.

"Morning, Tamara, is everything all right?" she called from outside.

"Eh, yes, thank you, Rosaleen. Did something happen downstairs?"

"No, nothing. I just dropped a pot."

The doorknob began to turn.

"Em, don't come in! I'm naked!" I dived and pushed it closed.

"Oh, okay . . ." Talk of bodies, particularly naked ones, embarrassed her. "Breakfast will be ready in ten minutes."

"Fine," I said quietly, wondering why on earth she had lied. Given her near-catatonic state, Mum going downstairs was *huge*.

That's when it struck me how important each line in the diary was. Each word was a clue, a revelation, of something that was happening right under my nose. When I'd written that I'd woken to Rosaleen dropping a pot and yelping, I should have read into it more. I should have realized that she would never normally do such a thing, that something must have happened to make her drop the pot. Why would she have lied about Mum going downstairs? To protect me? To protect herself?

I settled back down on the floor, my back to the door, and read the entry I'd discovered last night once again.

Sunday, 5 July

I shouldn't have told Weseley about Dad. I hate the way he looked at me, with such pity. If he didn't like me, he didn't like me. A dad who'd committed suicide wasn't going to make me any more likable—though seemingly that was the case—but how was he to know that? It's probably really hypocritical for all this to come from me but I don't want people's opinions of me to change just because of what Dad did. I always thought I'd want the opposite, to really milk the sympathy, you know. I'd have everybody's attention.

Immediately after Dad's death there were a lot of questions since I was the one who found him, lots of cups of tea and nice pats on the back, while I blubbered over my statements to the police; and, of course, at Barbara's house where Lulu was assigned to tend to our

*every whim, which for me was hot chocolate with extra marshmal-
lows on an hourly basis. But after that first month, I haven't been
getting any special attention.*

*Anyway, Weseley totally changed when I told him Dad killed
himself. I should have said something else, like he died in a war
or—I don't know—just something more common. Would it be too
weird if I said, "By the way, about the suicide thing? I was just
joking. He really died of a heart attack. Ha ha ha."*

No. Maybe not.

Who the hell was Weseley? I looked at the date. Tomorrow,
again. So between now and tomorrow evening I'd meet a Weseley.
Absolutely impossible. Was he going to climb up the wall of Fort
Rosaleen to say hello to me?

*So after zilch sleep all I wanted to do was lie in bed all morning—
actually, all day. This wasn't going to happen. The talking Rosaleen clock rapped on my door once before entering to tell me they
were off to Mass and the market. I mumbled something about not
being a Mass person and waited for a bucket of holy water to come
pouring down on me but there was no reaction of the sort. She gave
my room a quick look to make sure I hadn't spread feces all over the
walls and then said it was fine if I stayed home and kept an eye on
Mum. Hallelujah.*

*I drifted off again but awoke to the sound of a car horn. I ig-
nored it and tried to go back to sleep again but it honked louder
and longer. I scrambled out of bed and pushed open the window,
ready to shout abuse but instead started laughing when I saw Sister
Ignatius squashed into a yellow Fiat Cinquecento with three other
nuns. She was in the backseat, the window was rolled down, and
half her body was through the gap as though she'd suddenly spurted*

toward the sun. Her mission was to try to get me to go to Mass with her but her efforts were in vain. Eventually one of the other sisters pulled her back into the car and it immediately took off, not slowing or even signaling as they rounded the corner. All I could hear was Sister Ignatius shouting thanks for the booook, as they disappeared.

Book? I'm supposed to give her a book? What book?

I checked on Mum, nibbled at some fruit in the kitchen, and wandered around the house, picking up things, and studying the few photographs dotted around the living room. Arthur with a giant fish, a laughing Rosaleen wearing pastels and holding on to her hat on a windy day. Rosaleen and Arthur together, always side by side, but never touching. I read a little more of the book Fiona gave me. At one o'clock on the button, when Arthur and Rosaleen's car returned to the house, a sense of heaviness came over me. My space was gone, rooms would be shared again, weird games would be played, mysteries would continue.

What on earth had I been thinking?

I should have explored. I should have broken into the shed and seen how much space they really had. I think Rosaleen is lying about that. I should have called a doctor and had Mum looked at. I should have investigated across the road, or at least peeked in the back garden. I should have done lots of things, but instead I had sat in the house and moped. And it would be another week until I'd have that time again.

What a wasted day.

I'll write again tomorrow.

I put the diary back into the floor and replaced the board. I took a fresh towel from the cupboard and my good shampoo, which was almost empty and irreplaceable due both to convenience and, for the first time in my life, cost. I was about to get into the shower when I remembered yesterday's entry mentioning Rosaleen pretending the doorbell didn't ring while my head was under a towel and I was facedown in boiling water. It would be the perfect opportunity to test the diary. My heart drummed in my chest as I kept the shower running and waited on the landing. I wasn't sure if I wanted the diary to be right or wrong. While what had happened yesterday could have been just luck, a second confirmation would mean something more serious. But *what* would it mean, exactly? What was the purpose of all this? What if the diary was right again?

The doorbell rang and that simple sound spooked me.

"Sister, morning to you," Rosaleen said, her voice hushed.

I peeked around the corner and saw Rosaleen's back and backside only. Today's tea dress was sponsored by Fyffes, with clumps of bananas decorating it. The front of her was squeezed out of the small slit she'd made in the opened door, almost as if she didn't want Sister Ignatius to see past her. And had it not started to rain at that very moment I don't think Sister would have made her way into the house. They both stood in the hallway then, and Sister Ignatius looked around. I caught her eye from where I was hiding.

"Come in, come into the kitchen," Rosaleen said with urgency, as though the hallway ceiling was about to cave in.

"No, I can't stay." Sister Ignatius remained where she was. "I just wanted to come over and see how you are. I haven't seen sight nor heard from you for the past few weeks."

"Oh, yes, well, I'm sorry about that. Arthur's been terribly busy working on the lake and I've been . . . keeping things together here. You'll come to the kitchen, won't you?" She kept her voice down as though a baby was sleeping in the house.

Why wouldn't she mention us?

Then I heard a chair drag across the floor in Mum's bedroom.

Sister Ignatius looked up. "What's that?"

"Nothing. Come to the kitchen, come, come and tell me about honey season—it must be coming up."

She tried to take Sister Ignatius by the arm and lead her away from the hallway.

"Yes, I'll be extracting the honey on Wednesday if the weather holds up."

"Please God, it does."

"How many jars would you like me to drop by?"

Then something dropped in Mum's room.

Sister Ignatius stopped walking, but Rosaleen pulled her along and kept talking, boring small talk. Natter natter natter. So-and-so died. So-and-so was taken ill. Mavis from the town was hit by a car in Dublin after being out to buy a top for her nephew John's thirtieth. She died. She bought the top and all. Very sad, as her brother had died the previous year of bowel cancer, now there's no one left in the family. Her father is alone and had to move to a nursing home. He's taken ill over the past few weeks. Eyesight is in great decline and didn't he used to be an excellent darts player. And the thirtieth party was a very sad one as they were all devastated about Mavis. Blather blather blather about crap. Not once were Mum and I discussed. The elephant in the room again.

A few minutes later, after Sister Ignatius had left, Rosaleen momentarily leaned her forehead against the front door and sighed. Then she straightened up and twirled around to look up on the landing. I moved quickly. When I ducked my head around the corner I saw that Rosaleen's bedroom door was ajar. A shadow flickered by.

I couldn't stand to sit with Rosaleen and Arthur for breakfast. I'd have rather been anywhere but in that kitchen with the smell of frying food making me feel sick. But of course I knew what I'd do next. I'd read it in the diary. I went to Mum's room.

"Mum, come outside with me, please." I picked up her hand and gently tried to tug her up.

She was still as a rock.

"Mum, please. Come out to the fresh air. We can walk around the trees and the lakes, we can see the swans. I bet you've never even walked around these grounds before. Come on. There's a beautiful castle and lots of lovely walks. There's even a walled garden."

She looked right at me then. I could see her pupils dilate as she focused on me. She said, "Secret garden," and she smiled.

"Yes, Mum. Have you been there?"

"Roses."

"Yes, there's lots of roses."

"Mmm. Pretty," she said softly, then, as though she'd suddenly become from the North of England and dropped a few words, she said, "Prettier than rose." She said this while looking out the window, and then she looked at me and used her forefinger to trace the outline of my face. "Prettier than rose."

I smiled. "Thanks, Mum."

"She's walked around here before, hasn't she?" I exploded into the kitchen, full of energy, which startled Rosaleen.

She raised her finger to her lips. Arthur was on the phone, an old-fashioned thing that was stuck to the wall.

"Rosaleen," I whispered, "Mum talked."

She stopped rolling out dough and turned to me. "What did she say?"

"She said that the walled garden was a secret garden and that I was as pretty as a rose." I beamed. "Or prettier, actually."

Rosaleen's face hardened. "That's nice, dear."

"That's nice? That's fucking nice?" I exploded.

Rosaleen and Arthur both shushed me.

"Yes. That's Tamara," Arthur said.

"Who's on the phone?"

"Barbara," Rosaleen said, strands coming loose around the front of her pinned-back hair. She was really starting to sweat as she now put some elbow grease into rolling the dough.

"Can I talk to her?" I asked.

He nodded. "All right. All right. We'll come to some sort of arrangement. Yes. All right. Indeed. All right. Bye."

He hung up.

"I said I wanted to talk to her."

"Oh, well, she said she had to go."

"She's probably off to sleep with the pool boy. Busy, busy," I said cattily, unable to stop myself. "So what did she call about?"

Arthur looked at Rosaleen, instead of me. "Well, unfortunately they're having to sell the place where all your things are being stored, and so they can't keep them anymore."

"Well, there's no space here," Rosaleen said immediately, turning back to the counter and tossing flour on the worktop.

This conversation was familiar to me. I swallowed again, the diary proving itself once again.

"What about the garage?" I asked, knowing the answer already.

"There's no space."

"We'll find space," Arthur said to me.

"We won't because there is none." Rosaleen picked up the next dough ball and threw it down on the counter and started pushing her hands into it, squeezing it, punching it, making it into some sort of shape.

"There's room in the garage," Arthur said firmly.

Rosaleen stalled but didn't turn around. "There's not."

I looked from one to the other, initially intrigued by this—for once—public disagreement.

"Why, what's in there?" I asked.

Rosaleen kept rolling.

"We'll have to make room, Rosaleen," Arthur was saying, really firmly now, and just as she was about to interject he raised his voice: "There's nowhere else."

That was final.

I had a horrible feeling then that the conversation about me and Mum moving in with them wouldn't have gone too differently.

Rosaleen and Arthur didn't object when I brought the blanket outside to the garden with a plate of fruit and sat under the tree. The sun shower had left the grass wet but I wasn't planning on moving. The air was fresh and the sun was fighting its way back out again. From my place on the grass I could see Mum sitting at the window gazing outside. I willed her to come out, for the sake of my own sanity as well as hers. Not surprisingly, she didn't join me.

From where I was sitting I saw that Rosaleen still busied herself about the kitchen. Arthur was sitting at the table flipping through the paper. I watched Rosaleen leave the kitchen with the tray and a minute later she appeared in Mum's bedroom window. I watched her do her usual fussing about. Window, table, linen, cutlery.

Then I saw Rosaleen stand up straight and look at Mum. I sat up. It was unusual, whatever she was doing. Then her mouth opened and closed, clearly saying something.

Mum looked up at her, said something in response, then looked away. My heart thudded as I read her lips.

I stood up automatically, watching them both.

Then I ran inside, almost knocking Arthur over at the kitchen table, and charged up the stairs. I pushed open Mum's door and I heard a yelp and a smash as it smacked against Rosaleen and her tray. Everything dropped to the floor.

"Oh my!" Rosaleen hunkered down and grabbed everything in a panic. Her dress lifted up her thigh, and I saw that she had surprisingly youthful legs. Mum had twisted around in her chair to see, looked at me, smiled, and then faced the window again. I tried to help Rosaleen but she wouldn't let me, swatting me away and racing to pick up every item before I did. When she was done I followed her down the stairs like a puppy, nipping at her heels.

"What did she say?" I tried to keep my voice down so Mum wouldn't hear us talking about her.

Rosaleen, still in shock from my attack, was trembling and looking a little pale. She wobbled her way into the kitchen with the big tray.

"Well?" I asked, following her.

"Well, what?"

"What was that noise?" Arthur asked.

"What did she say?" I asked again.

Rosaleen looked from Arthur to me, her eyes wide and bright green, her pupils so tiny her green eyes glowed.

"The tray dropped," she said to Arthur, and then to me, "Nothing."

"Why are you lying?"

At that her face transformed. Morphed into something so angry, I wanted to take it all back right away: It was my imagination, I had made it up, I was looking for attention . . . I don't know. I was confused.

"I'm sorry," I stuttered. "I didn't mean to accuse you of lying. It just looked like Mum said something. That's all."

"She said thank you. I said she was welcome."

I forced myself to remember Mum's lips. "She said sorry," I blurted out.

Rosaleen froze. Arthur lifted his head from the newspaper.

"She said sorry, didn't she?" I asked, looking from one to the other. "Why did she say that?"

"I suppose she just feels she's being a nuisance," Rosaleen jumped in. "But she's not. I don't mind cooking for her. It's no bother."

"Oh," I said, realizing this was going nowhere.

Arthur clearly couldn't wait to leave, and as soon as he'd gone, the day returned to what it always was.

I still wanted to have a look around the garage when Rosaleen was gone. By now I learned the best thing to do was to pretend you didn't want her to go. That way, she was never suspicious.

"Can I bring something over with you to the bungalow?"

"No," she said, still clearly annoyed with me. "No, but thank you very much for offering, Tamara."

I rolled my eyes.

From the oven she took out the freshly baked brown bread and a fresh apple pie. A casserole dish of something else and a few Tupperware boxes. Enough for a week's dinner.

"So, who lives there, anyway?"

No answer.

"Come on, Rosaleen. I don't know what happened to you in your last life but I'm not the Gestapo. I'm sixteen years old and I only want to know because there's absolutely nothing for me to do here. Perhaps there's somebody over there who I could talk to that's not nearing death."

"My mother," she said finally.

I waited for the rest of the sentence. *My mother told me to mind my own business. My mother told me to always wear tea dresses. My mother told me never to reveal her apple pie recipe.* But nothing else came. Her mother. Her mother lived across the road.

"Why have you never mentioned it?"

She looked a little embarrassed. "Oh, you know . . ."

"No, I don't. Is she embarrassing or something?"

"No, she's . . . she's old."

"Old people are cute. Can I meet her?"

"No, Tamara. Not yet, anyway," she softened. "Her health isn't the best. She can't move around. She's not good with new people. It makes her anxious."

"So that's why you're always back and forth. Poor you always having to look after everybody else."

She seemed touched by that. "I'm all she has. I have to take care of her."

"Are you sure I can't help you? I won't talk to her or anything."

"No, thank you, Tamara. Thank you for asking."

"So did she move closer to you so you could take care of her?"

"No." She spooned chicken and tomato sauce into a casserole dish.

"Did you move closer to her so that you could take care of her?"

"No." She put two boil-in-the-bag rice sachets into another Tupperware box. "She's always lived there."

I thought about that for a minute while watching her.

"Hold on, so the bungalow's where you grew up?"

"Yes," she said simply, placing everything on a tray. "That's the house I grew up in."

"So, you didn't move far away, did you? Did you and Arthur move in here right after you were married?"

"Yes, Tamara. Now that's enough questions. You know curiosity killed the cat." She smiled briefly before leaving the kitchen.

"Boredom killed the fucking cat," I shouted at the closed door.

I sloped into the living room as I had done every morning and watched her scurry across the road like a little paranoid hamster anxious that a hawk was going to swoop down and grab her.

I saw her drop a dish towel and I waited for her to stop and pick it up. But she didn't. She didn't appear to notice. I quickly went outside and down the garden path, stalling at the gate like an obedient child as I waited for her to catch me and come running back out.

I bravely stepped beyond the gate. Once I'd done that, I walked to the entrance of the grounds, expecting by now for Rosaleen to have noticed the missing dish towel. Red alert; there was an apple pie somewhere emitting heat. The bungalow up ahead was a red-brick boring-looking thing, two windows covered in white netting, like two eyes with glaucoma, and separated by a snot-green door. The windows seemed dark and even though they weren't, the glass seemed tinted and only reflected the light from outside, showing no signs of life inside. I picked up the blue-checkered dish towel from the middle of the road, which was mostly always—mostly always, very dead—empty of traffic. The gate to the front garden was so low I could lift my leg over it. I thought it would be the safest way, since fifty years of rusted gate would probably give me away. I slowly walked up the path and looked through the window on the right of the building. I pressed my face up against the glass and tried to see through the horrific netting. After all the mystery I don't quite know what I was expecting to see. Some great secret, a crazy sect, dead bodies, a hippie commune, some weird sex thing . . . I don't know. Anything but an electric heater in place of a real fire surrounded by dodgy brown tiles and tiled mantel, green carpet, and jaded chairs with wooden handles and green crushed-velvet cushions. It was all a bit sad, really. It was like a dentist's waiting room, and I suddenly felt bad. Rosaleen hadn't been hiding anything at all. Well, other than the biggest home design disaster of the century.

I walked around the side of the house. Immediately as I turned the corner I could see that there was a small garden with a large garage, just like the one at the back of the gatehouse at the bottom of the land. From the window of the work shed something sparkled. At first I thought it was a camera flash, but then I realized that whatever had dazzled my eyes and momentarily blinded me only did so each time it caught the sunlight. As I neared the end of the side passage I yearned to see what was around the corner.

Suddenly Rosaleen stepped in front of me and I jumped, my scream echoing down the narrow alleyway. Then I laughed.

Rosaleen instantly shushed me, seeming more jittery than usual.

"Sorry." I smiled. "I hope I didn't scare your mum. You dropped this towel on the road. I just came to give it to you." Then I pointed. "What is that light?"

"What light?" She stepped a little to her right, blocking my view. "You best go back to the house," she whispered.

"Oh, come on, can I not at least say hello? This is all a bit too Scooby Doo for me."

"There's no mystery. I told you my mother isn't good in the company of strangers. Perhaps we'll have her over for dinner someday if she's up to it."

"Cool." Another over-fifty to add to my list of acquaintances.

Just then I heard a vehicle coming down the road, and, hoping it was Marcus, I saluted Rosaleen, turned around, and ran back to the house.

If it hadn't been Marcus, then that five seconds of hope still would have been the most exciting thing that had happened that day. But it turned out it was him. He was standing at the porch of the gatehouse by the time I ran across the road, running his hand through his hair and glancing at his reflection in the glass of the door.

"There's a hair out of place just over your ear," I called from the gate.

He spun around with a smile. "Goodwin. Good to see you."

"Have you come for the book?"

He smiled. "Eh, yeah, the book, of course. Couldn't stop thinking about . . . that damn book."

"Actually, there's a problem with the book."

"You lost it."

"No, I didn't lose it . . ."

"Don't believe you. Do you know what the punishment for losing library books is?"

"Spend a day with you?"

"No, Goodwin. If you do the crime you have to do the time. I'll have to revoke your traveling library card."

"Nooo, anything but my traveling library card."

"Yes. Come on, give it to me." He came close and started poking and prodding my body. "Where is it? Is it in here?" His hands were everywhere, in my jeans pockets, padding down my stomach.

"I refuse to give it up." I laughed. "Seriously, Marcus, I haven't lost the book but you can't have it back."

"I don't think you understand the rules of the traveling library. You see, you borrow a book, you read it, or dance around with it if that makes you happy, and then you return it to the handsome librarian."

"No, what happened was that somebody broke the lock and discovered that it wasn't a book, but in fact a diary. All the pages were totally blank."

Totally blank. Very dead.

"Then somebody wrote in it," I continued.

"Ah . . . *somebody*. That wouldn't happen to be you?"

"Actually, no. I don't know who wrote in it." I smiled to hide that

I was being serious. "It's just the first few pages. I could rip them out and give you back the book but . . ."

"You could just say you lost it. It would be easier."

"Stay there a minute."

I ran into the house and upstairs to my room, lifted the floorboard, and took the diary out. I brought it outside, hugging it close to my chest.

"You can't read it but here's proof that I haven't lost it. I'll pay or do whatever . . . I just can't give it back."

He realized I was serious.

"No, that's fine. One book isn't going to make a difference. Can I read it? Is there anything in there about me?"

I laughed and lifted it out of his reach. But he was too good for me, much taller, and he was able to grab it. I panicked. He opened the first page and I waited for him to read the embarrassing admittance that Dad had killed himself.

"'I shouldn't have told Weseley about Dad,'" he read. "Who's Weseley?" he asked, looking at me.

"I have no idea." I tried to grab the book from him, no longer laughing. "Give it back, Marcus."

He handed it back. "Okay, okay. By the way, you got the date wrong. The fifth is tomorrow."

I just shook my head. At least it wasn't just me imagining it. This diary thing was really happening. I shuddered and closed the book. I wanted so much to read it again. Then I remembered something from yesterday's entry.

"Oh, by the way, I found Sister Ignatius!"

"Alive, I hope."

"She lives on the other side of the grounds. I'll direct you."

"No, Goodwin, I don't trust you. The last residence you led me to was a dilapidated castle."

"I'll bring you to her myself. Come on, Bookman, to the Book-mobile!" I ran down the path and hopped on the bus. I had a book to deliver.

He laughed and followed me.

We soon pulled up outside the sisters' house and I pressed down on the horn.

"Tamara, you can't do that. It's a convent."

"Don't worry, this isn't a regular convent." I sounded the horn again.

A woman dressed in a black jumper and a black-and-white veil opened the door, looking very cross. She was older than Sister Ignatius. I jumped out of the car.

"What's all this racket?"

"We're looking for Sister Ignatius. She wanted to borrow a book."

"It's prayer time, she can't be disrupted."

"Oh. Well, hold on a minute." I rummaged around in the back of the bus. "Could you please give her this and tell her it's from Tamara. It's a special delivery. She ordered it last week."

"I will indeed." The nun took the book and closed the door immediately.

"Tamara," Marcus said sternly. "What book did you give her?"

"*Bedded by the Turkish Billionaire*. One of Mills and Boon's greats."

"Tamara! You'll get me fired."

"Like you care! Drive, Bookman! Take me away from here!"

We drove to the town and pulled over. But really we went to Morocco. He even kissed me by the Giza Pyramids.

"So what have you been doing the last few days?" Rosaleen asked happily, spooning three thousand calories onto my plate. The diary had been correct, shepherd's pie.

She'd grabbed me for dinner almost as soon as I'd got home. I'd had just enough time to hide the diary upstairs and come back down. I didn't want to mention I'd spent the day with Marcus in case she tried to stop me. But she couldn't complain about my hanging around with a nun, now could she? Remembering how the diary had stated she'd become unnerved when I mentioned Sister Ignatius, I decided to test the diary again.

"I've been spending most of my time with Sister Ignatius." Rosaleen dropped the serving spoons into the bowl and then, with awkward fidgeting fingers, she scooped them out.

"Sister Ignatius?" she asked.

"Yes."

"But . . . when did you meet her?"

"A few days ago. So how was your mum today? Is she coming over for dinner soon?"

"You never mentioned meeting Sister Ignatius a few days ago."

I just looked at Rosaleen. Her reaction was identical to the one I'd written about in the diary. Was I supposed to say sorry? Was I supposed to have tried to prevent this? I didn't know what to do, how to manage the information I was being given. What was the point of it?

Instead I said, "I never mentioned I got my period on Tuesday either but I did."

Arthur sighed. Rosaleen's face hardened.

"A few days ago you met her, you say? Are you sure?"

"Of course I'm sure."

"Maybe you just met her today."

"No."

"And does she know where you live?"

"Yes, of course. She knows I'm here."

"I see," she said breathlessly. "But . . . but she was here this morning. She never said anything about you."

"Really? And what did you say to her about me?"

Sometimes your tone can change things, I know that. Sometimes in text messages, people don't pick up tones, or they pick up tones that aren't there and completely misinterpret innocent messages. I've had countless arguments with Zoey over what she thought I meant by a five-word text. But this statement I made, it came with a tone, a deliberate one. And Rosaleen picked up on it. And being clever, she then knew that I must have heard her conversation with Sister Ignatius that morning. "Is there a problem with my friendship with her? Do you think she's a bad influence? Am I going to join some weird religious sect and dress in black every day? Oh no, hold on, maybe I will! She's a nun!" I laughed and looked at Arthur, who was now glaring at Rosaleen.

"What do you talk about?" Rosaleen asked.

I detected panic in her voice.

"Does it matter what we talk about?"

"I mean, you're a young girl. What would you have to talk about with a nun?" She smiled to hide her nervousness.

That was the point where I was going to talk about the castle, the fire, and the fact it had been lived in far more recently than I'd thought. I was going to ask Rosaleen the question about who died and where everybody was when I suddenly remembered the diary entry. *I wish I hadn't told her what I'd learned from Sister Ignatius about the castle.* Was this what I shouldn't have mentioned? Rosaleen was staring at me in the time it took me to think of an answer. I took a forkful of minced meat, to give myself some more thinking time.

"You know . . . we talked about a lot of different kinds of stuff . . ."

"*What* kinds of things?"

"Rosaleen," Arthur said quietly.

Her head snapped around to face him, like a deer who'd heard a trigger pulled back in the distance.

"Your dinner will get cold." He looked at her plate, which remained untouched.

"Oh. Yes." She picked up her fork and stabbed a carrot, but didn't lift it to her mouth. "Carry on, child. You were saying."

"Rosaleen." I sighed.

"Let her eat her dinner," Arthur said.

I looked to Arthur to thank him but he didn't look up, just continued shoveling food in his mouth. There was an awkward silence as we ate, and the sounds of munching and scraping cutlery took over the room.

"Excuse me, please. I'm just going to the bathroom," I finally said, leaving the room, unable to bear it anymore.

Only I stayed outside the kitchen door to eavesdrop.

"What was that all about?" Arthur barked.

"Ssh, keep your voice down."

"I'll not keep my voice down," he hissed back, but he lowered his voice.

"Sister Ignatius called here this morning and said nothing of Tamara," she hissed back.

"So?"

"So she acted as if she knew nothing about her. If Tamara had met her, surely she'd have said. Sister Ignatius isn't the kind to not say so. Why wouldn't she?"

"So what are you suggesting? That Tamara's lying?"

My mouth dropped and I almost barged back in there, except the next sentence from Rosaleen's lips, spoken with such bitterness, stopped me.

"Of course she's lying. She's just like her mother."

There was a long silence. Arthur said nothing.

CHAPTER THIRTEEN

Bouncing Castle

I lay in bed trying to block out Rosaleen's words. There was a history here I knew nothing of, that was certain, but it was also clear that there was nothing I could do about it. Yesterday was a closed book; tomorrow, however, was another story. I reread the entry for tomorrow over and over again, firing myself up. There was much to plan for. I lay in bed running through all the things I should do in my limited time tomorrow, before Rosaleen and Arthur returned to the house at one o'clock on the button. It was a humid July night, so it was either going to be a stormy night tonight or a scorcher tomorrow. I kicked off my covers and opened my bedroom window, hoping for some air. I lay in the blue light of the moon, watching the oily sky glisten with stars. I heard owls hoot, the occasional sheep and cow call for attention; the sounds of the country night that I'd grown used to drifted into my room. Now and then there was a welcome light breeze, and each time I heard the leaves on the trees gently rustle, they too thankful for the cool air. Eventually I became a little chilly and reached to close the window when I realized the sounds that I'd thought were birds chirping were actually voices in the distance. In the country who knew how far such sounds could carry, but as I listened out for them again, I heard the distinct rise and fall of conversation and sudden laughter, perhaps music and then silence again as the breeze stopped carrying their noise. It was coming from the direction of the castle.

It was eleven-thirty P.M. I threw on a tracksuit and sneakers, the floor creaking beneath my feet as I moved around as quickly as possible in my room. With each creak I froze, expecting the sleeping giant to awaken at any moment. I moved the chair away from the bedroom door and gently opened it. It would be a feat to get downstairs and out the front door without alerting the mistress of the house. I heard Rosaleen cough and I stalled, then immediately closed my door again. I'd never heard her cough at night before, so I took it as a warning.

I climbed on the bed to avoid walking on the creaky floorboards and crawled along the mattress to reach the window. It was an old springy mattress and it squeaked, but at least it sounded as though I was merely turning over. I took the flashlight from the bedside table and pushed the window open further. Sizewise, I could fit through it without a problem. My bedroom was directly over the front porch. Though the roof was pointed, I could, with great concentration, land on it. From there it would be a relatively easy climb down the wooden fencing on the porch and straight to the ground. Easy.

Suddenly Rosaleen and Arthur's bedroom door opened and there were quick footsteps down the corridor. I dived back into the bed and covered myself from head to toe with the duvet, making sure my tracksuit and sneakers, and the flashlight, weren't visible. I scrunched my eyes shut just as my bedroom door opened. The window was wide open and to my trained ear the voices from afar seemed so loud I was sure my intentions would be obvious.

My heart thudded loudly in my chest as the person was suddenly in my room. The floorboards creaked, one by one, as the figure came closer to me. It was Rosaleen. I knew by the way she held her breath, by the scent. The creaking stopped, which meant she was standing still. Watching. Watching *me*.

I fought hard not to open my eyes. I tried to relax my lids, and not allow my eyeballs to roll around too much. I tried to breathe normally, a little louder than usual to show my deep slumber. I felt Rosaleen hover over me and I almost jumped up to attack, but I heard the window close and realized she was leaning over me to reach it. I contemplated opening my eyes, catching her out, making a drama. But what could I gain from this?

"Rosaleen." I heard a hiss from my bedroom door. "What are you doing?"

"I'm just making sure she's all right."

"Of course she's okay. She's not a baby anymore. Come back to bed."

I felt a hand on my cheek, then fingers gently pushing my hair back to behind my ear just like my mother used to do. I waited for the duvet to be pulled off me and for my midnight prowl costume to be revealed, but instead I felt her breath on my face, felt her lips brush against my forehead in a gentle kiss, and then she was gone. The door closed.

She's not a baby anymore.

After she left I waited until Arthur's snores began again. Then I got out of bed, pushed the window open, and didn't think twice before climbing out and landing gently on the slate archway of the porch. It was only when I landed on the grass and looked up at the house, at my bedroom, at the closed window, that I understood the meaning behind my message to myself to leave the window open. Using the flashlight I made my way toward the castle, following the voices. I could see only a few feet ahead of me; the rest of the world had been swallowed up by the black hole of night. The trees seemed to hold even more secrets at night-time, and in the darkness their "ssh" sound to one another led me to believe there was more they weren't telling me. As I got closer to the castle and the voices, I smelled smoke, and heard music, heard the clink of glasses or bottles. I could see light coming from the castle's entrance hall and the room with the intact windows to the right. The rest of the rooms to the left and to the back were black. I turned off the flashlight and made my way around the back of the castle, passing two rooms that I'm sure had a grand view of the lake behind and the hundreds of steps that led down to it. I reached the window room I'd climbed out of the day before, and I listened.

A night light made up of stars circled the old wall. Yellow stars moved around and I leaned in to watch them. Then I heard the distinct slurping sound of kissing. Which was quickly followed by a scream.

There was lots of running, lots of shushing, lots of cans and bottles being knocked over. Lots of whispering. Then I felt a hand pull at my hair and grab me by the scruff of my neck and I was literally dragged all the way to the castle.

"Hey, let go." I kicked. "Get your fucking hands off me."

I swatted at the hands around my waist which were definitely male as I was half lifted and half dragged. I thanked Rosaleen for her carbohydrate-rich diet then and the extra few pounds I'd put on since arriving, or else I'd have been easily thrown over his shoulder. Once inside and placed fully on the ground, he kept his arm around my waist and remained behind me. I turned around a few times to see an ugly-looking thing with fluff on his chin. Then I realized six people were staring at me. Some were sitting on the stairs, others on crates on the floor. I felt like shouting at them to get out of my house.

"She was watching us," the screamer said, arriving at the doorway, panting as though about to faint from the ordeal.

"I wasn't watching." I rolled my eyes. "That's totally gross."

"She's an American," one guy said.

"I'm not American."

"You sound American," another one said.

"Hey, it's Hannah Montana."

Lots of laughs.

"I'm from Dublin."

"No, she's not."

"Yes, I am."

"You're a long way from Dublin."

"I'm just here for the summer."

"On vacation," someone said, and they all laughed again.

A guy appeared at the doorway behind the squealer. He listened for a while as I tried to defend myself with a screechy embarrassing voice that I just couldn't seem to control, and I wondered how on earth I had ended up being the uncool person in this room full of hicks.

"Gary, let go of her," the latest arrival finally said.

Fluffy Chin let go immediately. I'd identified the leader.

Once released, I gathered myself. "Can I take any more questions from the room? Perhaps you sir, in the fleece jacket and Doc Martens, would you like to ask a question about the days when Guns N' Roses were cool?"

Someone smirked, was elbowed, then cried out in pain. Fluffy Chin, still behind me, dug me in the back, which really hurt.

"I just heard you all from my room. You were loud. I was in bed." I realized I sounded like the most annoying person on the planet, like a child who'd interrupted her parents' dinner party.

"You live nearby?"

"She's lying."

"Well, where the hell do you think I live? I just flew over from L.A. for a midnight stroll?"

"Are you staying in the gatehouse?"

"The *royal* gatehouse," somebody else said, and they all started laughing again.

Okay, so it was far from being Buckingham Palace, but it was a lot better than the other shithole barn houses I saw as we drove over here. I looked from one face to the other, trying to decide my answer. How stupid would it be of me to tell them where I was staying?

"Oh no, I just live in a cowshed and sleep with the pigs just like the rest of you," I snapped back. "I don't know what your big problem is. It's not as if he looks like he's from around here either."

I was referring to the dark-skinned leader of the gang, who was still standing at the doorway, just staring at me. Go for the leader in hostage situations, take them all out. I knew it wasn't the cleverest idea.

They all looked at each other with wide eyes and I could hear "racist" being murmured over and over.

"That's not racist." I rolled my eyes. "He's wearing Dsquared. Last time I checked hicksville, population nil, it didn't stock Dsquared."

Really, I wasn't being very clever. I've seen *Deliverance*; I know what they can make you do, and I'd already accused them of sleeping with pigs, which wasn't a great beginning to what probably should have been an apology. I saw their leader's teeth flash as he smiled briefly and then he covered his mouth with his hand as the rest of the gang went into overdrive, squaring up to me with pointed fingers and calling me a racist over and over again. Then the leader called them all to stop, tried to reason with the squealer and a few drunken others, and then eventually grabbed me and pulled me outside and around the back of the castle, back to the scene of the crime; the window where I'd supposedly spied.

"Is this where you pretend to kill me but really let me loose?" I asked, a little nervously. Okay, a lot nervously. It crossed my mind that he was going to beat me up.

He smiled. "You're Tamara, aren't you?"

My mouth dropped open. "How did you . . ." And then the penny dropped. "You're Weseley."

It was his turn to look surprised. "Arthur told you about me?"

"Arthur? Eh, yeah, of course he did. He talks about you all the time."

"He told me about you too."

"He did?" It was my turn to look confused. I didn't think Arthur would speak of me at all. I couldn't even imagine what he'd say.

"Smoke?"

I took one of his cigarettes and he struck up a match. When he lit it I could see his face properly. His skin was a milky chocolate, not ebony, but beautifully dark. His eyes were big and brown, his eyelashes so long, I was momentarily jealous as in my previous life I spent a lot of my pocket money on false ones with glitter. His teeth were perfectly straight and white, with a nice jaw, perfect cheek-bones. He was incredibly good-looking. He was taller than me, a head taller. The match burned down to his finger and he dropped it. I realized then he must have been looking at me too. He lit it again and I inhaled. It had been too long since I had one of these.

"Thanks."

"No problem."

"What the hell are you doing, Wes?" The squealer appeared around the corner, another girl in her wake. "Oh, now you're having a smoke with her? She's related to that freak family, I hope you

159

know." They wobbled their way unevenly to us, filling the air with the fruity scent of a Body Shop gift basket.

"Calm down, Kate," he said.

"No, I will not fucking calm down . . ." She went on a tirade of drunken nonsense and then started to hit him over and over again with her purse. Her friend pulled her away.

"Fine." She shook her friend off, then grabbed her friend's arm before she fell, almost bringing her down with her.

"Ouch," I said, watching her struggle to get up.

"It didn't hurt," she insisted.

"A fake Louis Vuitton—are you joking? I felt the pain just looking at it."

"You're a snob," Weseley said to me, chuckling.

"You're a bad boyfriend."

"She's not my girlfriend."

"Whatever."

"You want a drink?"

I nodded way too enthusiastically. He laughed again, then disappeared headfirst through the window, back into the castle. I followed him in.

"Hey Weseley, you're not giving Hannah Montana our cans, are you?" one of his friends called out.

Weseley ignored the comment and handed me a can.

"What is this?" I asked.

"Diamond White."

"Never heard of it."

"How can I explain this so that you'd understand?" He thought hard. "Think of it as champagne, but made with apples."

I rolled my eyes. "If you think I drink champagne then you don't know me at all."

"Well, I don't, do I? It's cider. Americans call it hard cider."

"I'm not American."

"You don't sound Irish."

"And you don't look Irish. Maybe Irish as the world knows it has changed." I gasped sarcastically. "Oh my God, who should we tell?"

"My mam has red hair and freckles."

"So she must be Swedish."

He pointed at a crate behind me and I sat down. He sat opposite me.

"Where's your dad from?"

"Madagascar."

"Cool, like in the movie?"

"Yep, *exactly* like the animation," he said heavily.

"You ever go there?"

"No."

"How come he moved here?"

"Because."

"Ah." I nodded understandingly. "Always a good reason."

We both laughed.

Someone in the next room said something about me being a racist again.

"I only meant your clothes," I said quietly. "You're dressed better than John Boy in there, and Mary Ellen, who walked off in her fake Uggs in a puff of Dewberry."

He exhaled loudly, his eyes steady on mine. "She's not my girlfriend."

"So you said. But that's not what my super spy glasses told me."

"Yeah, well, that was just . . ." He stomped out his cigarette and then put the butt in a jar. I was thankful for that. I felt protective of the castle and didn't want these kids trashing it. "There are buses, you know," he said. "Things with wheels that carry people to the big smoke."

"From where?"

"Dunshaughlin. It's less than thirty minutes in the car. My dad drives me."

Well, mine is dead.

"By the way, is this yours?" He rooted around in a bag on the ground and handed me a pen. It was the one I'd stolen from Arthur's writing desk and had dropped yesterday.

I had a feeling someone was there. Someone was watching me.

"Were you here yesterday?" I asked.

"Em . . ." He thought hard.

"You shouldn't have to think about it," I snapped.

"I don't know. No. Yes. No, I don't know if I was. I found the pen tonight, if that's what you mean."

"You weren't here yesterday, when I was here?"

"I'm here most days with Arthur." He still didn't answer the question.

"You are?"

"Well, I have to be, don't I?"

"You do?"

"I work with the man."

"Oh."

"I thought you said Arthur told you."

"Oh . . . yeah. So does Rosaleen know you work with Arthur?"

He nodded. "I don't think she likes me being around, but since Arthur put his back out he needs a hand around here."

"How long have you worked with him?"

He thought hard and stared into the distance, "Ooh let's see. Me and Arthur go back about . . . three weeks now."

I started laughing.

"We only moved here last month," he explained.

"Really?" I felt my heart lift. He was one of my kind. "From where?"

"Dublin."

"Me too!" I knew my excitement was too much *Famous Five*. "Sorry," I felt my face flush. "Just a little overexcited to meet a member of the same species. So how did you rise to be leader so quickly? Did you cast a spell? Show them how to make fire?"

"I find that politeness goes a long way. Spying, party crashing, and insults is a bit of a no-no when you're trying to fit in."

"I don't want to fit in," I said sulkily. "I just want to get out of here."

We were silent then.

"Do you know anything about what happened here? In this castle?" I asked.

"You mean with the Normans and everything?"

"No, not that. What happened to the family who lived here, more recently."

"There was a fire or something, then they moved out."

"Wow, you should write history books."

"Well, why do you want to know?"

"I'm just wondering."

He studied me for a while. "We could ask them if you want." He nodded to the group next door, right before we heard an eruption of laughter. I think they were playing spin the bottle.

"No, it's okay," I said.

"Sister Ignatius would know. You know her, don't you?"

"How do you know that?"

"I told you, I work around here. I'm not blind."

"But I've never seen you."

He shrugged.

"She told me to ask Rosaleen and Arthur," I explained.

"You should. You know Rosaleen lived in the bungalow across the road from the entrance all her life? If anyone knows, she would. She could probably tell you everything that's happened around here for the past two hundred years."

I couldn't tell him that the diary stated I should not ask her anything. "I don't know . . . I don't think they want to talk about it. She's so secretive. They must have known the people and if somebody died, well, then, I don't just want to blurt it out. I mean, they probably knew them. Arthur can't be working for free. Actually"— I clicked my fingers—"who pays you?"

"Arthur does. Cash."

"Oh."

"So how come you're here?" he asked, shifting gears.

"I told you, I heard you from my bedroom."

"No, I mean, here in Kilsaney."

"Oh."

Silence. I thought fast. Anything but the truth. I didn't want his sympathy.

"I thought you said Arthur told you about me," I said, stalling.

"I'd deserve an award if I got anything more out of him. He just said that you and your mam are staying with them."

"We just, you know, we just had to move. Just for a little while. Probably only for the summer. We sold our house. And we're waiting to buy a new one."

"Your dad's not around?"

"No, no, he, em . . . he left Mum, for someone else."

"Oh, man, sorry to hear it."

"Yeah, well . . . she's a twenty-year-old model. She's famous. She's always in magazines. She brings me out clubbing with her."

He frowned at me and I felt like an idiot. "Do you still see him?"

"No. Not anymore."

I was following the rules of my diary. *I shouldn't have told Weseley about Dad.* But I didn't feel better for it. I was lying to Marcus as it was, and that was kind of justifiable because everything with Marcus was one big fat lie, but I didn't feel like lying to Weseley. Besides, he'd only find out from Arthur. In about ten years.

"Weseley, sorry, that's a lie." I rubbed my face. "My dad . . . he died."

He sat up. "What? How?"

I should have said something else, like he died in a war or—I don't know—just something more common.

"Eh. Cancer." I wanted us to stop talking about it now. I couldn't go there. I couldn't do it. I wanted him to stop asking me. "In his testicles."

"Oh."

That did it.

I'd left shortly after that. I thanked Weseley for the smoke and the drink and climbed back out the window. Halfway toward the house I stopped walking and turned around and ran back.

"Weseley," I whispered, slightly out of breath, standing at the window. He was tidying away all the cans and butts from the ground.

"Did you forget something?"

"Eh, yeah . . ." I whispered.

"Why are we whispering?" he whispered, smiling, and came toward the window.

"Because, em . . . I don't really like saying this out loud."

"Okay . . ." His smile faded.

"You'll think I'm weird—"

"I already think you're weird."

"Oh. Okay. Em. My dad didn't die of cancer."

"No?"

"No. I just said that because it was easier. Though the testicle part wasn't very easy. That was just weird."

He smiled gently. "How did he die?"

"He killed himself. He swallowed a bottle of pills and whiskey at the same time. On purpose. And I found him." I swallowed.

There it was. The face change that I wrote about. The pure look of sympathy. The nice look you'd give any horrible person. He was silent.

"I just didn't want to lie," I said, then started to move away.

"All right. Thanks for telling me."

"I've never told anyone."

"I won't tell anyone."

"Okay, thanks. I'm really going now." Cringe. "Good night."

He leaned farther out the window and raised his voice. "I'll see you around, Tamara."

"Yep. Sure," I called back over my shoulder. I just wanted to get out of there.

The gang in the entrance hall whistled and laughed as I disappeared back into the darkness.

I learned something important that night. You shouldn't try to stop everything from happening. Sometimes you're supposed to feel awkward. Sometimes you're supposed to be vulnerable in front of people. Sometimes it's necessary because it's all part of you getting to the next part of yourself, the next day.

CHAPTER FOURTEEN

One o'Clock

At one o'clock on the button, when Arthur and Rosaleen's car re-turned to the house, a sense of heaviness came over me. My space was gone, rooms would be shared again, weird games would be played, mysteries would continue.

What on earth had I been thinking?

I should have explored . . .

I reread the last diary entry over and over, sure of how I was going to spend my morning. I knew one important fact.

I had until one o'clock that day.

The morning played out exactly as I'd read the night before. Ro-saleen waking me, telling me to stay home. It seemed so obvious then—the second time around—that she just didn't want me vis-ible to the rest of her little world. Imagine the horror and shame of having to tell people that Mum and I existed; that a man she knew had taken his life, the worst sin of all. I'd felt angry about that and had to fight the urge to go to Mass too and stay under the covers.

As I listened to their car drive away, here's where my day differed from the diary. It was still weird, having things happen that I'd already read about in the diary, but I was sort of getting used to it.

Dying of curiosity about the bungalow, I wasn't about to waste the day like the diary predicted, so instead of falling back asleep after Rosaleen and Arthur had driven off, I got dressed and ran downstairs. I was sitting on the garden wall when the yellow Cinquecento came flying down the road, its windows rolled down, and came to a stop in front of me.

"Ah!" Sister Ignatius's eyes lit up as she leaned out the back. "Just the girl I wanted to see. Are you coming to Mass?"

I looked in the car at the four nuns squashed together.

"Oh, you can sit on Sister Peter Regina's knee," she teased, and I heard a "pah" from inside. "We sing at all the morning Masses. You should join us if the laryngitis isn't still at you."

Can't, I mimed, grabbing my throat and opening and closing my mouth.

"Gargle some salt and you'll be as right as rain," she said with a mock glare, then brightened. "Thanks for the book, by the way."

"You're welcome," I broke my silence. "I picked it especially for you."

"I thought so." She chuckled. "You know at the beginning, I didn't like her, Marilyn Mountrothman. She was stuck up and expected far too much, but by the end I grew to love her. Just like Tariq. It didn't seem an obvious pairing but the way he knew just what she was thinking all the time, particularly when she was crying about the message from her father but wouldn't tell him. Oh, that got me, I must admit. But he figured it out. He knew that she loved him. Smart man! I suppose that's how he made his millions and became the oil tycoon. I like it when they put the photos of them on the front covers. It helps me visualize them all the way through. Him with his hair slicked back and all those muscles . . ."

"You actually read the book?"

"Oh yes, of course, the whole thing. Sister Conceptua has started it now."

The nun in the front passenger seat twisted around. "Don't tell me what happens. He's just chartered the private plane to Istanbul."

"Oh, you've the best bits to get to yet." Sister Ignatius clapped her hands. "Two words, Turkish delight," she said.

"I said ssh," Sister Conceptua snapped. "You'll give it away."

"We have to go," one of the nuns barked from behind the wheel. "We'll be late."

"Think of coming next week, okay?" Sister Ignatius said to me.

"Okay." I nodded. "I'm thinking of going back to bed for the morning. If you see Rosaleen, you might just let her know that."

Her eyes narrowed. "Are you going back to bed?"

"Yes, I'm really thinking about it."

"I see. What are you getting up to, Tamara?"

"We really have to go." The sister at the driver's seat started up the engine.

"Wait." I panicked slightly. "I just need something from you. A name."

Moments later I was watching them fly around the corner, no signaling or brake lights visible, but Sister Ignatius's arm high in the air in a salute.

It was ten o'clock.

I had my priorities in order and Mum was at the top of my list. I flicked through the phone book and searched for the name Sister Ignatius had given me. The phone rang once, twice, three times, then just as it went to the answering machine a man answered.

"Hello?" he croaked, then cleared his throat. "Hold on." I could hear he was out of breath as he fought to turn the answering machine off.

I cleared my throat. Tamara Big-Girl had work to do.

"Hello, I'm calling to make an appointment with Dr. Gedad."

"Uh, he's not here." He sounded half asleep. "Can I take a message?"

"Em . . . no . . . will he be back before one o'clock?"

"His surgery isn't open on Sundays."

I paused. There was something familiar about this.

"It's actually a house call."

"Is it an emergency?"

I held my breath. Then: "Weseley, is that you?"

"Yeah. Who's this?"

Lie, Tamara, lie, make up a name.

"It's Tamara. Sorry for waking you."

"Tamara." He sounded a little more awake now. "Are you okay? You need a doctor? He's my dad."

"Oh . . . it's not for me, it's for my mum. But it's not an emergency or anything. Do you think he'll be back by one?"

"I don't know. They go to Mass and then the market. Usually they're back around one."

"What is it with the bloody Mass and market here?"

"I know, they all love it." He yawned. "I think my dad goes just to hand out business cards to anyone that coughs."

I laughed. "Did you stay out much later last night?"

"About another hour. Didn't you hear us?"

"It took me about a half hour to climb back into my bedroom. I closed the window by mistake and broke all my nails prying it back open."

He laughed. "You should have come back, I'd have helped you

get in. I know where Arthur's secret stash of tools are. Do you want me to get my dad to call you at one?"

"No, it's okay. Before one suits me best."

"What about tomorrow?"

I would have to wait another week for Rosaleen and Arthur to leave. Unless . . . I had to have one small window of opportunity when Rosaleen called on her mother.

"How about between ten and eleven tomorrow?"

"I'll run it by him. I'll get him to call you."

"No," I said quickly. "He can't call here."

"Well, do you have a *cell*?" he teased.

"No."

"Okay." He sighed. "It's far too early in the morning for me to have to think. Give me a second."

I waited.

"Right, I take it you don't want Rosaleen and Arthur to know, so when my dad gets back I'll find out if he's available and then I'll meet you at the castle at two to let you know."

I smiled. He could have phoned; I guessed he wanted to see me again.

I hung up, feeling fired up. One thing almost crossed off my list.

Mission two was to explore the bungalow. Or at least to have a look in the back garden; I didn't want to scare the life out of the old lady. With my alibi prepared, I emptied a few berries into a bowl, boiled the kettle, toasted a few slices of bread, scrambled a few eggs—very badly, managing to burn the bottom of the pan. I soaked it in the sink and dreaded the look on Rosaleen's face when she saw it. I put everything on a tray and covered it with a tea towel just as Rosaleen did each morning. Feeling proud of my first-ever attempt at breakfast, I left the house and made my way very slowly, so as not to spill the cup of tea I'd prepared. With two hands holding the tray, climbing over the gate proved to be difficult. The towel became soaked with tea but I pressed on. I passed the lace-curtained living room window and walked down the side passage. Again, my vision blocked as a bright light shone directly at my face. I closed my eyes tightly, then tried to balance the tray against one side of the bungalow so I could rub them. I almost dropped the tray, making a racket as cups and plates collided. When the light had left my eyes and my vision returned, I continued on, choosing to look down at the ground as I walked. As soon as I reached the end of the passageway, I stepped into the back garden and prepared to be blown away, prepared to see a little old lady tending her garden full of giant mushrooms and fairies and unicorns. But I saw nothing. Nothing but a long grassy field with trees on either side. Rosaleen's mother didn't have a green thumb, that was for sure.

The back of the bungalow was as deserted-looking as the front. Two windows—covered by the same lace curtains—flanked a back door.

I turned my attention to the nearby work shed, where an object in its window glistened and beckoned me forward. I began to make my way toward it. Halfway down I realized I should have left the tray behind, but I continued on. On closer inspection, the object that was glistening appeared to be a twisted piece of glass hanging from a piece of twine. It spiraled elegantly and smoothly to a sharp point, the same shape as a bunch of grapes, and was about six inches in length. As the draft from the window blew it, it spun in circles, twirling and giving the illusion that it was spiraling down, catching the light at different points over and over again. It was hypnotizing.

As I was staring at the glass, something else caught my eye. A movement. Thinking it was a reflection in the glass, I turned to see who was behind me, but there was nothing but the trees moving in the breeze. I thought I'd imagined it but on further inspection, there it was again. A figure inside the shed. I moved in closer to the work shed, trying not to make much noise with my tray and really wishing I hadn't bothered with it now, as the eggs and tea would surely be cold and the buttered toast, soft. The window ledge was shoulder height. I stood on my tiptoes to see inside. I didn't dare look around the rest of the room and kept my eyes on the figure—Rosaleen's mother—in case she saw me and came at me with a sharp piece of glass.

I could only see her back. Her figure, in a long brown cardigan, was hunched over a workbench. She had long scraggy hair, more brown than gray, and it looked like she hadn't brushed it for a month. I watched her for a while, trying to decide whether to knock or not. I didn't even know her name. I didn't even know Rosaleen's maiden name to be able to properly address her. Eventually I built up the courage. I knocked gently.

The figure jumped and I hoped I hadn't given her a heart attack. She half turned, slowly and stiffly. The side of her face that was toward me was covered mostly by her long tatty hair. Over her eyes were a pair of oversized goggles, protective glasses that covered half her forehead and pinched her cheeks. She was all hair and goggles, like a nutty professor.

I balanced the tray on one knee and while the cups and plates clinked and slid, wobbled and spilled, I quickly waved, giving the biggest smile I'd ever given a person just so she'd know I wasn't here to kill her. She just stared at me, no expression, no registering of any kind. I lifted the tray as high as I could, then balanced it on my knee again to quickly make an eating motion. There was still no response. I knew then that I was going to be in big trouble; this had not gone to plan. Rosaleen was right: Her mother was not ready for perfect strangers and even if she was, I should have waited for Rosaleen to introduce us. I took a few steps back.

"I'm leaving this here for you," I said loudly, hoping she'd hear me. I placed the tray down on the grass and backed away. As I was moving backward, I glanced down past the work shed at the rest of the garden. My mouth dropped and I sidestepped to take a closer look. Two dozen rows of washing lines filled the lawn. On each line were dozens of glass mobiles, all different shapes, twisted and turned glass to make unique shapes, some ridged, some smooth, dangling in the breeze, catching the light, sparkling and silently swaying. A field of glass.

I walked up to the lines to further investigate. They were all far apart enough for the glass pieces not to hit against one another. The lines were pulled tight, attached to a wall at the end of the garden and run tightly all the way to a pole at the other end. They stood taller than me so I was constantly looking up, seeing the light of the sky through the glass. They were the most beautiful things I had ever seen. Some appeared to drip from the twine, full and fluid like giant teardrops, but instead of falling, they'd frozen mid-air. Others had fewer swirls and curves and were more rigid, more angry and sharp, like hanging icicles or spikes. Each time the wind blew they swayed from side to side. I walked down the middle of one row and stopped to examine them. I'd never seen anything like them, so clear and pure. Some had bubbles trapped inside, others were completely clear. Fascinating and beautiful, some distorted and disturbing, others pretty and so fragile, as though they would shatter if touched.

I turned around to make sure I was still alone and saw that Rosaleen's mother had moved to the shed's second window that overlooked the garden. She was looking at me, her hand pressed up against the glass. I stopped walking and stood frozen in the middle of a row, feeling like a Cabbage Patch girl in a field of glass, and smiled back, wondering how long she'd been watching me. I tried to make out her face, to see her features, but it was impossible from where I stood. She was yet again showing only her silhouette, her long hair falling to her shoulders, not gray as I had thought earlier, but a mouse-brown with white streaks. She seemed to be ageless, faceless, even more mysterious to me now.

I left the field of glass mobiles, taking them all in one last time. Once I'd passed into the other garden, I could see her watching me still.

I waved again, pointed to the tray on the grass, and made more eating gestures, as though it was feeding time at the zoo. She continued to stare at me, making no reaction. Completely uncomfortable—hot sun, good win, very dead—I turned around and quickly walked away from the garden, feeling as I used to feel as a little girl walking in the dark, as though there was a witch behind me.

It was twelve o'clock.

I entered the gatehouse and paced the living room, back and forth, up and down, left and right. Sat down, stood up. Made my way to Mum's room, then left and went back to the room again. I wrung my hands and looked out the window now and then, expecting to see Rosaleen's mother come racing across the road on her wheelchair, doing wheelies and cracking a whip. Or Rosaleen and Arthur rounding the corner at top speed. Maybe Rosaleen had laid traps around the bungalow and I'd tripped a wire, moved a blade of grass out of place, walked through a beam and triggered an alarm in her handbag. She was going to tie me to a bed, break my legs with a sledgehammer, and force me to write her a novel. I didn't know what was going to happen. I broke the rules at home all the time; here it was different. Here it was all so strict and ancient, like living on an excavation site where everybody was tiptoeing around, speaking quietly so as not to crumble the foundations, using little brushes and tools to scratch at the surface and blow away dust, but never going any deeper. I'd arrived stomping through the place with a shovel and spade and ruined everything.

And now I'd have to go back and get the tray or else Rosaleen would know what I'd done. I hoped I hadn't poisoned her mother—oh God, what if I had? Eggs could be dangerous things and I'd forgotten to wash the berries. Was salmonella lethal? I almost picked up the phone and called Weseley again but I resisted. After spending far too long frantically worrying, I realized nothing was going to happen—not immediately, anyway—and I really hadn't done anything wrong either. I'd tried to be nice to an old woman. So shoot me. I hoped she was enjoying my eggs.

I calmed down then. Next on my list was the garage at the end of the garden. I opened the back door which led from the kitchen to the garden, then through Rosaleen's vegetable patch. I looked up at Mum's bedroom window, which was empty as she continued to sleep on.

As garages go, it was a fine one. It was clad in the same limestone as the house, or near enough to it, and looked better built than any of the new developments around Dublin. I say that with the greatest respect to my dad, who was proud of what he built—I just don't think he cared much for architecture. To him, it was more about space and how to give the least possible amount of it to everybody. This garage almost filled the full width of the garden, eighty-two feet long. To the right of the house, on the other side of the neatly manicured hedge, was a tractor trail, yet another path that meandered around the grounds. But before it left the house's vicinity there was a turn-off which led to the garage's double doors. I'd never seen Arthur park the tractor inside the garage. Perhaps Rosaleen was correct, perhaps there wasn't room inside for our possessions. I favored this way to the garage because I wouldn't be visible from the house, and saw there were two big doors to open, a big lock to pick. I looked in all of the windows but I couldn't see anything as they'd been covered on the inside by black sacks. I tried the single door on the side, which was also locked, and then I went around to the double doors again. I pulled and pushed, I kicked and banged. I used a rock to continuously hammer at the lock, but that did nothing but dent the metal.

It was twelve-thirty by the time I returned to the house, none the wiser on the garage. I washed my hands and changed my clothes, which were filthy from my breaking-and-entering attempt. I checked on Mum, who was finally awake and taking a shower. I took my time getting dressed, knowing exactly how long I had until Rosaleen and Arthur returned. I sat on my bed and looked across to the bungalow. Then something caught my eye.

On the pillar by the front gate was the tray. I stood up, examined the garden across the way, the bungalow. Nobody was in the garden, nobody watched from the bungalow's window. I checked to see if Rosaleen had returned but the car was still gone.

It was twelve-fifty P.M.

I ran downstairs and outside, across the road. The tray was covered by the tea cloth, just as I had laid it. Underneath, the food was gone, the teacup was empty. The dishes gleamed as though they had just been cleaned. On the plate sat the tiniest version of one of the glass mobiles that I had been studying earlier. Like a small teardrop, it was soft and smooth and fit perfectly into the palm of my hand. There was nothing else. No card, nothing to tell me it was for me. I waited, but nobody came. It was dangerously close to one o'clock and I couldn't wait any longer. I couldn't risk Rosaleen returning to find me on the wall with a tray and a glass teardrop. I put the piece of glass in my pocket. I ran across the road as quickly as I could without shattering the contents of the tray. Just as I closed the front door behind me, I heard Rosaleen and Arthur's car return. Shaking, I placed the cleaned cups and saucers and plate back in the kitchen cupboards. But the burned pan was beyond repair. Maybe it was a sign not to disturb tomorrow. Careful not to disrupt anything else, I put the tray back where it belonged. I grabbed my book from the living room, ran upstairs into my mum's room, and dived on the bed. Mum, who was coming out of the bathroom, looked at me in shock. Seconds later the door opened and Rosaleen looked in.

"Oh, sorry," she said, as Mum tightened her towel around her. Then Rosaleen stepped back further from the door so that she could only see me.

"Tamara, is everything okay?"

"Yes, thanks."

"What did you do all morning?" It wasn't an interested inquiry, it was a concerned one, and not concern for my boredom either.

"I was just here with Mum all morning, reading my book."

"Oh, very good." She stalled a bit, always afraid to leave a room. "I'll be downstairs if you need me."

She closed the door and when I looked at Mum, I realized she was looking at me and smiling. She laughed then and shook her head, and I almost felt like canceling the appointment with Dr. Gedad.

The door opened again. Rosaleen looked at Mum's breakfast tray.

"Jennifer, you didn't eat again."

"Oh," Mum said, looking up while putting on her cashmere robe. "Tamara will eat it for me." Then she smiled sweetly at Rosaleen.

"No, no," Rosaleen said hastily, coming inside and taking the tray. "I'll just take that away."

Mum kept watching her, blue eyes shining.

"Tamara, *your* lunch will be ready soon," Rosaleen told me nervously, and backed out of the room.

I looked at Mum in confusion, for an explanation, but she had disappeared again. Turtles either disappear into their shells because they're scared or because danger lurks and they're protecting themselves. Either way, as soon as turtles grow those shells, they never lose them because they're physically a part of them.

Mum would keep the new shell she'd grown over the past few months, and she would carry it around with her for the rest of her life, but that didn't mean she would disappear into it. I saw proof that day that Mum hadn't disappeared for good; I saw it in her eyes. I remember the exact moment when I saw her again. It was at one o'clock.

CHAPTER FIFTEEN

Things You Find in a Pantry

Rosaleen looked different today, having made an effort for Sunday Mass and market. Her Sunday clothes were a knee-length beige-colored skirt with a small slit up the middle at the back. She wore a slightly see-through cream blouse with puffy shoulders, which was tied in a bow at the neck, and underneath I could see a lacy bra, though I doubted she knew about the blouse's transparency. She'd worn a matching beige jacket with a peacock feather brooch on the lapel, and on her feet were nude patent slingback peep-toes. Only an inch or two high but she looked good. I said so and her face brightened and her cheeks pinked.

"Thank you."

"Where did you buy the outfit?"

"Oh." She was embarrassed about talking about herself. "In Dunshauglin. About a half hour away there's a place that I like. Mary's very good, God bless her soul . . ."

I awaited Mary's tragic news with bated breath. It involved a dead husband and lots of God blessing her.

I tried again with another conversation.

"Do you have any brothers or sisters?"

"A sister in Cork. Helen. She's a teacher. And I've a brother, Brian, in Boston."

"Do they ever visit?"

"Now and then. It's been a while. Usually Mammy would visit them, Helen in Cork at least, to give her a change of scenery, but now she can't. She has MS." She looked at me then, opening up a little more. "Multiple sclerosis—do you know what that is?"

"Kind of. Something about your muscles no longer working."

"Close enough. It's got worse over the years. It gives her awful trouble. That's why I'm back and forth. I can't travel, I don't like to leave her, you know. She needs me."

It seemed like a lot of people needed Rosaleen. But it struck me that with so many people needing one person, maybe it was more that she needed them to need her. I never wanted to need Rosaleen.

Her mother never arrived to point the accusing finger at me, but two o'clock did. I snuck out of the house unnoticed while Rosaleen was getting the makings of her tarts ready. I'd learned that the three thousand various pies she'd made during the week not only fed us and her mother, but she also brought them to the Sunday farmers' market where she sold them along with her homemade jam and organic homegrown vegetables. Earlier she'd carried a pouch stuffed with notes and coins to the table, turned her back to take something out of it, and then squeezed twenty euros into my hand. I was honestly so touched, I refused to take it but she wasn't having any of it.

When I reached the castle, Weseley was sitting on the stairs—my stairs. He was wearing blue jeans, a black T-shirt with a blue skull on it, and blue sneakers. Even in the daylight he was cool.

He looked up and pulled earphones out of his ear. "He can come tomorrow at ten."

There was no hello or anything. I was a little put out.

"Oh. Great, thanks." I waited for him to stand up and flutter away, like a little pigeon who'd delivered its message, but he stayed. "Actually," I said, "could he come at ten-fifteen, just in case Rosaleen is delayed leaving?"

"Yeah, sure, I'll tell him."

"Okay, great, thanks," I repeated.

He still didn't leave and so I stepped in further and leaned against the wall directly opposite him.

"Do you know the woman who lives in the bungalow?" I asked.

"Rosaleen's mother? I saw her the first week we moved here but not since then. She doesn't really go out much. She's old. I think she's got Alzheimer's or something."

"Have you ever been to her house?"

"I've dropped a few things off for Arthur. Firewood, coal, some furniture, that kind of thing. But Rosaleen always escorts me on and off the premises." He smiled. "It's not as if there's anything over there to steal, if that's what she's worried about."

"So Arthur never goes over to the bungalow himself . . ." I thought aloud. "He mustn't get along with Rosaleen's mother. I wonder why."

"Check you out, Nancy Drew. Or how about, I'm now Arthur's dogsbody so he couldn't be arsed carrying over dodgy rocking chairs to his mother-in-law when he's paying me next to nothing to do it for him."

"But he never even visits her."

"You're really looking for something, aren't you?"

It reminded me of what Sister Ignatius had said about my mind doing unusual things when it searches. She had known before I did that I was looking for something.

"It's just that . . ." I thought about it. "To be perfectly honest,

I'm so bored here." I sighed. "If I had some sort of life, or friends, or someone to talk to, then I wouldn't be making something out of nothing. I wouldn't care about Rosaleen and her secrets."

"What secrets?" he said with a laugh. "Rosaleen doesn't have secrets. She just doesn't understand the art of conversation. She's so used to spending time on her own, I don't think she knows to offer information about herself."

"I know, but . . ."

"But what?"

I don't know how or why but I suddenly started telling him everything about the past few days. All the odd conversations, the missing photo album, Arthur's unusual comment about thinking Mum didn't want to see him, the way Rosaleen couldn't stand for me to be in the room with anyone on my own, Rosaleen failing to mention me in her conversation with Sister Ignatius, Sister Ignatius wanting me to ask Rosaleen questions, the comment about Mum lying, Rosaleen wanting to keep Mum up in the room all the time, the secretive way she disappears to the bungalow, what I'd seen in the back garden, the tray being left on the wall, the argument about not wanting to put our belongings in the garage.

He listened patiently, making enough reactions to encourage me to keep going and not hold back.

"Okay . . ." he said as soon as I'd finished. "That does sound a little odd, and I get how you can be really suspicious, but it could probably all be explained too. Just by the fact that Rosaleen is a bit of a weirdo—no offense," he said quickly. "I know she's your aunt."

"None taken."

"I haven't been here long enough to know anybody properly but I know Rosaleen doesn't really speak to anybody in the town. Whenever my mam passes her, she always puts her head down and walks on. I don't know if she's just shy or what. And about how she is with you, what does she know about being a mother? But that's not to say that you're not right, Tamara. There could be something they're keeping from you. I don't know what the hell that could be, but if anything else weird happens, tell me."

"Something else hugely weird *is* happening," I said.

My heart drummed. I couldn't believe I was going to tell him about the diary. I just wanted him to believe me so much.

"Tell me."

"You'll think I'm psychotic."

"I won't."

"Just please believe me that I'm not lying."

"Okay. Tell me," he said, getting impatient.

I told him.

He leaned back from me then and folded his arms, all body language the equivalent to a computer shutting down. Oh God. He looked at me differently. Never mind the face change when I'd told him that Dad had died, this reaction was on a whole new level. The guy thought I was a nut.

"Weseley," I began, but I didn't know what else to say.

"Yoo-hoo," a voice called suddenly, and Weseley snapped out of it and looked toward the doorway. A beautiful blond entered. She looked directly at him, not noticing me along the wall.

"Ashley," he said, surprised, "you're early."

"I know, sorry, blame the excitement of wanting to see you. I brought a blanket." She shimmied the basket in her hand. She rushed toward him and dropped the basket by their feet, threw her arms around his neck, and kissed him, and not in a sisterly way. I felt a surprising twinge of envy, which I shrugged off. As though she'd sensed me then, she opened her eyes and saw me standing there, my arms folded, bored with their display.

"Cute PDA, but I'm bored now. Can I go?" I said.

185

Weseley broke their embrace and turned to me with a smile.

"Who are you?" The girl looked at me like I was a bad smell. "Who is she?" she asked him.

"I'm his secret lover. We love to do it in old castles fully clothed while I'm leaning against the wall and he's sitting on the stairs on the other side of the room. It's tough but we love a challenge. Kinky." I winked at him while walking to the door. "Later, lover."

"That's Tamara," I heard him say as I left the castle. "She's just a friend."

She's just a friend. Four words that could possibly kill any woman, but they made me smile. Not only had my freakish rendition of the weirdest story failed to send him charging at me with a torch, wanting to burn me at the stake, but also here, in this place, I had made a friend.

And the castle was my witness.

"Tamara," I heard him calling behind me a few minutes later, just as the house was coming into my view. I took a few steps back, moved closer to the trees so that a peeping Rosaleen wouldn't see us talking.

He was out of breath by the time he got to me.

"About the diary thing . . ."

"Yeah, I'm sorry, forget it—"

"I want to believe you, but I don't."

I was both complimented and insulted at the same time.

"But if you tell me what's going to happen tomorrow, and then it happens, then I'll believe you. That's fair, isn't it?"

I nodded.

"And, if you're right, then I'll help you do whatever it is you're supposed to be doing."

I smiled.

"But if you're making this up"—he shook his head and he looked at me oddly again—"then you know . . ."

"I know. Then you'd like to be my boyfriend. I understand."

He laughed. "So what's going to happen?"

"I haven't read the next entry yet."

I'd been so busy all morning with my missions that I hadn't had time to read the diary.

He looked doubtful. I mean, even I barely believed myself and I knew I wasn't lying.

"I'll read it when I get back to the house and then I'll call you later. Or will you be home? I don't want to disturb you and *Yoo-hoo*."

He laughed. "All right, call me later." He started to leave. "By the way, she's not my girlfriend."

"Sure, she's not," I called back.

Once in the house I made a point of sitting with Arthur and Rosaleen in the lounge, pretending to read the book Fiona had given me. Then I could wait no longer. I yawned, stretched, excused myself from the room and went upstairs. I removed the diary from underneath the floorboard, moved the chair up against the door, and sat down next to it. I opened the book in more hope than expectation, hoping the new entry had already arrived in the early hours of the morning.

As soon as I opened the cover, I saw the words of the previous day disappear as though the new day had drained the ink away, and in their place the neatest writing—*my* neatest writing—began to appear in loops and lines, word after word, so quickly I could barely keep up. The first line made me nervous.

Monday, 6 July

What a disaster! Rosaleen left at ten o'clock for feeding time at the zoo just as I predicted. I watched to make sure nothing fell from her tray that would cause her to come running back early. Dr. Gedad showed up at ten-fifteen on the button. I prayed she wouldn't look out the window of the bungalow and see his parked car but there was nothing I could do about that. I just needed to get him in and out of the house as quickly as possible. He seemed such a warm and lovely man. I shouldn't have been surprised, really, with Weseley as his son. We were still in the entrance hall when the front door opened and Rosaleen stepped in. Honestly, the look on her face when she saw him, it was like she'd been caught by the police. Dr. Gedad didn't seem to notice. He was as friendly as anything and introduced himself. Rosaleen just stared at him as though an unearthly thing had been beamed into her precious house. She went on a nervous rant about an apple pie; she'd tasted the apple pie and she'd added salt instead of sugar, which was the first time she'd ever done that. She seemed really upset, as though it was the worst thing in the world that anybody could ever do. She'd come home to get the other pie that she'd made for dinner. She was sure me and Arthur would understand if we allowed her to bring it to her mother to eat instead. I mean, it was only an apple pie, but she was practically shaking. I don't know if it was because she'd made a mistake or because I'd arranged a doctor for Mum behind her back. Dr. Gedad asked after her mother, who he'd heard was unwell, and in the most bizarre twist ever, he ended up talking to Rosaleen in the kitchen without my being allowed to sit with them, and when they'd finished, Dr. Gedad said to me that he was sure that his presence wasn't needed at all. He was very sorry for my loss, gave me a pamphlet about some counseling, and then left.

Now things are worse than they were before I started all this. I can't stand this anymore. I can't stand being here anymore. Next time Marcus comes along in his bus, I'm hijacking it and I'm forcing him to take me home. Wherever that is now, it's not here.

Don't count on my writing tomorrow.

With shaking hands I returned the book to under the floorboard and knew that I had to fix this situation. I went downstairs to the kitchen, where Rosaleen was making her pies for the next day.

I sat and watched her, nervously biting my nails and trying to decide what to do. If I stopped her from using the salt in the pie then that would mean that I could stop her from returning to the gatehouse too early. But if I changed everything then Weseley would never believe me about the diary. Which did I need more, a doctor for Mum or an ally here to help me?

"Tamara, would you mind fetching me the sugar from the pantry, please?" Rosaleen broke into my thoughts.

I froze.

She turned around. "Tamara?"

"Yes." I snapped out of it. "I'll get it now."

"Can you just fill this up to there? That'll make it easier." She smiled pleasantly, enjoying the bonding.

I took the measuring cup from her and walked slowly to the pantry. I looked at the floor-to-ceiling shelves stocked with everything a person could possibly need for ten years. Condiments separated into Mason jars with screw-on lids, labeled in perfect penmanship with contents and expiration dates. A shelf of root vegetables: onions, potatoes, yams, carrots. A shelf of canned goods: soups and broths, beans, tinned tomatoes. Below that the grains, all in their glass jars: rice, pasta of all kinds of shapes and colors, beans, oatmeal, lentils, cereals, and dried fruits—sultanas, raisins, apricots. Then there were the baking supplies—flour, sugar, salt, and yeast—and so many jars of olive oil, sesame oil, balsamic vinegar, oyster sauce, and rails and racks of spices. There were even more jars of honey and jam: strawberry, raspberry, blackberry, and even plum. It was endless. The sugar and salt had both been emptied from their boxes and poured into jars. The jars were labeled, of course, in that perfect handwriting. My hand shook as I reached for the salt jar. I remembered my lesson from last night: I could change the diary. I didn't need to follow its story. If I hadn't found it, life would be going on as if it was supposed to.

But then I thought of Weseley. If I gave Rosaleen the sugar, she wouldn't return home early tomorrow, she wouldn't catch the doctor before he went upstairs, she wouldn't convince him not to see Mum. If I changed the diary, then I would have absolutely no idea what would happen, so I wouldn't be able to tell Weseley and he wouldn't believe me about the diary. I'd have lost a new friend and look like the biggest weirdo on the planet.

But if I went forward with the salt and told Weseley what was to happen tomorrow, then Mum wouldn't see a doctor. How much longer could I wait here while she sat upstairs sleeping and waking as though there was no difference between either?

I made my decision and reached for a jar.

CHAPTER SIXTEEN

Total Abstraction

I got very little sleep that night. I tossed and turned, felt too hot and kicked off the covers, then felt too cold and covered up again, one leg out, one arm out. Nothing was comfortable. I couldn't find a happy medium. I daringly went downstairs to the kitchen to phone Weseley about the diary entry. No need to wait for tomorrow. I didn't use the stairs, instead I did my gymnastics teacher proud by climbing over the banister and landing gently on the stone floor. I thought I did pretty well not making a sound going down the stairs and *still*, just as I reached for the phone in the kitchen, Rosaleen appeared at the door in a nightdress from the 1800s, which went to the floor and hid her feet, making her appear as though she was floating like a ghost.

"Rosaleen!" I jumped.

"What are you doing?" she whispered.

"I'm getting a glass of water. I'm thirsty."

"Let me get that for you."

"No," I snapped. "I can do it. Thank you. You go back to bed."

"I'll sit with you while you—"

"No, Rosaleen." I raised my voice. "You need to give me space, please. I just want a glass of water, then I'm going back to bed."

"Okay, okay." She raised her hands in surrender. "Good night."

I waited to hear the creaks on the steps. Then I heard her bedroom door close, her feet moving across her bedroom floor, and then the springs in her bed. I rushed to the phone and dialed Weseley's number, which I'd already memorized. He picked up after half a ring and knew it was me.

"Hi, Nancy Drew."

"Hi," I whispered, then froze, suddenly so uncertain about what I was doing.

"So, did you read the diary?"

I searched for any sign that I shouldn't tell him. I listened for a suspicious tone in his voice—was he playing with me? Was he setting me up? Was I on speakerphone in a room full of his hillbilly friends—you know, the kind of thing I would have done if some dork that had moved to my area crashed my party and started spurting crap about a prophesying diary.

"Tamara?" he asked, and I could hear nothing in his voice, nothing to make me change my mind.

"Yes, I'm here," I whispered.

"Did you read the diary?"

"Yes." I thought hard. It wasn't too late to tell him this had been a *hilarious* joke, just like the one about my dad dying. Oh, how we'd laugh.

"And? Come on, you've made me wait until eleven o'clock," he said. "I've been trying to guess all day what it said. Will there be any earthquakes? Were there any lotto numbers? Anything we can make money out of?"

"No," I said, "just boring old thoughts and emotions."

"Ah," he said, and I could hear his smile. "Right, then, out with it. The prophecy, please . . ."

Later that night, I continued to wake up every half hour, the preview of the day to come keeping me on edge. At three-thirty A.M. I couldn't take it any longer and I reached for the diary to see what the events of tomorrow would hold, and if they'd been affected.

I reached for the flashlight beside the bed and with a pounding heart opened the pages. I had to rub my eyes to make sure what I was seeing was correct. Words were appearing, then disappearing, sentences half forming, then vanishing again as quickly as they'd arrived. The letters seemed to jump off the page, and everything was jumbled, without order. It was as though the diary was as confused as my mind, unable to formulate thoughts. I closed the book and counted to ten, and full of hope, I opened it again. The words continued to jump around the page, finding no meaning or sense.

Whatever plans I had put in place with Weseley, tomorrow had certainly been altered. In exactly what way was still unclear, as it obviously depended on how I lived the day when I awoke. The future hadn't been written yet. It was still in my hands.

In the moments that I did manage to sleep, I dreamed of glass shattering, of me running through the field of glass on a windy day, the pieces blowing, and scraping my face, my arms and my body, piercing my skin. But I couldn't get to the end of the garden, I kept getting lost among the rows. The figure stood at the window watching me, hair in front of her face, and every so often lightning would flash and I could see her face: She looked like Rosaleen. I woke up in a sweat each time, my heart thudding in my chest, and I was afraid to open my eyes. Then I'd eventually go back to sleep, only to walk myself straight back into the same dream. At six-fifteen I couldn't force myself back to sleep again, and I was up.

For the first time since I'd moved here I was the first person downstairs, at six forty-five. I sat in the living room with a cup of tea and tried to force myself to concentrate on the book about the invisible girl that Fiona had given me. I was averaging about a paragraph a day but I must have gotten lost in the story without noticing because I didn't see or hear the postman approach the house; I only heard the envelopes land on the mat in the front hall. Always happy to do something different in a house where everything went like clockwork, I went to the hall to retrieve them. They were literally within my grasp when a hand came in and stole them away from me, like a vulture that had flown down and scooped up its prey.

"No need for you to do that, Tamara," Rosaleen said brightly, shoving the envelopes into the front pocket of her apron.

"I don't mind. I was only picking them up, Rosaleen. I wasn't going to read them."

"Of course you weren't," she said. "You just relax and enjoy yourself." She smiled and rubbed my shoulder.

"Thanks." I smiled back. "You know, you should let somebody do something for you for once." I followed her to the kitchen.

"I like doing everything," she said, getting to work on breakfast. "Besides, Arthur is good at a lot of things but he'd be boiling an egg till September if you let him." She chuckled.

"Speaking of September, what's going to happen?" I asked. "The plan was for us to stay for the summer. It's July now, and, well, nobody's talked about September."

"Yes, and it's almost your birthday." Her eyes lit up. "And we need to talk about what you'd like to do for that. Have a party? Go stay with some friends in Dublin?"

"Actually, I might like a few friends to come stay with me here," I said. "I'd like them to see where I live now, see what I do every day."

Rosaleen looked a little shell-shocked by that. "Here? Oh . . ."

"It was only a thought," I backtracked quickly. "Actually, it's so far for Laura and Zoey to come, and it would probably be too much hassle for you . . ."

I waited for her to jump in and reassure me that it wasn't, but she didn't.

"Anyway, I'd rather talk about my future than about my birthday," I said. "If we're still here in September, which is looking likely, how am I going to get to St. Mary's from here? There aren't any buses, or at least none that pass by here. I doubt Arthur would want to drive me to and from school every day . . ." I waited for her to tell me that's exactly what was going to happen. But again, she didn't. Instead she started getting breakfast ready, taking out the pots and pans that usually served as my wake-up call.

"Well, that's something you'll have to discuss with your mother, I suppose."

"But, Rosaleen, how am I supposed to discuss anything with Mum?"

"What do you mean?" Clatter, clatter, bang, crash. All systems go in the kitchen.

"You know what I mean." I jumped up and stood beside her, but she still wouldn't look at me. "She doesn't talk. She's completely catatonic. I don't get why you refuse to admit this."

"She's not catatonic, Tamara." She finally stopped and looked at me. "She's just . . . *sad*. We need to give her space and time and let her figure it all out herself. Now, be a good girl and fetch me the eggs from the fridge and I'll show you how to do a nice big omelette." She smiled. "How about I put a few peppers in it for you?"

"Peppers," I said perkily, and her face lit up. "Lovely, juicy, problem-solving *peppers*." I dragged my feet to the fridge to fetch them. I took out a green one and a red one. "Oh, hello, Mr. Green Pepper. How's about you solve the problem for me? Where am I going to go to school in September?" I held it to my ear and listened. "Oh no, it mustn't be working." I shook it. "Maybe I'll try the red one. Hello, Mr. Red Pepper. Rosaleen seems to think you can solve the problems of my life. Shall we send Mum to a madhouse or should we leave her upstairs forever?" I listened again. "No. Nothing." I tossed the peppers down on the counter. "Looks like the peppers can't help us out today. Maybe we should try some onions," I said, faking excitement. "Or grated cheese!"

"Tamara," I heard Arthur say, as he walked in the kitchen, a warning in his tone, and I stopped. I trudged out and sulked in the living room. Even though we're not allowed to eat in the living room, Rosaleen brought the omelette out to me. A decent person would have apologized, but instead, I just asked for some salt.

At ten o'clock I watched Rosaleen scurry out of the house with the tray loaded with enough food to feed an entire family, and among all of my worries about the day, one of them was that her mother would reveal my recent visit to her. Then, at ten-fifteen, Dr. Gedad's car pulled up outside the house. I took a deep breath and opened the door.

"You must be Tamara." He beamed while walking up the path. He immediately made me smile. He was tall, slender, fit-looking. His hair was graying and was tight on his head. He had high cheekbones and soft eyes which gave him a slightly feminine look, but he was also masculine and handsome. I welcomed him in and shook his hand.

"Well, good morning to you. Isn't it a great summer we're having." He spoke from the back of his throat, as though he'd a piece of bread stuck there, slightly muffled, but in a lovely singsong way. His Madagascan accent was mixed with some words that were spoken with a pure Irish *blás*. It was a lovely, peculiar sound.

"Can I take your briefcase?" I was nervous, jittery, unsure what to do. I looked anxiously at the door.

"No, thank you, Tamara. I'll need this with me."

"Oh yes. Of course."

"I believe I'm here to see your mother?"

"Yes, she's upstairs. I'll show you the way."

"Thank you. I'm very sorry to hear about your father. Weseley shared the sad news with me. It must be a very difficult time for you both."

"Yes, thank you," I said, and tried to swallow that lump that always arrived whenever anybody mentioned Dad.

I started to lead Dr. Gedad upstairs and was almost beginning to believe that I was going to get away with it when the front door opened. Rosaleen stepped into the hall with a tinfoil-covered plate in her hands. She looked at Dr. Gedad as though he was the Grim Reaper. Her face went white.

"Good morning," Dr. Gedad said pleasantly.

"Who . . . ?" She looked from the strange man on her staircase to me, then back to the man again. Her eyes narrowed. "You're the new doctor."

"I am indeed," he said cheerfully, going back down the stairs.

No! I shouted at him in my head.

"It's very nice to meet you, Mrs.—"

"Rosaleen," she said quickly, glancing at me, then back to him again. "Rosaleen will do fine. Well, welcome to the town."

They shook hands.

"Thank you very much. And I must thank you and your husband for giving young Weseley a job here."

Rosaleen's discomfort was all over her face. "Well, yes, he's a great help," she said, brushing him off. "Doctor," she then said, looking confused. "What's . . . why . . . Tamara, are you sick?"

"No, I'm fine, thank you, Rosaleen. If you'll just follow me, Dr. Gedad," I said quickly, heading back upstairs.

"Where are you going?"

"To my mum's room," I said as politely as possible.

"Oh, you won't want to disturb her, Tamara," she said with a smile to me and a little frown to Dr. Gedad, hinting to him that I was some kind of weirdo. "You know how important her sleep is to her." She looked at the doctor. "She hasn't been sleeping much, which is understandable, of course, under the circumstances."

"Of course." He nodded gravely. He looked at me then. "Well, perhaps I should let her have her rest. I can come back another time."

"No!" I interjected. "Rosaleen, she's been sleeping nonstop most days for the past week." I couldn't control my voice, shrieking like a squeaky violin.

"Because of her restless nights, of course," Rosaleen said firmly. "Won't you have some tea, Doctor? You wouldn't believe it but it seems I used salt in the baking rather than sugar. My mother almost fell over. Though she shouldn't have been having pie for breakfast, I know that," she said apologetically.

"How is your mother?" he asked. "I hear that she's unwell."

"I'll tell you over a cup of tea," she said chirpily, and he followed her into the kitchen.

"You're a difficult woman to say no to, Rosaleen."

I stood on the stairs, my mouth agape at what was occurring. I had read all about it but didn't believe that the doctor would so easily obey Rosaleen when an apparently sick patient was upstairs.

"I'll just give your mother a little more rest, Tamara," Dr. Gedad said over his shoulder, "and then I'll see to her."

"Okay," I whispered, trying to hold back my tears, because I knew that because of whatever Rosaleen was going to say to Dr. Gedad, he wouldn't make it up those stairs. Despite knowing the outcome, I tried to join them in the kitchen, but Rosaleen stopped me at the door.

"If you don't mind, Tamara, I'm going to have a few private words with the doctor about my mother. Just to make sure everything's okay. She's been slightly off for the last few days."

I gulped, initially guilty that perhaps my visit to the bungalow had made her worse, but soon my anger returned. I really didn't care about her mother, I was worried about mine.

"Yes, of course I understand, Rosaleen. I was just trying to do exactly the same thing for my own mother," I replied bitchily. I turned my back on her before she had a chance to respond and I stormed upstairs. I went into Mum's room. She was still asleep, curled in a ball in the womb of her bed.

"Mum," I whispered gently, falling to my knees and pushing back her hair.

She groaned.

"Mum, wake up."

Her eyes fluttered open.

"Mum, I need you to get up. I called a doctor for you. He's downstairs but I need you to go down to him, or else call to him. Please, do that for me?"

She groaned and closed her eyes again.

"Mum, listen, this is important. He'll help you get better."

She opened her eyes again. "No," she croaked.

"I know, Mum, I know you miss Dad more than anything else in the world. I know you loved him so much, and you probably think that nothing can ever make you feel better, but it *can* get better and it *will* get better."

She closed her eyes again.

"Mum, please," I whispered, tears welling. "I need you to do this for me."

Mum's breathing was slow and deep again as she fell back asleep. I knelt beside her, crying.

Below the bedroom floor, I heard Dr. Gedad and Rosaleen's muffled conversation. Then the kitchen door opened and I wiped my tears away and shook Mum again to wake her.

"Okay, Mum, he's coming. All you have to do is go as far as your door. That's all, no further."

She woke up and looked alarmed

"Please, Mum."

Now she seemed confused. I swore and left her side to run downstairs just as Rosaleen was opening the front door.

"Ah, Tamara, I had a few words with Rosaleen and I think it's best that I leave your mum for the time being and return again if she needs me. If you feel any need to call, here's my card."

"But I called so you'd see her today."

"I know, but after speaking with Rosaleen I realize that it is not necessary. There's really nothing to worry about. Your mother is indeed going through a difficult time but there is little cause for you to worry so much for her health. I'm sure she'd just want you to relax and have a clear mind," he said in a fatherly tone.

"But you haven't even seen her," I said angrily.

"Tamara . . ." Rosaleen had a warning in her voice.

Dr. Gedad looked uncomfortable, then uncertain about his decision. What reason was there not to trust Rosaleen? I could see him asking himself. Rosaleen could too, so she moved quickly.

"Thank you so much for calling around, Doctor," she said gently. "Please pass on my regards to Maureen and your boy . . ."

"Weseley," he said. "Thank you. And thank you for the tea and buns. I did not taste a bit of salt in it."

"Oh no, that was in the apple tart." She laughed like a child.

And then he was gone. She closed the door and turned to face me but I marched past her to the front door, opened it, and slammed it loudly behind me. I charged up the road. Outside the air was warm and smelled sweet with cut grass and cow manure. I could hear Arthur's lawnmower in the distance. I spotted Sister Ignatius to my left in the far distance on the other side of the grounds; a navy-and-white figure in the middle of green. I ran to her, anger rushing through my blood. As I approached I saw she had set up an easel and stool in the middle of the grasslands in front of the castle, which was a quarter of a mile away, and she stood directly in front of one of the swan lakes, in the shade of a giant oak tree. The morning was already hot, the sky perfectly indigo without a cloud visible. She must have been concentrating intently, her head close to the page, her tongue moving around her lips as she moved the brush around.

"I hate her," I shouted, breaking the silence and sending a flock of birds up from a nearby tree into the sky where they tried to regroup and relocate. I stomped across the scorched grass in my flip-flops.

Sister Ignatius didn't look up as I neared. "Good morning, Tamara," she said brightly. "Another lovely morning."

"I hate her," I said louder, coming close, my voice still raised.

She looked at me then, eyes wide in panic. She shook her head quickly, and waved her arms about as if she was in the middle of a railway track trying to stop an oncoming train.

"Yes, that's right, I *hate* her," I kept shouting.

She put her finger in front of her lip, jiggling around like she needed to go to the toilet.

"She is Satan's spawn," I spat.

"Oh Tamara!" she finally exploded, and threw her hands up in the air, looking distraught.

"What? I don't care what *he* thinks. I *want* him to strike me down. Get me out of here, God, I'm fed up and I want to go *home*," I whined in frustration, then fell back onto the grass. I lay on my back and looked up at the sky. "That cloud looks like a penis."

"Oh, Tamara, would you stop it," she snapped.

"Why, do I offend you?" I asked sarcastically, just wanting to hurt absolutely everybody I came into contact with, no matter how good and gentle they were.

"No! You chased off the squirrel," she said, the most frustrated I'd ever seen her. I sat up, shocked, and listened to her long, vehement speech. "I've been trying to get him all week. I laid out some treats on a plate and finally got him—he didn't want nuts so all those stories about squirrels and nuts need to be changed. He wouldn't touch the cheese, but he loves the Toffee Pops, would you believe. But now look, he's gone and he'll never come back and Sister Conceptua will eat me alive for taking her Toffee Pops. I think you and your dramatics gave him a heart attack." Then she sighed, suddenly calmed, then turned to me. "You hate who? Rosaleen, I suppose."

I looked at her painting. "That's supposed to be a squirrel? It looks like an elephant with a bushy tail."

Sister Ignatius looked angry first. Then, as she examined her piece, she began to laugh. "Oh, Tamara, you really are the perfect dose, you know that."

"No," I huffed, getting to my feet. "Apparently I'm not. Otherwise I wouldn't have to call a doctor for Mum. I could just fix her all by myself." I paced up and down on the grass.

She turned serious then. "You called Dr. Gedad?"

"Yes, and he came this morning. I planned his visit for when Rosaleen was over at her mum's stuffing her with food—and by the way, I've seen her mum and there's no way in the world she's putting away all that food every day unless she's got worms. But Rosaleen came home early before Dr. Gedad even got up the stairs because—stop the press—she put salt in her apple tart instead of sugar and yes, you're right to look at me like that because I did it and I don't care and I'd do it again tomorrow and I'll know soon enough whether I do or not actually." I took a breath. "Anyway, she came back to get the apple pie that was supposed to be for me and Arthur, not that I care because all her food makes me fart fifty times a day, and she managed to talk the doctor out of seeing Mum. So he's gone now and Mum is still in the bedroom, probably drooling and drawing on the walls."

"How did she send him away?"

"I don't know. I don't know what she said to him. He just said that right now Mum just needed to rest and if I needed him again for an emergency or whatever, I should call."

"Well, the doctor would know," she said uncertainly.

"Sister, he didn't even *see* her. He just listened to whatever Rosaleen said."

"So why shouldn't he trust Rosaleen?" she asked.

"Well, why *should* he? I'm the one that called him, not her. What if I'd seen her try to kill herself and I never told Rosaleen?"

"Did she try?"

"No! But that's not the point."

"Hmm." Sister Ignatius went silent as she dabbed her brush in a mucky brown color and applied it to the paper.

"Now it looks like an inbred animal who's just eaten a bad nut," I said.

She snorted and laughed again.

"Do you ever, like, pray? All I see you do is make honey, or garden, or paint."

"I enjoy creating new things, Tamara. I've always believed the creative process is a spiritual experience where I cocreate with the divine creative spirit."

I looked around, wide-eyed. "And is the divine creative spirit on his lunch break?"

Sister Ignatius was lost in thought. "I could go see her, if you like," she said quietly.

"Thank you, but she needs more than just a nun. No offense."

"Tamara, do you know what it is that I actually do?"

"Uh, you pray."

"Yes, I pray. But I don't only pray. I have taken vows of poverty, chastity, and obedience like all Catholic sisters, but on top of that, I vow to help service the poor, sick, and uneducated. I can talk to your mother, Tamara. I can help."

"Oh. Well, I suppose she's two out of the three."

"And besides, I'm not 'just a nun,' as you say. I'm also trained in midwifery," she said, dabbing at the paper again.

"But that's ridiculous, she's not pregnant." Then I registered what she'd said. "Hold on, you're a what? Since when?"

"Oh, I'm not just a pretty face." She chuckled. "That was my first job. But I always felt that God was calling me to a life of spirituality and service and so I joined the sisters, and with them I traveled the world with the great gift of being able to be both nun and midwife. I spent most of my thirties in Africa. All around. Saw some harsh things but also wonderful things. I met the most special and extraordinary people." She smiled at the memory.

"Did you meet somebody there who gave you that?" I nodded at her gold ring with the tiny green emerald. "So much for your vow of poverty. If you sold that you could build a well somewhere in Africa. I've seen it on the ads."

"Tamara," she said, shocked. "I was given that almost thirty years ago for twenty-five years' service as a nun."

"But it looks like you're married—why would they give you that?"

"I *am* married. To God," she said.

I screwed up my face in disgust. "Gross. Well, if you'd married a real man that exists, I mean one that you could actually see, then you'd have got a diamond for twenty-five years' service."

"I'm perfectly happy with what I have, thank you very much," she said. "Did your parents never bring you to Mass?"

I shook my head and imitated my father. "'There's no money in religion.' Even though Dad's totally wrong. We were in Rome and saw the Vatican. Those guys are loaded."

"That sounds like him all right." She chuckled.

"You met my dad?" I was shocked to hear it.

"Oh yes."

"When? Where?"

"When he was here."

"But I don't remember him ever being here."

"Well, he was. So there you go, Miss Know-It-All."

"So did you hate him?"

Sister Ignatius shook her head.

"Go on, you're allowed to say that you hate him. Most people did. I did too sometimes. We used to row a lot. I was nothing like him and I think he hated me for that."

"Tamara." She put down her brush and took my hands in hers, and I was mildly embarrassed. She was so sweet and so soft, it was like a bit of reality would blow her over, but with all her travels and her daily work, she'd probably seen more of it than I. "Your father loved you very much, with all of his heart. He was good to you, blessed you with a wonderful life, was always there for you. You were an extraordinarily lucky girl. Don't speak of him like that. He was a great man."

I immediately felt guilty and with old habits dying hard, I did what I always did. "You should have married him then," I snapped. "You'd have had a gold ring on every finger."

After a long silence in which I was supposed to apologize, but didn't, Sister Ignatius went back to her crap painting. She dabbed her brush in the green paint and flattened the bristles on the paper where she embarked on a journey of unusual jerking motions with her wrist, like a music conductor with a paint brush, to make the green blob look like leaves, or something close to that.

"There's no tree in front of you."

"There's no squirrel either. I'm using my imagination. Anyway, it's not a tree, it's the ambience my poor little squirrel inhabits that I'm trying to depict. Think of it as abstract art; a departure from reality in depiction of imagery," she said. "Well, it's partially abstract, as artwork that takes liberties."

"Like your brown elephant having a huge tail instead of a trunk."

She ignored me. "Total abstraction, on the other hand," she continued, "bears no trace of any reference to anything recognizable."

I studied her work a little more closely. "Yeah, I'd say yours is a little more like total abstraction. Like my life."

She chuckled. "Oh, the drama of being seventeen."

"Sixteen," I corrected her. "Hey, I went over to Rosaleen's mum yesterday."

"You did? And how is she?"

"Well, she gave me this." I took the glass teardrop out of my pocket and moved it around in my hand. It was cold and smooth, calming. "She has loads of them over there. It's so weird. In her back garden there's a shed, that's like her factory, and behind the shed there's an entire field of these glass things. Some are totally freaky and pointy but most of them are beautiful. They're hanging from clotheslines, about ten of them, all tied on with wiry cords, and they catch the light. I think she makes them. She certainly doesn't grow them. But it's like a glass farm."

Sister Ignatius stopped painting and I dropped the teardrop into her hand. "She gave this to you?" she asked.

"No, well, she didn't exactly hand it to me. I saw her in the shed. She was working on something, all bent over, wearing goggles, doing something with glass, and I think I gave her a fright. So I left the tray down in the garden for her. I'd made her some food."

"That was nice of you."

"Not really. You should have seen the state of it. And Rosaleen didn't know I went there so I had to go back to collect the tray. When I did all the dishes were clean and all the food was eaten and everything. And this was sitting on the plate." I took the drop back from her and examined it again. "Sweet of her, wasn't it?"

"Tamara . . ." Sister Ignatius reached her arm out and held on to the easel, which was so light it offered her no support.

"Are you okay? You look a little . . ." I didn't get to finish as Sister Ignatius looked so weak. I immediately wrapped my arms around her and remembered that despite her youthful aura and her childish giggles, she was in her seventies.

"I'm fine, I'm fine," she said, attempting to laugh it off. "Stop fussing. Tamara, I need you to slow down when you speak, and go back over what you just said. You found that on the tray when you went to collect it?"

"Yes, the tray that she placed on the front garden wall," I said slowly.

"But that's impossible. Did you see her put it there?"

"No, I just saw the tray from my bedroom window. She must have put it there when I was elsewhere in the house. Why are you asking so many questions? Are you mad at me for going over? I know I probably shouldn't have, but Rosaleen was being so secretive."

"Tamara." Sister Ignatius closed her eyes and she looked more tired when she opened them. "Rosaleen's mother, Helen, has multiple sclerosis, which has unfortunately been getting worse over the years. She's wheelchair bound, which is why Rosaleen has become her full-time carer. So you see, she couldn't have wheeled herself out to the front garden with this tray." She shook her head. "Impossible."

"She could have," I replied. "If she just put the tray on her lap, then she'd have her hands free to wheel herself—"

"No, Tamara, there are steps in the front garden."

I looked in the direction of the bungalow, and even though I couldn't see it from where we were, I visualized the steps. "Oh, yeah. That's odd. So who else lives in the bungalow?" I asked.

Sister Ignatius was quiet, her eyes moving around as she thought hard. "No one, Tamara," she whispered. "No one."

"But I saw someone. Think, Sister," I barked, panicking now. "Who did I see in the work shed? A woman all hunched over with goggles, work goggles, and long hair. She had all these glass things all over the place. Who could she be?"

Sister Ignatius just shook her head over and over.

"Rosaleen has a sister—she told me about her. She lives in Cork. She's a teacher. Maybe she came to visit. What do you think?"

Sister Ignatius continued to shake her head. "No. No. It couldn't be."

Shivers ran down my spine and my body was covered in goose bumps. The look on Sister Ignatius's usually calm face was as though she'd seen a ghost.

CHAPTER SEVENTEEN

Possessed

I stopped interrogating Sister Ignatius. She had become gray in the face and had lost all of her color.

"Sit down, Sister. Come on, sit here on the stool. You're okay, it's just hot out today." I tried to remain calm as I helped her to the wooden stool. I moved it nearer to the tree trunk so that she was completely shaded. "Let's just rest here for a minute and then we'll go back to the house."

She didn't respond and just let me guide her, one hand around her waist, the other holding her hand. Once seated, I pushed back some loose strands of hair from her face. She didn't feel hot.

Then I heard my name being called in the distance and saw Weseley running. I waved my hands wildly to let him know I could see him. By the time he reached me he was breathless and had to hunch over, hands on his knees, to catch his breath.

"Hi, Sister," he finally said, giving her a goofy wave even though he was right beside her. "Tamara." He then turned to me, alert. "I heard it all."

"Heard what?" I asked impatiently.

"Rosaleen." Pant. "In the kitchen." Pant. "With my dad." Pant. "You were right. About it all. About the sugar and the salt and"—pant—"her coming home early. How did you know?"

"I told you." I quickly looked at Sister Ignatius but she was staring distantly into space, looking as though she was going to faint at any moment. "It was written in the diary."

He shook his head disbelievingly and I became angry. "Look, I don't care if you don't believe me, just tell me what—"

"I believe *you*, Tamara, I just don't believe *it*. You know?"

"Yeah, I know."

"So today I broke away from Arthur at ten o'clock this morning. I went to take care of the walnut trees on the south of the grounds. We're having a problem with walnut blight"—at that, he looked to Sister Ignatius—"so we're trying to maintain the soil pH above 6.0, cut out all the affected shoots—"

"Weseley, shut up about the walnut trees," I interrupted.

"Right, sorry. I couldn't stop thinking about what you'd said and so I went to the gatehouse and hid outside the kitchen window in the back garden. I heard it all. Rosaleen started talking about her mum first of all, saying her health had deteriorated. She has MS. She asked my dad a few questions about her, some advice, that kind of thing. I could tell she was just trying to delay him."

I nodded for him to continue.

"My dad really annoyed me. I felt like yelling at him and telling him to go upstairs. But just as he said he was going up to your mam, Rosaleen started talking about her. My dad was keen to get upstairs to see her, but Rosaleen was insistent. She said that . . ." He paused.

"Come on, Weseley, tell me."

"Just promise to be calm when I tell you, till we work something out."

"Okay, okay," I hurried him.

"Right." He spoke slower now, studying me as he spoke. "She said that this had happened before. That your mum was prone to depression and that she regularly goes into states like this where she withdraws from everybody—"

"That's bullshit!"

"Tamara, listen. She said that your dad and your mum kept it from you all of your life and so you weren't to know about it. She said your mum was on antidepressants and that the best thing to do was to leave her alone in her room until the depression passed. She said that's what they always did."

"Bullshit!" I interrupted again. "That's a lie! That's a fucking lie! My mother has never been like this before. She's, she's—uughh, Rosaleen's a lying bitch! How dare she make something like this up? I would know. I was home with them every day. My mum was never like this. Never!"

I was pacing, I was shouting, my blood was boiling. I felt so angry I wanted to tear the sky down. I felt so out of control, like there was nothing I could do to make everything okay again. Then I questioned myself. Was there some way that I could have missed Mum's behavior? Had she been like this before and I just couldn't remember? Was I such a terrible daughter that I didn't notice? I thought about her faint smiles to Dad, the fact that she was never overenthusiastic like other mums, the fact that she never gave anything away. No, that meant nothing. She just wasn't emotional—sure, she never cried, but it didn't make her *depressed*. No, no, no. It was wrong. It was all wrong.

Weseley tried to take hold of me and calm me down but I was

screaming, that much I can remember. And then I remember Sister Ignatius finally coming to, standing and coming toward me with open arms and that sweet, sad, but older, so much older face than a few minutes ago. She looked so sad and pitying that I could hardly look at her.

"Tamara, you have to listen to me now . . ." she was saying, but I didn't want to hear. I thrashed and squirmed away from them. And then I remember running, running so fast while I heard them shouting my name. I fell a couple times, felt Weseley behind me, then trying to grab me. I screamed and kept running, faster and faster, thinking he was on my heels. I don't know when he stopped running, when he decided to let me go, but I kept on going despite feeling an ache in my chest and finding it hard to breathe. Hot tears ran from the corner of my eyes and straight back to my ears. I ran out of the woods and straight onto the road, and the roar of an engine and a screech of tires and a long car horn sounded in my ear and I froze. I absolutely froze. I waited to be hit, for the bumper to crash into my side and for me to go flying up over the windshield, but it didn't happen. Instead I felt the heat of the car's grid beside my leg, so close, too close, as the car stopped right next to me. Then the door opened and there was shouting. A man. My hands were over my ears, I was crying, unable to catch my breath, and I could hear my name being yelled over and over. Angry, aggressive, accusing. Like it was my fault.

Finally it got quiet and arms were around me and I was being rocked gently, and I realized I was in Marcus's arms, the traveling library was beside us, and I was sobbing uncontrollably onto his shirt.

I finally looked up at him. His face was concerned, afraid.

"So where should we go now? Paris? Australia?" he asked softly, smiling.

"No," I sobbed. "I want to go home. I just want to go home."

* * *

I was silent in the bus on the way to Killiney. Marcus had tried to ask questions but gave up after a while. I finally stopped crying and I felt weak from the emotion, tired from it all. I wiped my eyes with my snotty tissue one last time and took a deep breath and exhaled.

"That sounds better," Marcus said, looking at me as we stopped at a red light. "Are you going to talk to me now?"

I cleared my throat. "Hello, Marcus. I want to get really drunk."

"You know what, that's exactly what I was thinking." He smiled mischievously and pulled the bus over outside a convenience store. "You're a woman after my own heart," he said before closing the door and running into the shop.

I should have told him then. Again. My age, that is. I could have saved a lot of heartache. Less than three weeks to go till my seventeenth birthday, and that was probably still too young for him. I'm not quite sure what I was thinking, if I was really able to think at all. I felt numb, and wanted to be more numb. I didn't want to feel, I didn't want to have to think. My life felt so out of control that I wanted to lose control of me too. Just for a little while, at least.

We were only an hour away from Killiney. An hour was nothing, but it was a world away for me. I'd been ripped away from my home, my place; I felt like my identity had been taken away with it. Sure, you can be homesick, or you can move away and miss a place. But we were forced to move. Some bank, some institution had chased my father, had tormented him so much he'd taken his own life. Then, after they'd done that, they'd taken our home, our sense of place, the foundation of our family. And while we were cast out, forced to live with people we barely knew, it just sat here, huge and empty with a "For Sale" sign, while we had to sit outside and watch it like strangers, without being able to return.

"Do you still have the keys to this place?" Marcus asked as we weaved through the windy roads that led through my old neighborhood.

I nodded. Another lie.

"Hey, slow down there, Tamara." He looked at me knocking back my third can of beer. "Leave some for me," he said with a laugh.

I finished it and burped loudly.

"Sexy," he said, keeping an eye on the road.

If you ask me now, I'll honestly say that's the first moment that I consciously decided what I wanted to do. Of course I can blame him for putting it in my head, but really it was me. Perhaps I'd known from the second I ran out onto the road and he put his arms around me that we'd end up at the house and I'd end up on the floor with him in my old bedroom. Maybe I'd decided it the first day I met him. Maybe I did have it all planned. Maybe I was more in control than I thought. Or maybe the third beer had played havoc with me in my emotional state. I pointed out places to Marcus as we drove to the house, telling him stories, telling him the names of people who lived in the neighborhood. I didn't wait for responses. I didn't really care if he answered or not. I was saying all this for me. I had given up pretending to be the person I'd kept trying to be, the same as Zoey and Laura, the same as everybody else around us. Because it wasn't working. It wasn't working for Laura, it hadn't worked for Zoey, and it most certainly hadn't worked for me.

We finally pulled up outside the house. I told Marcus to park the bus down the street so that it wouldn't be seen directly in front of the house from the road. The last thing we wanted was for the neighbors to come looking for books. I'm not sure why I bothered; the house wasn't even visible from the road. And the large black gates locked between ten-foot walls were enough to dissuade anyone from bothering us. Dad had put so much time and effort into those gates: drawn up plans over and over again, asked me and Mum what we thought, so proudly walked me to the entrance to ask my opinion, and I remembered saying once that I didn't care.

I think I was telling Marcus this as we walked along, but I wasn't sure. "I don't have the zapper for the gate on my keys," I heard myself say. "I'll have to climb over and open the gates from the house."

I had a system, one I'd use so many times. Mum and Dad had taken my keys most evenings after school so that I wouldn't escape, but despite its height I'd navigated the gates safely on many an occasion. I could hear Marcus warning me, pointing out which way to go, but I didn't follow his advice. On autopilot I just scaled the gate and landed safely on the other side. I heard him applauding as I walked the long driveway to our house.

Our house—glass, stone, wood, bright, light, modern, airy. It was like something from a catalog. Stone to camouflage parts of the house to match the rock it was built into, wood to blend into the woodlands surrounding it, glass to give us views of the sea that stretched on forever. Dad had tried to create the most perfect place that neither of us would ever want to leave. He did that right. I knew the front door would be locked, and still on autopilot I made my way around the back of the house.

I saw a tennis ball in the back garden, lying soggy and wet. It had recently flown over from our nearby tennis court and I'd been too lazy to collect it. I'd been playing with Dad that day. Spring had arrived, we'd started using the outdoor court again, but I was playing horrendously. After a winter of having not picked up a racket, I was rusty. I kept missing the ball, kept hitting it over the fence, and had grown tired of searching for it in the garden. Dad had been patient, he hadn't yelled, he hadn't said anything. He'd even gone to fetch the ball himself a few times. But when he purposely fluffed a few shots, that had angered me. I remember him in his little white tennis shorts, his white-collared T-shirt, his sport socks that he pulled up too high, which embarrassed me even though I was the only one who could see them. My lovely dad . . .

In the back there were the same garden statues—an old chubby couple with gardening tools in their hands, the man revealing the crack of his behind—that my granddad, my dad's dad, always used to talk to before he died. He called the woman Mildred and the man Tristan, for no particular reason, but it had made me laugh since I was a child and Mildred and Tristan had become part of the family. But Mum obviously hadn't arranged for them to be moved and so Mildred and Tristan remained the only inhabitants of the house. Near the washing line there was a red plastic peg in the grass, dropped there from the last wash.

I climbed up onto the swimming pool roof, where the old weather-beaten wooden ladder was still lying. I'd stored it there for my midnight escapes. In the newest addition to the house, the pool was covered over by a blue canvas, our six pool loungers lay diagonally by the window, still with their pink cushions waiting for me and my morning swim. A deflated swimming ring sat on one of the sun loungers. I'd brought it back from Marbella. It was a pink flamingo. Manuel, a boy I'd kissed last year, had given it to me and I was intent on bringing it home. It lay there now with nobody to use it. A discarded kiss.

I used the ladder to climb up my bedroom balcony. Nobody ever locked my bedroom balcony door. It was supposedly too high up, too inaccessible for any burglar to reach. My head was spinning as I finally pulled myself up onto the balcony. The weather had cooled now, since we were closer to the coast. The sea air was cold, the wind took away the July heat and brought the scent of seaweed and salt. I looked out to the beach and took in the view, remembered sixteen years of summers with Mum and Dad here. I don't know how long I'd been standing there, reminiscing, when I remembered Marcus at the gates.

As soon as I opened the balcony door to my room, the alarm went off. I ran immediately inside, hoping they hadn't changed the code. They hadn't, of course. What owners in their right minds would ever want to break back into their repossessed house?

After failing on the first attempt, due to shaky fingers, I punched in the right numbers and the alarm finally stopped. I took a few breaths, waited till the ringing died down in my ears, pressed the button for the gate, and went downstairs and opened the front door. While I waited for Marcus to make his way up the driveway, I wandered around the house. I ran my fingers over all the surfaces. Some were slightly dusty. Then I heard Marcus behind me, his voice echoing in the entrance hall. I heard him whistle, impressed.

I went into the kitchen, saw family meals at the table, rushed breakfasts at the breakfast counter, Christmas dinners in the nearby dining area, noisy parties, birthday parties, New Year's Eve. I remembered fights, Mum and Dad, me and Dad. I remembered dancing. Dancing with my dad. I remembered Dad's party trick, a long story that I never really understood but loved to hear him tell. He would come alive while telling it, loving the limelight. His cheeks would be flushed with alcohol, his blue eyes glazed, but he would recant the tale perfectly and confidently, just dying to get to that final line to make everybody erupt in laughter. I could see Mum's area where she'd prop herself with her lady friends for the night, all huddled together, elegant women with expensive shoes, thin ankles, tanned skin, and highlighted hair.

As I turned away, I saw Dad wander through the halls, wink at me, cigar in hand, as he went to the only room Mum would let him smoke in. I followed him in there now. I watched him enter and greet his friends. They all cheered as he opened his best brandy as they settled down for a chat or to play snooker. I looked around the walls and remembered the photographs. His achievements, his degrees, his sports trophies, his family photographs. Me teary-eyed on my first day of school, me on his shoulders in Disney World, wearing a Mickey Mouse T-shirt with my hair in pigtails, a silly smile with missing front teeth. Dad and his friends on the top of a ski slope in Aspen. Dad playing golf with Padraig Harrington at a celebrity charity event.

I moved into the television room and saw him sitting in his favorite armchair watching television. Mum in the other corner, legs curled up underneath her, her arms wrapped around her legs protectively, the two of them laughing at some comedy show. Then he looked at me and winked again. He stood up and I followed him once more. We walked through the entrance hall, past Marcus, who was watching me, and then he walked through the closed office door. He disappeared. I couldn't go in there.

The fight. The horrible fight we'd had. I'd slammed that door in his face and run upstairs. I should have told him instead that I loved him. I should have said sorry and hugged him.

"I never want to see you again. I hate you!"

"Tamara, come back!" His voice. His lovely voice. Oh, Daddy, I'm here, I'm back. Please come out of the office.

Then the next morning, seeing him, my beautiful dad. My handsome dad on the floor. Not the way he was supposed to end up. He was supposed to live forever. He was supposed to take care of me forever. He was supposed to interrogate my boyfriends and walk me down the aisle. He was supposed to gently persuade Mum when I couldn't get my way; he was supposed to watch me proudly for the rest of my life. And then when he got old I was supposed to protect him, I was supposed to be there for him, paying it all back.

It had been my fault. It had all been my fault. I'd tried to save him but I didn't even know how to do that properly. If I'd learned how, if I'd paid attention, if I'd tried to be an interested, better person than the selfish one I'd been, then maybe I could have helped. They'd said I got to him too late, that there was nothing I could possibly have done, but you never know. I'm his daughter—that should have helped.

That room, his room, that smelled of him. Of his aftershave, of cigars, of wine and brandy, of books and wood. The room he'd taken his life in, with the stained rug on which I'd thrown up after his funeral. I couldn't go in there.

I heard the clink of cans and the rustle of a plastic bag, and I turned around. Marcus was watching me.

"Nice house."

"Thanks."

"You okay?"

I nodded.

"Must be weird being back here."

I nodded again.

"You're not very chatty today."

"I didn't really bring you here to talk."

He looked at me then. I could see it in his face.

Tell him. Tell him now.

"So come on, let me show you the best room in the house," I said. I took him by the hand and I led him upstairs.

Back in my bedroom, I lay down on my bedroom floor, on the soft plush cream carpet where my king-sized bed used to sit with its white leather headboard. My head spun from the alcohol and from all that had been going on. I wanted to forget everything that had happened that day—Sister Ignatius, Weseley, Rosaleen, Dr. Gedad, the mystery woman in Rosaleen's mother's house. I wanted to forget my mother as I'd tried to drag her limp, frail body out of bed. I wanted to forget Kilsaney and all the people in it. I wanted to forget we'd ever left this house and that Dad had ever done what he'd done. I wanted to go back to the night I'd snuck out of the house and then had the fight with him. I wanted everything to change.

And then everything changed.

Everything.

The dominoes started to fall again.

CHAPTER EIGHTEEN

RIP

Though two years ago our house in Killiney could have fetched a whopping eight million euros, it stood for sale for half of that now. I know how much it had been worth because Dad regularly had it valued. Each time the new appraisals would come through, he'd surface from the cellar of his multimillion-euro home with a 450-euro bottle of Château Latour to share with his perfect model wife and his perfectly hormonally imbalanced teenage daughter.

I don't begrudge Dad his success, not just because his success was inevitably our success—ironically, his failures became ours too—but because he worked hard, early mornings, late nights, weekends. He cared about what he did: He donated regularly to charities. Whether he did it in a tuxedo, in front of flashing cameras, or with his hand raised high at a charity auction was entirely irrelevant. He gave and that's what mattered. There was nothing wrong with having an expensive home, nothing wrong at all. There's pride in building something up, working hard to achieve something. But it shouldn't have been his manhood that increased with each new success, it should have been his heart. His success was like the witch in the

"Hansel and Gretel" fairy tale: It fed him for all the wrong reasons, fattening him in all the wrong places. Dad deserved his success, he just needed a master class in humility. I could have done with one too. How special I thought I was in the silver Aston Martin in which he drove me to school some mornings. How special am I now, now that somebody bought it from a depot of repossessed cars for a fraction of the price. How special indeed.

Even at half its asking price, the house was still a priority sale for the real estate agent. Little did I know that when I opened the balcony door to my bedroom and set off the alarm, it sent an automated response phone call to the agent, who immediately jumped into her car and came to check the premises. By the time I was three flights upstairs, I didn't hear the electric gates open half a mile down the driveway. I also didn't hear her open the front door and step into the entrance hall.

But she heard us.

And so the next people that paid us a visit were the police. Three flights of heavy pounding on the stairs allowed us time to stop what we'd been previously doing on the floor of my bedroom, but not enough to clothe ourselves, and so, huddled behind Marcus with my clothes scattered around me, that's how I met Officer Fitzgibbon, an overweight man from Connemara, with a redder face than mine, who I'd regularly been acquainted with on the beach with my friends. This was not the time for reunions.

"I'll give you a minute to get dressed, Miss Goodwin," he said, immediately looking away.

Twenty-two-year-old Marcus, who'd been invited to an eighteen-year-old girl's house which hadn't yet been sold, found the entire thing mildly embarrassing, but mostly amusing. He didn't know that the girl he'd just slept with was a few weeks away from her seventeenth birthday, and so not only were the bottles of beer highly illegal, but half of what they'd done on the carpet. He kept looking at me and snorting while we quickly got dressed. I was panicked, my heart thudding so loudly I could barely think, feeling so queasy I was afraid I'd vomit right there in front of them all.

"Tamara, relax," he said cockily. "They can't do anything. It's your house."

I looked at him then, and I hated myself more than he was ever going to.

"It's not my house, Marcus," I whispered, my voice refusing to work.

"Well, your parents', whatever . . ." He pulled his jeans up one leg.

"The bank took it," I said, now dressed but now sitting there, feeling completely out of it. "It's not ours anymore."

"What?" A giant domino fell. I felt the floor vibrate as it thudded to the floor, like a great big skyscraper crashing down.

"I'm sorry," I said, and started crying. Then the words I wanted to say to him for so long finally came out, but all in the wrong way and totally at the wrong time. "I'm sixteen."

Thankfully Officer Fitzgibbon, who'd been standing at the door, was on alert and heard the entire conversation. He at least would believe Marcus didn't know, but it was up to Marcus to prove that in court. He stepped back into the room just as Marcus came flying at me in anger, shouting with such ferocity I wanted him to throw more at me, call me everything under the sun. I knew that I'd ruined everything for him. Whatever arrangement he'd made with his dad with that traveling library, it'd probably been his last chance. We'd never spoken about it but I recognize somebody on their last chance. I used to see it in the mirror every day.

We were brought to the police station. Went through the humiliation of giving statements of the entire account. I was hoping the first time I finally had sex I could write all the juicy and embarrassing details in a diary, not confess them at a police station. Tamara Fuckup, ripping things apart as usual.

Rosaleen and Arthur had to drive to Dublin to collect me from the station. As soon as Marcus's dad found out, he sent a car for him. I tried to apologize to Marcus over and over again, trying to cling to him so he'd stop and listen, but he wouldn't. He wouldn't even look at me.

Arthur stayed in the car while Rosaleen met with the police, the next most embarrassing thing that happened to me that day. Rosaleen seemed more concerned about Marcus, what would happen to him. They told her the maximum sentence for sleeping with a "child" under seventeen was two years. I broke down crying at that. Rosaleen seemed as distraught as I was, and I don't know if it was because I'd soiled their name, even more so than my father's suicide, or if she was genuinely fond of Marcus. She asked question after question until Officer Fitzgibbon calmed her with the news Marcus would most likely be able to argue in court that he truly didn't know my age. It seemed to be enough for Rosaleen but it wasn't enough for me. How long would this take him? How many sessions in court? How much humiliation? I'd ruined his life.

Rosaleen didn't even try to talk to me, just curtly told me that Arthur was waiting outside, and then she left the station. I eventually followed her. There was the most horrific tension in the car when I sat inside. I was mortified, absolutely mortified. I couldn't look at Arthur. He said nothing when I got in the car and we pulled away and headed back to Kilsaney. I was actually relieved to be going so far away, to be so disconnected from what had just happened. It had finally ripped through the umbilical cord that tied me to this place. Maybe that had been my intention.

I cried the entire way home, so embarrassed, so disappointed, so angry. All of those emotions were directed at myself. About thirty minutes in, Arthur pulled the car over outside a convenience shop.

"What are you doing?" Rosaleen asked.

"Could you get some bottles of water and some headache tablets?" he asked quietly.

"What? Me?"

There was a long silence.

"Are you all right?" she asked him.

"Rose," he merely said.

I'd never heard him call her that, though it sounded familiar—I'd seen it somewhere, heard it somewhere—but I couldn't think. Rosaleen looked back at me and then at Arthur, reluctant to leave us two alone. Eventually she got out of the car and practically ran into the shop.

"Are you okay?" Arthur asked, looking at me in the rearview mirror.

"Yes, thanks." My tears welled again. "I'm so sorry, Arthur. I'm so embarrassed."

"Don't be embarrassed, child," he said softly. "We all do things when we're young. It will pass." He gave me a small smile. "Just as long as you're okay?" He gave me a worried, paternal look then.

"Yes, I'm fine, thank you." I rooted for my tissues again. "It wasn't . . . he didn't . . . I knew what I was doing." I cleared my throat awkwardly. I could see Rosaleen at the end of a long checkout line, anxiously looking out at us in the car.

"Arthur, this depression that Mum has, does it run in the family?"

"What depression?" he asked, turning around in his seat.

"You know, the depression that Rosaleen told Dr. Gedad that Mum has, this morning."

"Tamara." He looked right at me, then checked Rosaleen in the shop. There were three people in front of her. "Tell me straight."

"I made an appointment with Dr. Gedad to see Mum this morning. She needs help, Arthur. There's something *wrong*."

He seemed extremely worried by this. "But she has her daily walks, at least. She gets some fresh air."

"What?" I shook my head. "Arthur, she hasn't left the house since we arrived."

His jaw hardened and he gave another quick glimpse—good win, very dead—at Rosaleen in the shop. "What did Dr. Gedad say when he saw her?"

"He didn't even get up the stairs. Rosaleen told him that Mum has suffered from depression for years and that Dad knew about it but he decided never to tell me and . . ." I started crying, unable to finish. "It's all lies. He's not even here to defend himself, or to be able to tell me . . . It's all lies. Though I know I'm not one to talk."

"Here, Tamara, hush now. Rosaleen is just trying to care for her the best that she can," he said, almost whispering, as if she'd hear him from the shop. There was only one person in front of her in the line now.

"I know, Arthur, but what if it's the wrong way? That's all I'm saying. I don't know what happened between them years ago but if there's anything—anything—that Mum did to Rosaleen to hurt her or annoy her, do you think that this could be . . ."

"Could be what?"

"Could be Rosaleen's way of maybe getting her back? If Mum did something to her . . ."

The door opened and we both jumped.

"Gosh, you'd think I was the bogeyman," Rosaleen said, getting in. "Here." She dumped a bag in Arthur's lap.

He looked at her then, a cold long stare that chilled me, made me want to look away. He passed the bag back to me without a word and started up the engine.

None of us spoke for the next hour.

When we arrived back at the gatehouse the sky had clouded over and darkened the bright day. There was a chill in the air and the clouds promised rain. The breeze was welcoming to my muffled head. I took a few deep breaths before going into the house and making my way upstairs.

"You'll know you won't be going anywhere for a long time to come," Rosaleen said.

I nodded.

"There'll be a few tasks for you to do around here," she added.

"Of course," I said quietly.

Arthur stood by and listened.

"Stay within the grounds when you're out," he added, and it seemed to take a great effort for him to say it.

Rosaleen looked at him, surprised and then annoyed that he'd stepped in. He didn't meet her eye. Obviously her plan had been to keep me inside the house where she could keep a close eye on me.

"Thank you," I said, then went upstairs to Mum.

She was asleep in bed. I crawled in beside her and wrapped my arms around her, squeezing her tight to me. I breathed in the scent of her freshly washed hair.

Downstairs a storm brewed as I heard Rosaleen and Arthur's voices in the living room. First they were just talking, then the volume grew louder and louder. Rosaleen tried to hush him a few times but he shouted over her and she gave up. I couldn't hear what they were saying, I didn't even try to. I'd given up poking my nose in where it didn't belong. All I wanted was for Mum to get better, and if Arthur's raised voice was going to get me that, then fine. I scrunched my eyes shut and wished that today had never happened. Why hadn't the diary warned me?

The argument between Rosaleen and Arthur became worse. Unable to listen anymore, I decided to leave, to give them and me the space we needed. I hated that I'd brought this upon them too.

Before we'd arrived, they'd been so happy with their life, their little routines, just the two of them. My arrival had caused a rip in their relationship and it was slowly tearing more and more with each day. As soon as there was a break in their argument, I went downstairs.

"Sorry to disturb you," I said quietly. "I'm just going out for a walk to clear my head. Around the grounds. Is that okay?"

Arthur nodded. Rosaleen had her back to me and I could see her fists clenched by her side. I quickly left the house. It would be light for another hour or so, which gave me enough time for a brief walk and the opportunity to clear my head. I wanted to go to the castle but I could hear Weseley and his friends had gathered there. I wasn't in the mood for them, I just wanted to be alone. I turned in the opposite direction and headed toward Sister Ignatius's, despite knowing I wouldn't call on her. At this hour I didn't want to cut through the woodlands. I stayed on the path and kept my head down as I strode by the dark gothic entrance, still chained up and left to rot.

As soon as I had the chapel in sight I realized I'd been holding my breath. It was only big enough to hold ten people at most. Half the roof had caved in, but above it the oak trees bent their branches to protect it. It was quaint. No wonder Sister Ignatius was so fond of it. As I peeked inside I saw there were no pews. Above the altar, a simple but large wooden cross had been secured to the stone wall. I guessed Sister Ignatius had something to do with hanging it there. The only other thing that stood in the chapel was a large oversized—good win, very dead—marble bowl, chipped and cracked in places around the rim, yet still solid and firmly fixed to the concrete floor. Spiders and dust lived in it now, but I imagined generations upon generations of Kilsaneys all gathering here to baptize their children. There was a wooden door that led to the small graveyard next door. I chose not to go through that but instead returned through the main door where I'd entered. From behind the gate that protected the graveyard, I strained my eyes to read the headstones, though many were covered in moss, ravaged by time. In an oversized crypt rested an entire family: Edward Kilsaney; his wife, Victoria; their sons Peter, William, and Arthur; and their daughter, something beginning with B. Maybe Beatrice, or Beryl, or Bianca, or Barbara. For Florie Kilsaney: "Farewell thy mother, we mourn thy loss." Robert Kilsaney died at one year old, 26 September 1832, then his mother, Rosemary, followed him ten days after. For Helen Fitzpatrick in 1882, "Husband and children bear her in tender regard." Some were just names and dates and were all the more mysterious for it: "Grace and Charles Kilsaney, 1850–1862." Only twelve years old, both born and died on the same day. So many questions.

Some of the gravestones had various symbols on them: arches, doves, arrows; others had spooky-looking animals, the symbolism of which I had no understanding of but wished to know. I planned to ask Sister Ignatius whenever I felt I could face her. I scanned the headstones again, no longer feeling as scared as I had been the first time I'd passed by. A large cross climbed high up to the sky, with various names added as family members joined one another, their names and inscriptions more legible as the years went by. On the ground before it was a bunch of flowers—fresh flowers—tied together with long grass. The newest and freshest inscription was at the bottom and as soon as my eye rested upon it, I couldn't believe I hadn't noticed it earlier. I climbed up on the fence to see the engraving. "Laurence Kilsaney, 1967–1992, RIP."

Only seventeen years ago. He must have died in the fire in the castle. Which made him only twenty-five. How sad. Even though I didn't know Laurence, or any of his family, I started to cry. I picked a few wildflowers, tied them together with my hair ribbon and, against my better judgment, jumped over the fence. I laid the flowers on the grave and reached out to touch the gravestone, but just as my fingers touched the cold stone, I heard a noise behind me: a click. The hairs rose on the back of my neck. I spun around, expecting to come face to face with a stranger, so close I swore I could feel their breath on the back of my neck. I looked in every direction, almost dizzy with the effort of trying to focus. Just trees, trees, and more trees as far as my eye could see. I tried to tell myself I was spooked because I was standing in an ancient graveyard surrounded by generations of a family who'd been lost to plague, war, suffering, fire, and, more humanely, to old age. I tried to tell myself that, but somebody was there all right, I was sure of it. I heard a twig snap and my head darted around to follow the sound.

"Sister Ignatius, is that you?" I called. The response was merely my trembling voice echoing back to me. Then I saw the trees move, heard the rustle moving farther away, as somebody pushed their way through the trees in the opposite direction.

"Weseley?" I called, the tremble in my voice echoing back.

Whoever it was had left in a hurry. I swallowed hard and rushed from the grave, climbed over the fence, and moved quickly away, brushing myself off as though I'd walked through a giant spiderweb.

I hurried back to the gatehouse, turning back over and over again to make sure I wasn't being followed. It was dusk by the time I got back to the house. Rosaleen was in the living room, knitting, with the television on quietly in the background. Her face looked haggard, weary from fighting. Arthur was in the garage in the back garden, making an angry racket. My curiosity about the garage had been killed with these recent events. I no longer cared what they had in there. I felt I was chasing a secret and now the secret was chasing me. I was afraid. I just wanted the time to pass so that Mum would stop her grieving, get better, and we could move on from this place that felt so haunted by the ghosts of the past, a past that, despite my having nothing to do with it, was dragging me further and further into it.

CHAPTER NINETEEN

Purgatory

I was grounded for the next two weeks, going up and down the stairs namely for breakfast, lunch, and tea, and doing whichever chores Rosaleen decided would be appropriate punishment, such as vacuuming the living room, polishing the brass, removing all the books from the shelves and dusting, watching her tend to her vegetable and herb garden while explaining to me what she was doing. I think she enjoyed the entire thing, babbling away as though I was a toddler and everything she said was the first time I'd ever heard it. I think it gave her a new lease on life to have so many drained souls living around her. The more exhausted we got, the stronger she grew, like a vampire. I couldn't even bring myself to read the diary anymore. It was as if I had given up on everything. Strangely, every day that went by I felt there was more life coming from Mum's room than from mine. The more energy I lost, the more she gained. I would hear her pacing the room like a caged lioness.

In fact, I was rebelling against the diary. I held it responsible for getting me in this position in the first place. I wanted control over my days again, even if I just wanted to lie in bed and let the world pass by under my nose, just like it had before.

Every day I waited for Marcus to call. He didn't.

Every day Sister Ignatius came by. I was so mortified, I refused to see her. I'm sure she knew what had happened; I'm sure the whole town knew. So much for my new start. I didn't want a lecture. I didn't want a stern stare. I missed the honey extraction, which I should have been helping her with, but instead I lay in my bedroom, hiding under my bedclothes, still mortified at the very thought of what had happened. While in bed, I could hear Arthur making a few attempts to see Mum. He'd wait until Rosaleen was out in the back garden and he'd knock lightly on her bedroom door. If he thought she was going to call out to him to enter, then it was clear he really didn't get it. After a minute or two he'd just walk away.

One night, Rosaleen and Arthur had another fight. I heard Arthur say, "I can't do this anymore." Then he stormed up to Mum's bedroom, where he stayed for fifteen minutes. Rosaleen listened outside the door the entire time. I couldn't hear what was going on.

On Sundays I stayed in bed all day. I heard the sisters honking the horn to entice me out, but I didn't move. I didn't even look out the window. I just wanted to hide away from them all. I wondered if maybe I should contact Marcus, or even write to him. But I didn't know what on earth I should say. All I could think of was "sorry," and that wasn't enough.

One day a van arrived with all of our stuff from Barbara's husband's warehouse. I watched them back the van down the trail that led to the garage and didn't feel an ounce of excitement. Those things didn't belong to me anymore. They belonged to that girl who used to live in that house. I didn't know who I was anymore. I fell back asleep again. I woke up when I heard the doorbell ring. It was Sister Ignatius again. She was being very persistent. At first

I just thought she was friendly, then concerned, but that day she sounded a little frantic. I listened to her from my bedroom. It was all mumbling, but then Sister Ignatius raised her voice.

"Are you just going to *muffle muffle* lie up there and let her think she's done something wrong, let that poor boy *muffle muffle* all that?"

Muffled words.

"Tell her that she must come to see me."

Muffle, muffle.

Then the door slammed. I looked out the window, peered above the windowsill and saw Sister Ignatius, wearing a floral shirt and skirt, walking away with her head down. My heart broke for her but it also lifted in a weird way. She was telling Rosaleen to make sure I didn't feel guilty. Maybe she'd forgiven me after all. Even thinking that that was possible lifted my spirits. It gave me hope, made me think I was overreacting and that maybe I should just get over it.

That night I couldn't settle, I couldn't sleep at all. I took the diary from the floorboards and waited and waited for the words to appear, hoping that by ignoring it I hadn't made it all disappear. When it finally arrived it made me sit up and take notice.

Wednesday, 22 July

I called Marcus today. I found his name in the phone book. There aren't many Sandhursts in Meath. Turns out his dad is a big legal eagle and has a famous firm in Dublin. How much more embarrassment could I have caused his family? I was terrified I was going to have to speak to his parents first but some woman answered, sounded all official, and then put me straight through to Marcus. As soon as he heard my voice I had to plead with him not to hang up. Then when I'd convinced him, I had no idea what to say. I apologized so much, going on and on and on, that he eventually stopped me. He said that all the charges had been dropped. Hadn't I been told?

No.

I asked him if his dad had arranged that. He couldn't believe I'd asked him that. He said I'd far more problems than he'd thought if I didn't know. He wished me well and hung up.

What on earth was he talking about? If I didn't know what?

I called Marcus the next day, feeling less nervous knowing his dad wouldn't answer. It all went exactly as I'd written except instead of my asking if his dad had arranged for the charges to be dropped, I asked how they had been dropped. An entire night to think about it and that's the best I could come up with. I still didn't get any answers. In fact, I think he hung up even sooner. If I didn't know *what*? What was he talking about? I needed to find out.

Thursday, 23 July

I spent time with Mum in her bedroom before I went to bed. She was humming a tune to herself. I don't know what it was but it made her smile. I told her I'd something for her and I took the glass tear out of my pocket and laid it down on the bedside table. She stopped humming as soon as she saw it. Then she lay on the bed, her eyes still turned enough for her to see it. She just kept staring at it.

"It's pretty isn't it?" I said.

She looked at me, a sharp look that took me aback a little, then she stared at the glass tear again. It seemed like its very presence offended her and so I reached to take it back. Her hand came up quick and landed on mine. It didn't hurt but I got a shock and so I just left it with her.

Later that night I was fast asleep, dreaming of visiting Marcus in prison when I felt a hand on my shoulder. In the dream it was a prison guard but I quickly woke up and it was Mum's face that was close, her nose almost touching mine. I swallowed my scream. She whispered into my ear, "Where did you get it?"

I was still half asleep, I didn't know what she was talking about. I didn't know if she meant the diary, or if it was the packet of cigarettes I'd hidden in my wardrobe.

"The tear," she whispered again, with urgency in her voice.

I panicked, to be honest. I thought I was going to be in trouble for going over to Rosaleen's mother's house when I wasn't supposed to. I was half asleep, like I said, and in shock that Mum was here in my room—talking—in the middle of the night. I could hear the springs in Arthur and Rosaleen's bed move and I just felt frozen in some kind of strange fear. And so, well, I lied. I told her that I found it around the house, that I thought it was nice so I kept it.

As soon as I'd said that, I immediately knew what was different in her, apart from the fact that she was talking. It was the light that had suddenly arrived in her eyes, making them alive again. I had missed that. But as soon as I said those words, as soon as I lied, the light faded again. Her eyes were dull, empty, lifeless again. I'd killed whatever excitement was rushing through her. I'd thrown water on the fire. She left the room silently and returned to her bedroom.

Then Rosaleen's door opened. Footsteps down the corridor. My bedroom door opened. The long white nightie was illuminated in the moonlight. She interrogated me for a few minutes about hearing a door close but I denied it. She stared at me in a long silence, as if trying to decide whether I was telling the truth or not, nodded, then closed the door. I heard her bedsprings and then, silence.

I couldn't sleep after that. I just kept thinking about whether my lie to Mum was right or wrong. By the time morning light had *flooded my room, I realized I had made a mistake. I should have just told her the truth.*

I'll write again tomorrow.

After reading that entry, I had the day to plan what I was going to say to Mum. I felt anxious, watching Mum's silent living and knowing that soon enough that spell would be broken. I tried to remember the diary entry word for word. I didn't want to get it all wrong. I wanted to do and say exactly the same things as I'd written so as to summon the same response. I wanted her to come to my room in the middle of the night. Then I wanted to tell her the truth about the glass teardrop.

Finally after dinner I went upstairs to her bedroom. She was lying in bed, examining the ceiling, humming softly.

"I have something for you," I said, my voice so croaky that the words were barely audible. I started again. "I have something for you."

She kept humming as I reached into my pocket and felt around for the glass, which was warm from my body. I placed it on the bedside table. The gentle tapping sound made her eyes turn, but not the rest of her head. When her eyes landed on the glass teardrop, she instantly stopped humming.

"It's pretty, isn't it?" I asked.

She looked at me then, and I recognized the moment that the spark entered her eyes. She returned her stare to the teardrop. Not wanting to but knowing I should follow protocol, I reached for it, and just as I'd written, out came her hand and it landed on mine to prevent me from taking it.

"No," she said firmly.

"Okay," I said. "Okay."

I went back to my room and sat up in bed, unable to sleep, knowing she would awaken me. I read the diary entry for the next day, unsure whether it would be accurate, as events that were about to unfold would probably alter the day that Tamara of Tomorrow would have.

Friday, 24 July

Happy Birthday to me. Seventeen. I decided to get out of bed early this morning and Rosaleen was surprised to see me. I think I almost gave her a heart attack in the pantry when I entered the kitchen. I thought she was up to something, because she looked as guilty as sin and shoved something in the pocket of her apron. It could have been something for the cake but I don't know . . .

She gave me an awkward hug and kiss, and then danced off with Mum's breakfast tray and to get my gift from her bedroom. She returned with a perfectly wrapped gift, pink paper with white and pink ribbon. It was a basket of strawberry bubble bath, soaps, and shampoo. She was practically hyperventilating while I opened it, leering over me with a nervous smile to see if I liked it or not. I told her I did. I told her it was perfect and I genuinely did like it. Though it was different for me. Last year for my sixteenth birthday, I'd received a Louis Vuitton handbag and a pair of Gina shoes. But weirdly I was more grateful for this bath set because I actually needed it. I was running out of shampoo and the red squirrels here aren't easily impressed by Louis Vuitton bags.

Then she said an extraordinary thing—"I saw it last month, would you believe, and thought to myself and I even said to Arthur, 'That's got Tamara's name written all over it.' I've been hiding it in the garage since then and I was so terrified you'd find it." Then she giggled nervously.

That comment chilled me. Rosaleen was cleverer than I gave her credit for. There was no way that she would have avoided my going to the garage, or tried to stop us from storing our belongings in there because she was simply hiding a little soap basket. She was either clever or she thought I was stupid. She stirred my hunger to get inside that garage even more.

Mum slept all day again. Zoey and Laura both phoned the house. I told Rosaleen to tell them I was out. Sister Ignatius came by with a present for me. Rosaleen offered to pass it to me but Sister wouldn't give it to her. The longer I ignore her, the worse I'm making it. Now I've so much more to apologize for. She's been the best friend I've had here but I just feel like hiding from the world. I can't bear being seen.

After dinner, Rosaleen emerged from the pantry with a chocolate cake with candles singing "Happy Birthday." That must have been what I almost caught her doing in the pantry this morning. It's probably too late to check that apron pocket now.

I'll write again tomorrow.

I must admit I hadn't thought much about my birthday during the past couple of weeks, and the times I did, it was with a heavy heart for poor Marcus. If only we'd just waited. If only I'd just told him. I hadn't thought about what kind of celebration or presents I could have. But after reading today and yesterday's entry, I was fired up. I was excited.

It was as though I'd spent the past days wandering through a misty glen and I couldn't see past my own nose. But now the fog had lifted. My mind seemed to have come to the end of its wander because I was sitting up in bed, fully alert, my heart racing, and feeling breathless as though I'd run for miles. I was intent on figuring out what on earth Rosaleen had been doing, or was about to do in the pantry tomorrow morning.

As I was working out a plan, I heard Mum's door open. I quickly lay down and closed my eyes. She closed the door behind her ever so quietly, aware that she needed to be silent. She sat on the edge of my bed and I waited for her hand on my shoulder. There it was. The urgent squeeze.

I opened my eyes, not feeling the panic I'd written about, but instead feeling totally prepared.

"Where did you get it?" she whispered, her face close to mine.

I sat up.

"Across the road. In the bungalow," I whispered back.

"Rosaleen's house," she whispered, and immediately looked out the window. "The light," she said, and it was then I noticed a kind of light flashing on my bedroom wall opposite the window. It had the same effect of trees swishing from side to side across the moonlight, causing the light to appear and disappear in the room. Only it wasn't the trees because the light seemed to sparkle more, like glass, releasing prisms of color. It reflected against Mum's pale face and she seemed caught in its field, entranced. I got up and looked out my window and across to the bungalow. Hanging in its front window a glass mobile caught the light, sending beams flashing outward, like a lighthouse.

"There are hundreds more of them over there," I whispered. "I wasn't supposed to be there, but she . . ." We both looked to the wall as we heard the springs in Rosaleen and Arthur's bed. "She was being so secretive. I just wanted to say hello to her mother, that's all. I brought over some breakfast a couple of weeks ago and I saw someone in the shed in the back garden. It wasn't her mother."

"Who was it?"

"I don't know. A woman. An old woman, with long hair. She was working in there. Making them. She must blow the glass herself. Do you think she's allowed to do that? Legally?" I looked at the teardrop in my mum's hand. "There were hundreds of them. All hanging on lines. Then when I went back to collect the tray, this drop was sitting on it."

We both looked at the teardrop.

"What does it mean?" I broke the silence.

"Does she know?" Mum asked, not answering my question.

I took the "she" to mean Rosaleen. "No. What's going on?"

She squeezed her eyes shut and covered them with her hands. She rubbed her eyes fiercely, then ran her hands through her hair as though trying to wake herself up.

"I'm sorry. I feel so fuzzy. I just can't seem to . . . wake up," she said, rubbing her eyes again. Then she looked at me directly, her eyes shining. She leaned in and kissed me on the forehead. "I love you, sweetie. I'm sorry."

"Sorry for what?"

But I was asking her back view as she rose and quietly left my bedroom. I looked outside again at the light, the jagged glass twirling around as though being blown from inside. Then, as I was concentrating on that, the curtain across the way moved, and I realized someone had been watching me. Or had been watching us.

Then I heard Rosaleen's door open, footsteps down the hall and my door opened. There she stood in her vision of white.

"What's wrong?" she asked.

"Nothing," I said, following the diary's script.

"I heard a door close."

"Nothing's wrong."

After a long stare, she left me alone to ponder what I had achieved by telling Mum the truth. Something good had to come of it, surely, and I was about to find out. I went to check the diary to see if the entry had changed. I held my breath.

As I opened it, the pages started to slowly curl inward at the edges, becoming browned and charcoaled, as though they were burning before my very eyes. Eventually they stopped retreating and the burned stained pages stared back at me, hiding tomorrow's world from me.

CHAPTER TWENTY

The Housewife in the Pantry with the Cocoa Powder

I hardly slept after the incident in the early hours of the morning. I lay with my covers up to my chin, rigid with a cold fear that had me jumping in my bed every time I heard the slightest noise. I was pretty sure that the woman in the bungalow was the person who'd followed me to the graveyard the week before last, and as the morning moved in and the sun shed light on the shadows, I became less frightened of her. Perhaps she wasn't dangerous, perhaps just a little odd. By the look of her hair and clothing, she wasn't somebody who saw people regularly. Besides, she'd given me a gift of the small tear-shaped glass. She was obviously reaching out.

But the burned diary pages gave me a sense of impending doom.

When I did sleep I dreamed of fire: of castles on fire, and books on fire. I dreamed of glass being made, blobs of molten hot glass. After waking up with my heart beating wildly in my chest, I tried hard to stay awake. I watched the pages of the diary for the rest of the morning, waiting for the burned pages to uncurl themselves, for the writing to magically reappear in its neat loops and crosses. But they remained the same.

I was up early, determined to catch Rosaleen do whatever she was doing. Catching the Housewife in the Pantry with the Cocoa Powder wasn't exactly the most exciting thing in the world, but I had realized that the diary was leading me somewhere, was trying to show me something, pointing me to the way out—just as I had been trying with the bluebottle. I would be a fool to ignore the miracle of what was occurring. Every word was a clue, every sentence an arrow, a signpost for me to get out of here.

The radio was blaring in the kitchen, Arthur was having a shower, and so Rosaleen thought she had the downstairs entirely to herself. She turned and headed to the pantry, and I ducked out of sight behind the hall door just in time. I could see her in the pantry through the crack in the door.

She had Mum's breakfast tray on the counter and she reached into a box, hidden behind another box, and took out a container of pills. My heart hammered. I had to block my mouth to make sure I didn't scream. I watched her tip two capsules into the palm of her hand, open them, and sprinkle the powder into the porridge, and mix it around. I fought with whether to jump out then and confront her. I had her. But I had to stop myself. They could merely be headache pills, and my pouncing on her would backfire, *again*. I had to find out if they were something more serious, which were making Mum sicker. I leaned in closer to the crack in the door but as I did so, the floorboard under my foot creaked. Rosaleen immediately dropped the container into her apron pocket, picked up the tray, and swiveled around as though nothing had happened. I quickly stepped out from behind the door.

"Oh, good morning," she said with a bright smile. "How is the birthday girl today?" I might have been paranoid but I was convinced her eyes were searching my face to see if I'd witnessed her actions.

"Old." I returned the smile, doing my best to regain my composure.

"Oh, you're not old, child." She laughed. "I remember when I was your age." She threw her eyes to heaven. "It's all ahead of you yet. Now I'll bring this up to your mother and I'll be back down to give you a special birthday breakfast."

"Thanks, Rosaleen," I said sweetly, and watched her race up the stairs.

As she disappeared into Mum's bedroom and the closed door behind her, the mail landed on the mat by the front door. I stalled, waiting for Rosaleen to come flying down on her broomstick to snatch it, but she didn't. She didn't hear it. I walked over and reached for the post—only two white envelopes, probably bills— and rushed into the kitchen with them. I didn't know what to do. I looked around quickly for somewhere to hide them. I wouldn't have time to read them now. I heard Rosaleen's feet on the stairs again and my heart slammed in my chest. Last second, I decided to tuck the envelopes into the back of my tracksuit bottoms and covered them over with my baggy boyfriend cardigan. I stood in the center of the kitchen with my hands behind my back looking as guilty as sin.

She slowed when she saw me. The muscles in her neck protruded.

"What are you doing?" she asked.

"Nothing."

"You're not doing nothing. What's in your hands, Tamara?" she said forcefully.

"Fucking thongs," I said, pulling at the back of my trousers.

"Show me your hands." She raised her voice.

I took my hands out from behind my back; waved them at her cockily.

"Turn around." Her voice quivered.

"No," I said defiantly.

The doorbell rang. Rosaleen didn't move. Neither did I.

"Turn around," she repeated.

"No," I repeated, stronger, firmer.

The doorbell rang again.

"Rose!" Arthur shouted down the stairs. Rosaleen didn't answer and we heard boots on the stairs as he made his way down. "I'll get it," he said, glancing at us with frustration. He opened the door.

"Weseley," I heard Arthur say.

"I couldn't back the van up any more, is that okay? Is it in far enough? Oh, hi, Tamara," he said, as he stepped into the hall, in view of the kitchen.

Rosaleen's eyes narrowed even more.

I smiled. Yes, I had a friend that she didn't know about.

I looked at Weseley with wide eyes, willing him to pick up that something was wrong. I didn't want him and Arthur to leave.

"We'll see you two later," Arthur said.

The front door closed behind them and Rosaleen and I were left facing one another in the kitchen.

"Tamara," Rosaleen said gently. "Whatever you are hiding, and I think I know what it is, just give it back."

"I'm not hiding anything, Rosaleen. Are you?"

She twitched.

On that note we heard a bang from upstairs, a crash of plates, and then feet on the floorboards. We both snapped out of our staring match and immediately looked up.

"Where is he?" I heard my mother screech.

I looked at Rosaleen and ran past her.

"No, child." She pulled me back.

"Rosaleen, let go, she's my mother."

"She's not well," she said nervously.

"Yes, and I wonder why that is!" I yelled in her face, and ran upstairs.

I didn't make it that far. Mum had flung the door open and with wide eyes, terrified eyes, was searching the hallway.

"Where is she?" she said, unable to focus on me.

"Who? Rosaleen?" I started, but she pushed by me when she saw her at the bottom of the stairs.

"Where is he?" she demanded, standing at the top of the stairs in her dressing gown.

Rosaleen, wide-eyed, was wringing her hands in her apron. I could still see the outline of the container of pills in the pocket. I looked from one to the other, not understanding what was going on.

"Mum, he's not here," I said, trying to hold her hand. She shook it away.

"He is. I know it. I can feel him."

"Mum, he's not here." I felt tears welling. "He's gone."

Her head twisted around to me then and her voice lowered to a whisper. "He's not gone, Tamara. They only said he was but he's not. I can *feel* him."

I was crying now. "Mum, stop, please. That's just . . . that's just . . . his spirit that you feel around you. He's always going to be with you. But he's gone . . . he's really gone. Please . . ."

"I want to see him," she demanded of Rosaleen.

"Jennifer," Rosaleen said, her hands reaching out even though she was too far away to touch her. "Jennifer, just relax, go back and lie down."

"No!" Mum shouted, her voice trembling now. "I want to see him! I know he's here. You're hiding him!"

"Mum," I cried, "she's not. Dad's dead, he's really dead."

Mum looked at me then, and for a moment she seemed so sad. Then she was angry and ran down the stairs. Rosaleen ran for the door but couldn't stop her.

"Arthur!" Mum yelled, heading outside.

Arthur, who was still in the driveway with Weseley, loading equipment into the Land Rover, jumped to attention.

Mum ran out to the garden, shouting, "Where is he?" over and over.

"Jen, stop it now. Relax, it's okay," Arthur called to her calmly.

"Arthur," Mum cried, running for him and throwing her arms around him. "Where is he? He's here, isn't he?"

In shock, Arthur looked to Rosaleen.

"Mum!" I cried. "Arthur, help her. Do something to help her, please. She thinks Dad is still alive."

Arthur looked at her with what seemed to be a broken heart. He took her in his arms, and as Mum's skinny body shook with tears and she asked over and over again where he was and why, he rubbed her back soothingly.

"I know, Jen, I know, Jen, it's okay. It's okay . . ."

"Please help her," I cried, standing in the middle of the garden, looking from Rosaleen to Arthur. "Send her somewhere. Get somebody to help."

"My dad's at home now," Weseley offered quietly. "I can call him and tell him to come around."

Something twisted inside me. A cold fear. An instinct of some sort. I thought of the burned diary, of the fire in my dreams. I had to get Mum out of the house.

"Take her to him," I said to Arthur.

Arthur looked at me in confusion.

"To Dr. Gedad," I said softly so that Mum couldn't hear.

In Arthur's arms, Mum twisted and slid downward, grief over-taking her.

Arthur nodded at me then, solemnly. Then he looked at Rosa-leen.

"I'll be back soon."

"But you—"

"I'm going," he said firmly.

"I'm coming too," she said hurriedly, swiftly taking off her apron and rushing into the house. "I'll get her coat."

"Weseley, stay with Tamara," Arthur instructed.

Weseley nodded and took a few steps closer to me.

Moments later the three of them were all in the Land Rover, Mum in the back, crying and looking so lost.

Weseley put his arm around my shoulders protectively.

"It's going to be all right," he said gently.

When we arrived here I felt like me and Mum were all washed up, two people who'd landed on the beach coughing and spluttering after our boat had gone down. We were a mess. We had nothing, belonged to nothing, and felt aimless, as though we were trapped in a waiting room with no doors.

I've realized, though, that when people are washed up, they haven't just been torn apart—they're the survivors. The other night I was forced to watch some nature documentary with Arthur about the South Pacific islands, how they're so far apart it was difficult to explain how life spread from one to another. Then these coconuts came bobbing along. All washed up, the narrator said. Two lost things that had survived the seas and arrived on a coastline. What did they do? They implanted themselves in the sand and grew into trees and lined the beaches. Sometimes a lot can come of being all washed up. You can really grow.

Even though Mum had a fit, thought that Dad was still alive, and she appeared to be falling apart, I felt like it was the start of something new, something better. And as we watched them drive away, Rosaleen looking back at us with concern, not wanting to leave us but not wanting to leave Arthur and Mum alone, I really couldn't help it. I smiled and I waved.

CHAPTER TWENTY-ONE

K Is for . . . Kangaroo

As soon as they were gone, I raced into the house. On the coat stand, Rosaleen's apron had been messily strewn across the top in her effort to hurry outside. I grabbed it and dug my hand into the pocket.

"Tamara, what are you doing?" Weseley was close behind me. "Maybe I should make you a cup of tea or something, to calm you dow— What the hell is that?"

He was referring to the container of pills I held up in my hand.

"I was hoping you could tell me." I held up the pills. "I caught Rosaleen putting these in Mum's breakfast."

"What? Whoa, Tamara," Weseley said. "She was putting *pills* in her food?"

"I saw her opening them and emptying the powder into the cereal and then mixing it around. She doesn't know I saw her."

"Well, maybe they're prescription pills."

"You think? Let's see, shall we? Despite the fact Rosaleen likes to pretend that I know nothing of my own mother's medical history,

I do know that her name isn't . . ." I read the label on the container. "Helen Reilly."

"That's Rosaleen's mother. Let me see them." He took it from me. "They're sleeping pills."

"How do you know?"

"It says it on the label. Oxazepam. That's a sleeping pill. She's putting these in your mum's food?"

I swallowed, tears springing in my eyes.

"Are you sure you saw her do this?"

"Yes, I'm sure. And Mum hasn't stopped sleeping since we arrived. Nonstop."

"Does your mum usually take them? Is Rosaleen just trying to help her, maybe?"

"Weseley, Mum is so drugged she can barely remember her own name. These are not *helping* her. It's almost like Rosaleen's trying to make her worse. These are making her worse."

"We have to tell somebody."

The relief at hearing "we" came like a tidal wave.

"I have to tell my dad. He'll have to tell somebody, okay?"

"Okay."

I felt hope now that I was no longer alone. I sat on the stairs while Weseley phoned his dad to tell him.

"Well?" I jumped up as soon as he'd hung up.

"They were in the room with him so he couldn't comment on it. He just said he'd take care of it. We'll just have to keep these safe in the meantime."

"Right." I took a deep breath. "So will you help me get Arthur's toolbox, please?"

"What do you need that for?" he asked, completely baffled now.

"To break open the lock on the garage."

"What?"

"Just . . ." I searched for the words. "Help me, please. We don't have much time and I'll explain everything later. But for now can you please, please help me? They're rarely out of the house. This is my only opportunity."

He thought about it in a long silence, turned the container of pills around in his hand while thinking. "Okay."

While Weseley ran into the work shed beside the house, I paced the garden, hoping they wouldn't return before I'd had a chance to have a good look around. I stopped pacing to peer across at the bungalow, wanting to see if the glass that had shone directly into my bedroom was still there. It was gone. But something on the garden wall caught my attention. A box. I moved closer.

"Weseley," I called.

He immediately heard the warning in my voice and jogged over, following where my finger was pointing.

"What's that?" he asked.

I crossed the road and examined it. Weseley followed me. The package was covered in brown paper and my name was written on the front, along with "Happy Birthday."

I picked it up and looked around. There was nobody at the windows, behind the net curtains. I opened the brown paper to reveal a brown shoe box. I lifted the lid. Inside was the most beautiful glass mobile, a series of different-sized tears mixed with hearts, joined together with wires through tiny holes. I lifted it up and raised it to the light. It sparkled against the sun and spun around in the breeze. I smiled and looked to the house to wave, to smile, to thank somebody.

Nothing.

"What the hell . . ." Weseley said, examining it.

"It's a gift. For me."

"I didn't know it was your birthday."

"Well, she did."

"Who? Rosaleen's mother?"

"No." I stared at the bungalow again. "The woman."

He shook his head. "And I thought my life was weird. Who is she? My mam and dad didn't think anybody other than Mrs. Reilly lived there."

"I have no idea."

"Let's go in and meet her. To say thanks."

"You think I should?"

He rolled his eyes. "You were given a present—it's the perfect opportunity to go in there."

I chewed on my lip and looked at the house.

"Unless, of course, you're afraid."

That's exactly what I was.

"No, we've got more important things to do right now," I said. I crossed the road with the box and hurried to the back garden, to the garage, with Weseley following me.

"You know, Sister Ignatius has been going crazy trying to see you. You just ran off that day and you gave her a fright. You gave us both a fright."

I glared at Weseley while he poked around in the toolbox for the correct tool to break the lock.

"I heard about what happened," he continued. "You okay?"

"Yes, I'm fine. I don't want to talk about it," I snapped again. "Thank you," I added more gently.

"Heard your boyfriend is in a bit of trouble."

"I said I don't want to talk about it," I snapped. "And he's not my boyfriend."

He started laughing at that. "So you know just how I feel."

Despite all that had gone on that morning, I smiled.

It didn't take Weseley long to pick the lock. As soon as we were in the garage I was immediately faced with my old life, all of it piled up, out of order, the kitchen with the living room, my bedroom piled on top of the games room, the spare bedroom with the bathroom towels. It fit together as perfectly as the thoughts in my head. Leather couches, plasma TVs, ridiculously shaped furniture that seemed so gaudy and soulless now.

I was more interested in seeing what Rosaleen and Arthur had hiding in here. As Weseley threw the dustsheets off the far end of the garage I was highly unimpressed. Just more old furniture, destroyed by time, eaten away by dust mites and smelling of mothballs. I don't know what I'd been expecting—a dead body or two, a money printer, boxes of guns and weaponry, a secret entrance to Rosaleen's Batcave. Anything other than this stinky old furniture.

I made my way back to my belongings. Weseley soon followed, oohing and aahing at a few items as he rooted around in the boxes. Taking a break, we sat on my once-upon-a-time living room couch, looking through my photo album while Weseley laughed at the various stages of my adolescence.

"Is that your dad?"

"Yeah," I said, and smiled, looking at a photo of his happy, animated face, while on the dance floor at a friend's wedding. He loved dancing, even though he was crap at it.

"He's so young."

"Yeah."

"What happened?"

I sighed.

"You don't have to talk about it if you don't want to."

"I don't mind." I swallowed. "He just . . . borrowed so much money, he couldn't pay it back. He was a developer, very successful. He had properties all over the world. We didn't know but he was in big trouble. He'd started selling everything to pay back the debts."

"He didn't tell you there was a problem?"

I shook my head. "He was too proud. He would have felt he'd failed us." My eyes filled. "But I wouldn't have cared, I really wouldn't have." But I knew I was protesting too much. I imagined Dad trying to tell me he was selling off everything. Of course I would have cared—I would have moaned and whined. I wouldn't have understood, I would just have been embarrassed about what everyone thought of us. I would have missed Marbella in the summer, Verbier for New Year's. I would have shouted at him, called him everything under the sun, and I would have stormed off to my bedroom and slammed the door. Greedy little pig that I was. But I wish he'd have given me the opportunity to understand. I wish he'd have sat me down and talked about it, and we could all have worked it out together. I'd live anywhere—in one room, in the castle ruin— if it meant we could all just be together.

"I don't care about losing anything. I'd rather have him back." I sniffed. "We've lost everything now, including him. I mean, what was the point?"

I turned the page of the album and we both laughed. Me, two front teeth missing as I hugged Mickey Mouse at Disney World.

"Aren't you . . . I don't know . . . angry at him? If my dad did that, I'd . . ." Weseley shook his head, unable to imagine it.

"I was," I replied. "I was so angry at him for so long. But over the last few weeks I've been thinking about what he must have been going through. Even in my lowest days I never could do what he did. He must have felt so much pressure, he must have been so miserable. He must have felt so trapped. And . . . well, when he died they couldn't take anything else. Mum and I were protected."

"You think he did it for you?"

"I think he did it for a lot of reasons. For all the wrong reasons, but for him they were all right."

"Well, I think you're very brave," Weseley said, and I looked up at him and tried not to cry.

"I don't feel brave."

"You are," he said, his eyes locking with mine.

"I've made the most stupid embarrassing mistakes," I whispered.

"That's okay. We all make mistakes." He smiled wryly.

"Well, I don't think I make as many as you," I added, trying to lighten the atmosphere. "You seem to make different mistakes with different people almost every night."

He laughed. "Okay, let's see what Rosaleen's hiding under here."

Unable to take my eyes off the photos, I opened another album and found my baby photos. I got lost in another world and lost track of time. In the background I could hear Weseley commenting on things he was finding, but I ignored him. Instead I stared at my beautiful dad, happy and handsome, with Mum. Then there was a photo of my christening day. Just me and Mum. Me so tiny in her arms—all that was visible beneath the white blanket was a little pink head.

"Holy shit, Tamara, take a look at this."

I still ignored him, lost in the photo of me and Mum in the church. She was holding me in her arms, a big smile on her face. Whoever had taken the picture—Dad, I assume—had left their finger over the corner of the lens, blocking the priest's face. Knowing Dad, it was probably on purpose. I touched his big white finger in the photo, bright from the flash, and chuckled.

"Tamara, look at all this stuff."

The photograph captured half of the priest, Mum, me in her arms, and another person cut off on the right-hand side, thanks to the dodgy photo skills. Then I noticed somebody else's hand was resting on the top of my head. A woman's hand, I could tell from the ring on her finger. Probably Rosaleen, my godmother, who

255

never seemed to do what my friends' godmothers did, which was just send cards at every occasion with money inside. No, my godmother wanted to spend time with me. Puke.

"Tamara." Weseley grabbed me and I jumped. "Look at this." His eyes were wide. He took me by the hand and a tingle shot up my arm.

I shoved the christening photograph in my pocket and followed him.

Any funny feelings for him quickly evaporated as I looked around the section that Weseley had unveiled.

"What's the big deal?" I asked, unimpressed. It was hardly as exciting as he was making it out to be. Old furniture as dated as anything I'd ever seen. Books, pokers, crockery, paintings all covered up, fabrics, rugs, fireplaces leaning up against the wall, all kinds of bric-a-brac.

"What's the big deal?" he repeated. His eyes were wide as he jumped about the place, picking things up, unveiling more oil paintings of evil-looking children with collars up past their earlobes and fat, unattractive ladies with big boobs, wide wrists, and thin lips. "Look at all this, Tamara. Look, don't you notice anything?"

He knocked down a rug and kicked it with his foot. It unrolled onto the dusty floor.

"Weseley, don't make a mess," I snapped. "We don't have long before they get back."

"Tamara, open your eyes. Look at the initials."

I studied the rug, a dusty-looking thing that might belong on the wall as a tapestry instead of on the floor. It had Ks all over it.

"And look at this." Weseley uncovered a box of china. It too had Ks stamped all over the plates, the teacups, the knives and forks. A dragon draped around a sword, climbing up from flames. Then I remembered the same emblem on the fireguard in the living room of the gatehouse.

"K," I said dumbly. "I don't get it. I don't . . ." I shook my head, looking around the garage, which at first had felt like a rubbish bin and now seemed like a treasure chest.

"K is for . . ." Weseley said slowly as though I was a child, and looked at me, holding his breath.

"Kangaroo," I said. "I don't know, Weseley. I'm confused, I don't—"

"Kilsaney," he said, and chills rushed through me.

"What? But it can't be." I looked around. "How could they have all this stuff?"

"Well, they either stole it . . ."

"That's it!" It all made sense to me. They were thieves—not Arthur, but Rosaleen. I could believe that.

"Or they're storing it for the Kilsaneys," Weseley interrupted my thoughts. "Or . . ." He grinned at me, eyebrows going up and down.

"Or what."

"Or they *are* the Kilsaneys."

I snorted, dismissing it immediately, then became distracted by a flash of red beneath a roll of carpet that Marcus had knocked over. "The photo album!" I said, seeing the red album I'd found the week I'd arrived. "I knew I wasn't imagining it."

We sat down and looked through it, though probably getting dangerously close to the moment when Arthur and Rosaleen would return. Inside there were black-and-white photographs of children, some sepia-colored.

"Recognize any of them?" Weseley asked.

I shook my head and he speeded up as he flipped through.

"Hold on." One photo caught my eye. "Go back."

There was a photograph of two children surrounded by trees. One little girl, and a little boy a few years older. They stood facing one another, holding hands, their foreheads touching. An image of Arthur and Mum's bizarre greeting on our first day here flashed through my mind.

"That's Mum and Arthur," I said, smiling. "She must be only around five years old there."

"Look at Arthur. He wasn't even handsome as a child," Weseley teased, squinting and studying it closer.

"Ah, don't be mean," I said with a laugh. "Look at them. I've never seen Mum as a child."

On the next page there was a photograph of Mum, Arthur, Rosaleen, and another boy.

I gasped.

"Your mum and Rosaleen knew each other as kids," Weseley said. "Did you know that?"

"No." I was breathless, dizzy. "No way. Nobody ever mentioned it."

"Who's the guy at the end?"

"I don't know."

"Does your mum have another brother? He looks the oldest."

"No, she doesn't. Not that she ever mentioned . . ."

Weseley slipped his hand underneath the plastic covering and pulled the photo from the paper.

"Weseley!"

"We've gone this far—you want to know all this or not?"

I swallowed and nodded.

Weseley turned the photograph over.

It read: "Artie, Jen, Rose, Laurie. 1979."

"Laurie, apparently," Weseley said. "Ring any bells? Tamara, you look like you've seen a ghost."

"Laurence Kilsaney, 1967–1992, RIP" on the gravestone.

Arthur had called Rosaleen "Rose" in the car on the way back from Dublin.

"Laurie and Rose" engraved on the apple tree.

"He's the man who died in the fire in the castle. Laurence Kilsaney. His name is on a grave in the Kilsaney graveyard."

"You're kidding."

I stared at the photograph of the four of them, all smiling, the innocence on their faces, everything ahead of them, a future of possibilities. Mum and Arthur were holding hands tightly, Laurence had his arm draped coolly around Rosaleen's neck; it dangled limply across her chest. He stood on one leg, the other crossed it in a pose. He seemed confident, cocky even. His chin was lifted and he smiled at the camera with a grin.

"So, Mum, Arthur, and Rosaleen hung around with a Kilsaney," I thought aloud. "I didn't even know Mum lived here."

"Maybe she didn't. Maybe she just came here on holidays." Weseley continued flipping the pages. All of the photographs were of the same four people, all at different ages, all huddled close together. Some pictures were of them on their own, some in couples, but most of them together. Mum was the youngest, Rosaleen and Arthur closer in age, and Laurence the oldest, always with a great smile and a mischievous look in his eye. Even as a young girl Rosaleen had an older look, a hardness in her eye, a smile that never grew as large as the others.

"Look, there they all are in front of the gatehouse." Weseley pointed at the four of them sitting on the garden wall. Nothing much had changed apart from some of the garden trees, which were now big and full. But the gate, the wall, the house, everything was exactly the same.

"There's Mum in the living room. That's the same fireplace." I studied the photo intently. "The bookcase is exactly the same. Look at the bedroom," I gasped. "That's the one I'm in now. But I don't understand. She lived here, she grew up here."

"You really didn't know any of this?"

"No." I shook my head, feeling a headache coming on. My brain was overloaded with so much information and not enough answers. "I mean, I knew she lived in the country but . . . I remember when we visited Arthur and Rosaleen when I was young, my granddad was always here alone, since my grandma died when my mum was young. I thought he was just visiting Arthur and Rosaleen too but . . . My God, what's going on? Why did they all lie?"

"They didn't really lie though, did they?" Weseley tried to soften the blow. "They just didn't tell you they lived here. That's not exactly the most exciting secret in the world."

"And they didn't tell me that they'd known Rosaleen practically all their lives, that they lived in the gatehouse and they once knew the Kilsaneys. It's not a big deal, but it is if you keep it a secret. But why did they hide it? What else are they keeping from me?"

Weseley looked away from me then, continued going through the photo album as if to find my answers. "Hey, if your granddad lived in the gatehouse, that made him the groundskeeper here. He had Arthur's job."

A startling image flashed through my mind. I was young, my granddad was down on his knees with his hands deep in muck. I remember the black beneath his fingernails, a worm in the soil wriggling around, Granddad grabbing it and dangling it near my face, me crying and him laughing, wrapping his arms around me. He always smelled of soil and grass. His fingernails were always black.

"I wonder if there's a photo of the woman." I flipped through the pages further.

"What woman?"

"The woman in the bungalow who makes the glass."

We studied the following pages, my heart thudding so loudly in my chest, I thought I was going to keel over. I came across another photograph of Rosaleen and Laurence together. "Rose and Laurie, 1987."

"I think Rosaleen was in love with Laurence," I said, tracing their faces with my finger.

"Uh-oh," Weseley said, turning over a page. "But Laurence didn't love Rosaleen."

I looked at the next photograph, eyes wide. It was a picture of Mum as a teenager, beautiful, long blond hair, big smile, perfect teeth. Laurence had his arms thrown around her and was kissing her cheek by the tree with the engraving.

I looked at the back of the photograph. "Jen and Laurie, 1989."

"They could have been just friends . . ." Weseley said slowly.

"Weseley, look at them."

That's all I had to say. The rest was plain to see. It was right there in front of us. They were in love.

I thought about what Mum had said to me when I'd returned from the rose garden the first day I'd met Sister Ignatius. I'd thought she hadn't been speaking properly, I thought she was telling me that I was prettier than a rose. But what if she'd meant exactly what she'd said: "Prettier than Rose"?

And away from them, at the other edge of the photograph, Rosaleen sat on a tartan rug with a picnic basket beside her, staring coldly at the camera.

CHAPTER TWENTY-TWO

Dark Room

I didn't know how long we had until Rosaleen and Arthur returned with Mum, if they were returning with her at all, but I had given up caring about being caught. I was done with their secrets, tired of tiptoeing around and trying to peek underneath things when nobody was looking. Weseley, in full support of my next move, led me back to the bungalow across the road. We were both looking for answers and I had never in my life met anybody like Weseley who was going out on a limb to help me so much. I thought of Sister Ignatius and my heart tugged. I had abandoned her. I needed to see her too. I remembered how during one of our first meetings she had grabbed my arm and told me she'd never lie to me. That she would always tell me the truth. She knew something. She had practically told me then, now that I look back, had quite obviously asked me to question her about it, and I hadn't realized it until now.

Weseley led me down the side passage. My knees trembled as I walked and I expected them at any time to give way and send me to the ground like a house of cards. The morning was darkening and the wind was picking up. It was only noon and already the sky had clouded over, great big gray clouds gathering as though the sky's eyes were covered by bushy eyebrows, its forehead furrowed in concern as it watched me.

"What's that noise?" Weseley asked as we neared the end of the passageway.

We stopped and listened. It was a tinkling sound.

"The glass," I whispered. "It's blowing in the wind."

Unlike the tinkling of a chime, it sounded as though the glass was smashing as the little pieces, the round and the jagged, hit against each other in the wind. Multiplied by hundreds, it was an eerie sound.

"I'm going to go down and check it out," Weseley said once we'd stepped into the back garden. "You'll be fine, Tamara. Just tell the woman you came over to thank her and take it from there. She might tell you more after that."

I nervously watched him walk across the lawn, past the work shed, and he disappeared into the field of glass.

I turned to the house and looked in at the windows. The kitchen was empty. I lightly rapped on the back door and waited. There was no answer. With a shaky hand, which I admonished myself about being so dramatic, I reached out and pulled down the handle. The door was unlocked. I pulled it open a crack and peered inside. There was a narrow hallway, which turned sharply to the right. Then there were three doorways off the hallway, all closed, one on the right, two to the left. The first on the left led to the kitchen—I already knew there was nobody in there. I stepped inside, trying to keep the door open so that I wouldn't feel so trapped, and so it wouldn't feel like I was totally breaking and entering, but the wind was so strong it blew shut. I jumped and once again told myself how stupid I was being. An old woman and the woman who'd given me the gift were hardly going to hurt me. I rapped lightly on the door to my right. There was no answer and so I gently turned the handle and slowly opened the door. It was a bedroom, definitely the bedroom of an old lady. It smelled damp and of talcum powder. There was an old dark wood bed with floral duvet cover, slippers by the bed, and a duck-egg-blue carpet that had seen more than a few Shake 'n' Vacs. There was a freestanding wardrobe probably containing all of her worldly outfits. A small dresser with a tarnished mirror sat against the door wall, with a hairbrush, medication, the rosary, and the Bible all neatly laid out on its surface. Facing the bed was the window overlooking the back garden. There was nothing else, nobody inside.

I closed the door gently and continued down the hall. The carpet was covered by an unusual kind of plastic mat, as if to keep it clean. It made a scraping noise beneath my feet and I was surprised nobody had heard me coming. Unless the woman was in the work shed again, which meant that she'd see Weseley. I froze and almost went back outside but I'd come this far and there was no going back. I reached the end of the hall, where it turned to the right. There was another door at the end of the hall, which led to the television room, which I had already seen through the window. The television was up loud enough so that I could hear the *Countdown* clock ticking, so I assumed that was where Rosaleen's mother was. But after all my wondering about her now wasn't the time for me to introduce myself; it wasn't her I was looking for. To the left of me there was another door, behind which I guessed was the second bedroom.

I knocked so gently the first time I barely even heard it myself. My knuckles brushed against the dark wood as though they were just feathers. The second time around I knocked harder and I waited longer, but there was no sound inside.

I turned the handle. The door was unlocked and it opened.

With my overactive imagination, I had envisaged much about Rosaleen's secrets over the past few weeks, possibly years, but in reality they had all disappointed me. The findings in the garage, while intriguing and surprising for me not to have known that Arthur and Mum were friends of Rosaleen since childhood, didn't live up to the scenarios I had created in my mind. The initial mystery behind the house turned out to be Rosaleen's ailing mother; the dead bodies in the garage had actually been everything the castle had been stripped of. It was all slightly disappointing because it didn't match up to the level of tension I felt around Rosaleen. It didn't match up to the level of secrecy she was shrouded in.

But this time I wasn't disappointed.

This time I wished for seventies carpets and dark wood, for the smell of a damp and badly designed bedroom. Because what I saw shocked me to the core so that I just stood there, frozen, my mouth agape, unable to breathe properly.

On each of three walls, covered from floor to ceiling, were photographs of me. Me as a baby, me at my Communion, me on a visit to the gatehouse when I was three years old, then four years old, six years old. Me at my school plays, me at my birthday parties, as a flower girl at my mum's friend's wedding, dressed as a witch at Halloween. A scribbled drawing I'd done during my first year at school. Then me at the age of eight, standing in the middle of the road to the castle by the house, bored as my mother talked with Arthur and Rosaleen over sandwiches and tea. There was a photograph of me at the entrance to the gatehouse from only last week, sitting on the wall, swinging my legs, my face up to the sun. And of me and Marcus, the first time he called to the house, of another day when we climbed into the bus and went on a journey. There was a photograph of the morning Mum, Barbara, and I arrived at the gatehouse for the first time. Another one of me only a fortnight ago at the gravesite, placing flowers by Laurence Kilsaney's grave. Me walking toward the castle. Photographs of me with Sister Ignatius, walking, talking, lazing on the grass, and one of me in the castle, sitting on the steps the morning I first discovered the diary entry, with my eyes closed face up to the sun. I had known somebody was watching. I had written it. The photos were endless, like a history of my whole entire life, scenes that I'd long forgotten and some which I never knew had been captured on celluloid.

In the corner of the room there was a single bed, unkempt, and untidy. There was a small locker beside that, its surface filled with pills. Before I turned around to leave, my eye caught sight of a familiar picture. I walked to the far wall and took the now-crumpled photograph out of my pocket. I held it up to the wall and saw that they were almost a perfect match, though the one on the wall was much clearer. Gone was the finger before the lens and so the priest's face was visible, Mum beside him with me in her arms. On my pink head was a hand with the ring. This photograph on the wall was much bigger than the one I had found. It had been blown up and zoomed in so the ring was very clear, very much in focus, and the person to whom it belonged was obvious.

Sister Ignatius.

Beneath the christening photograph was my mother holding me over the basin, and the priest trickling water on my head. I recognized that basin. It was now in the chapel in the grounds filled with spiders and dust, beside that was the flushed face of my mother lying in bed, hair sticking to her damp forehead, me wrapped up in her arms, just born. Another photograph of Sister Ignatius holding me. Just born.

I'm not just a nun. I'm also trained in midwifery. She'd said that only days ago.

"Oh my God." I trembled, my knees buckling from under me.

I reached out to the wall but there was nothing for me to cling to apart from photographs of myself. My fingers caught on them and pulled them down as I fell to the floor. I didn't pass out but I couldn't stand. I wanted to get out of here. I put my head between my legs and slowly breathed in and out.

"You're lucky today," I heard a voice say behind me and I snapped to attention. "Usually this door is locked. Even I have never seen inside this room. He's been busy."

Rosaleen was standing at the door, leaning against the doorway, her arms behind her back. So calm.

"Rosaleen," I croaked, "what's going on?"

She chuckled. "Oh, child, you know what's going on. Don't pretend you haven't been snooping." She looked at me coldly.

I shrugged nervously, knowing how guilty I looked.

Then she threw something at me and it landed on the floor.

The envelopes I'd taken that morning and left in the kitchen when I'd found the pills in Rosaleen's apron pocket. Then she threw something else, heavier, which thudded when it hit the carpet. I knew what it was right away. I reached out to grab the diary. I fumbled with the lock in an effort to open it and see if the burned pages were gone. Perhaps I'd changed the course of events already. But my questions were answered before I'd time to find out for myself.

"You spoiled my fun, burning those pages." She smiled a crooked smile. "Arthur and your mother are at the house. I probably shouldn't have left them . . ." She looked off toward the house while chewing on the inside of her mouth. She appeared so vulnerable then, the sweet aunt who was trying to carry the world on her shoulders, that I almost reached out to her, but when she turned to me the coldness was back in her eyes. "But I had to leave them. I knew you'd be here. I've an appointment to meet with Officer Murphy later today. You don't know what that's about, I suppose?"

I swallowed hard and shook my head.

"A bad liar," she said quietly, "just like your mother."

"Don't you dare talk about my mother like that." My voice trembled, but I was suddenly angry.

"I was only trying to help her, Tamara," she said. "She wasn't sleeping. She was tormenting herself. Going over and over the past all the time, starting to ask questions every time I brought a meal . . ." She was speaking to herself now, almost as though she was trying to convince herself. "I did it for her. Not for me. And she was barely eating, so it's not as though she took much of it. I did it for her."

I frowned, not knowing whether to interrupt or let her talk it out with herself. While she was deep in thought, I reached for the envelopes. Looked at the name on the outside.

Arthur Kilsaney
The gatehouse
Kilsaney Demesne
Kilsaney
Meath

The next envelope had the same address but it was addressed to both Arthur and Rosaleen.

"But . . ." I looked from one envelope to another. "But . . . I don't—"

"But, but, but," Rosaleen mimicked me, and it sent shivers running down my spine.

"Arthur's surname is Byrne. Just like Mum's," I said in a shrill voice.

Rosaleen's eyes widened and she smiled. "Well, well, well. The cat wasn't quite as curious as I thought."

I tried to gather the energy to stand. When I did, Rosaleen seemed to ready herself, while doing something with one arm still behind her back.

I looked at the envelopes again, trying to figure out what was going on.

"Mum isn't a Kilsaney. She's Byrne."

"That's right. She isn't a Kilsaney, was never a Kilsaney, but she always wanted to be." Her eyes were as cold as her voice. "She only wanted the name. She always wanted what wasn't hers, thieving little bitch," she spat. "She was a bit like you, always showing up when she wasn't wanted."

My mouth dropped. "Rosaleen," I breathed. "What's . . . what's wrong with you?"

"What's wrong with me? Nothing's wrong with me. I've only spent the past few weeks cooking and cleaning, doing everything, looking after everybody, holding everything together, as usual, for two ungrateful little"—then her mouth opened wide and she shouted with such anger I had to block my ears—"*LIARS!*"

"Rosaleen!" I shouted back. "Stop! What's going on?" I was crying now. "I don't know what's going on!"

"Yes, you do, child," she hissed.

"I'm not a child, I'm not a child, I'm not a child!" I finally yelled the words that I'd been saying over and over in my head.

"Yes, you are. You should have been *MY CHILD*!" she shouted. "She took you from me! You should have been mine. Just like him. He was mine. She took him from me!" Then, as if those words took all the energy out of her, she seemed to collapse in on herself.

I was silent while I searched my brain hard. She couldn't have been talking about Laurence Kilsaney anymore—that was years ago, before I was born—so she must have been talking about . . .

"My dad," I whispered. "You were in love with my dad."

She looked up at me then, such hurt in her face I almost felt sorry for her.

"That's why Dad never came back here with Mum. That's why he always stayed in Dublin. Something happened between all of you all those years ago."

Rosaleen started laughing. Quiet chuckles at first, but then she threw her head back and laughed loudly.

"George Goodwin? Are you serious? George Goodwin was always a loser, ever since he came here in his pretentious little car with his equally pretentious father, offering to buy the place. 'It'll make a great hotel, it'll make a great spa,'" she mimicked, and I could see him saying it, could imagine him arriving in his pinstripe suit with Granddad Timothy. Only short of calling in a bulldozer to knock the castle down, he must have been the devil to these people who wanted to protect their castle and their land. "He had to have everything, including your mother, even if she did already have a child. Best thing he did was to take you and your mother away from here. No! The best thing he ever did was end his life so those *suits* couldn't take this land away too. That's the only good thing George Goodwin ever did. And he knew it too. I bet he knew it right up until he took that first sip of whisk—"

"*STOP IT!*" I shrieked. "*STOP IT!*" I ran up to hit her, slap her, anything to stop her from saying all these lies, these horrible nasty dirty evil lies, but she got to me first. Those arms, toned from punching dough and rolling apple pies all day, toiling in her organic vegetable patch, carrying trays up and down those stairs every morning, were strong. With one arm held out she pushed me so hard I instantly felt winded, as though my chest had been crushed. I went flying backward and hit my head against the corner of the bed. I lay on the floor gasping. Then I started to cry. My vision was blurred, I tasted blood in my mouth. I was disoriented, couldn't stand up, couldn't find the door.

After a time, I don't know how long, my eyes focused and finally saw Rosaleen at the doorway, her image blurred. Feeling woozy I sat up and touched my head, finding blood on my trembling fingers.

"Now, now," Rosaleen said gently, "why did you make me do that, child? We'll have to work out what we're going to say," she said. "We can't have you going back like this, after seeing all of this. No, I must think. I must think now."

I mumbled something so incoherent I have no idea what I was trying to say. All I could think of was that Rosaleen had said my dad had taken me and my mum away from here, and that Mum had already had me. It was impossible. Nothing made sense. Mum and Dad had met at a banquet dinner, a posh meal with lots of people, and as soon as he'd laid eyes on her he had to have her. He said it himself, he said it all the time. They fell in love right away. Then they had me. That was the story, that's what Dad had told me. I had such a headache now and I was so tired, my eyelids so heavy, I just needed to close them. I realized then that Rosaleen was talking again, but not to me. I opened my eyes. She was looking down the hall, looking a little fearful.

"Oh." She had her small voice on again. "I didn't hear you come in. I thought you were in the work shed."

The woman who made the glass. If I shouted out I could get some help but I heard a man's voice instead and that made me nervous. It wasn't Arthur's voice, and it wasn't Weseley— Oh, where was he? Had he been hurt? He'd gone to the field of glass. All that glass—I'd had nightmares about that glass almost every night. Blowing in the wind, it would scrape and scratch, pierce and stab as I ran up and down the field, trying to get out, and the woman would be watching me. Where was the woman now?

"Why don't you go into the kitchen and I'll make you a cup of tea? Wouldn't that be nice?" I heard her pause. "What do you mean? How long have you been standing there?" Another pause. "But she ran at me. I was only trying to defend myself. I'm going to bring her back to the house as soon as I sort her out."

The man said something else and I could hear the sound of the plastic floor. A footstep followed by a dragging sound, a step again, then another dragging.

I pulled myself up to a sitting position and then I held on to the bed to try to stand up. Rosaleen was so busy talking to the man that she didn't notice me stand. I couldn't hear what the man was saying then but her voice got harder. It lost its nervous sweet edge and was back to the Rosaleen from moments ago. Possessed.

"Possessive," Sister Ignatius had said, pondering my surmise of Rosaleen weeks ago. "That's an interesting choice of word."

"Is this why you never let me into the room?" Rosaleen continued. "Is this how you intended me to find out? This isn't right, you know."

His voice again, followed by a stamping sound, then the dragging.

"And what's this?"

Finally Rosaleen's arm came out from behind her back and she whipped out the glass mobile that had been given to me. I wanted to shout out that it was mine but there was already too much commotion in the hallway.

"This wasn't part of the deal, you know, Laurie. I was happy to let you play around with the glass because you wanted to so much. I thought the fire and the glass would be healing after . . . well, after everything, but you've taken it too far. You've ruined everything, you've ruined absolutely everything. Things have to change now. Things most certainly have to change."

Laurie. Laurence Kilsaney RIP.

I was chilled. She was imagining him. Or she was seeing a ghost. No, that wasn't right, I could hear him too.

There were some angry words at that, and then Rosaleen swung her arm back and flung the glass mobile down the hall. I heard a scream. Then she dived at him and I saw a walking stick being swung and it knocked her away, and she fell back against the wall with a thud. She looked at him fearfully and I backed away into the corner, huddled my head into my legs tightly, just wanting to get out of there, wanting to be anywhere else but there but not being able to move.

"Rose?" I could hear a voice call.

"Yes, Mammy," she said, scrambling to her feet, her voice trembling. "I'm coming, Mammy." She gave the man one last look, then ran down the hall to the television room.

The man stepped into the doorway then and I prepared myself, but I still screamed when I saw him. Beneath long scrawny hair, a distorted face stared back at me. One side of the face looked as though it had melted and the skin had been put back in the wrong place. He quickly lifted a hand to his hair and tried to cover his face. He was wearing a long-sleeve shirt, but as he lifted his hand to his face it revealed a stump. His entire left side drooped downward. His eyes were big and blue, the right one perfectly framed against soft smooth skin, the other was pulled down so much that it appeared to leap from its socket. He started to come toward me and I began to cry.

Then I heard the back door open and the wind whooshing in. I heard steps on the plastic covering, and the man Rosaleen had called Laurie turned in fright.

"Leave her alone!" I heard Weseley shout, and Laurie raised his hands in the air, looking shocked, sad, shaken. Then Weseley came in and saw me. I must have looked a mess because his face changed, anger took over, and he pushed Laurie up against the wall, his hand around his neck.

"What did you do to her?" he growled in his face.

"Leave him," I heard myself say, but I couldn't get sounds out right.

"Tamara, get out of there," Weseley said, his face red, the veins throbbing in his neck from the effort it was taking to hold the man off.

I don't know how but I finally stood up, grabbing the diary, and pushed myself forward. I managed to lay a hand on Weseley to stop him. He let go of the man, grabbed me and pulled me from the room, slamming the door and locking it. He took the key and put it in his pocket, while I heard the man shouting to be let out.

CHAPTER TWENTY-THREE

Bread Crumbs

Just as Weseley and I reached the end of the hallway toward the front door, Rosaleen swung herself around the corner to block us. She reached out and grabbed my arm, but I moved almost outside her grasp and her nails dug into my skin as she pinched me and tried to hold on. I screamed.

"Follow me," Weseley said, and turned and ran the other way.

I started running but was abruptly jerked backward, feeling a pain in my neck as Rosaleen grabbed my hair and tried to pull me back. I elbowed her hard in the stomach and she released me. Despite her evil behavior I still felt bad and stopped to see if she was okay. She was doubled over, winded.

"Tamara, come on!" Weseley shouted.

But I couldn't. This was ridiculous. I didn't understand why we were fighting, why she had turned on me. I had to see if she was all right. As I came near her, she looked up, pulled back her right arm, and slapped me hard across the face. I felt the sting long after her hand left my face. Weseley tugged on me and I had no choice but to run.

We ran out the back door, down the back garden and past the work shed which separated the bungalow from the secret field of glass. Once in the field I realized how much the wind had picked up. It was blustery and my hair was billowing around my face wildly, sometimes blinding me, sometimes stuffing my mouth with a lock of hair. Weseley was squeezing one of my hands so tightly I needed the other to balance myself as we ran across the lumpy grass. The glass was swinging violently in the wind, back and forth, and it was hard to judge whether it was going to come flying at our faces as we darted past.

I held on tightly to Weseley's hand and I just remember thinking, *Don't let go, don't ever let go.* Every now and then he turned around to make sure I was still there, even though his hand was wrapped so tightly around mine it was crushing my fingers. I saw the worry in his face, the panic in his eyes. We were in this together and I had never been so grateful to have such a friend. We ducked under the lines of glass mobiles and made our way to the edge of the garden. Weseley began to figure out a way we could get over the wall. I stood there keeping watch for Rosaleen, who quickly appeared at the work shed and was scanning the garden for us. Our eyes met. She surged forward.

Weseley moved quickly, gathering crates and concrete blocks, building them up so that we could get over the wall. He stepped up to the top block.

"Right, Tamara. I'll lift you up."

I put the diary down on the block and he lifted me up from the waist. I scrambled to pull myself to the top, my bare elbows scraping the concrete, my knees banging against the wall, but finally I was there. Weseley handed me the diary and I jumped into the field on the other side. Pain shot through my ankles and up my legs as I landed. Weseley wasn't far behind. He grabbed my hand again and we ran.

Across the road and straight into the gatehouse, I screamed for Arthur and Mum between heaving breaths. There was no answer and the house stared back silently at us, the ticking of the grandfather clock in the hall the only response as we entered. We both ran up and down stairs, flinging open doors, shouting into every eave. Now I really started to panic. I sat on my bed, the diary in my arms, not knowing what to do. Then, as I hugged it tightly and started to cry, it became clear.

I opened the diary. Slowly but surely the burned pages began to uncurl right before my eyes, unfolding and lengthening, and words no longer neatly looped and lined appeared in jagged and messy scrawls as though written in blind panic.

"Weseley," I called.

"Yes!" he shouted up the stairs.

"We have to go," I shouted.

"Where?" he yelled. "We should call the police. Who was that guy? My God, did you see his face?" I could hear the adrenaline pumping through his words.

I stood up quickly. Too quickly. All the blood rushed to my head and I felt dizzy. Black spots formed before my eyes and I tried to keep walking, hoping they'd eventually disappear. I made my way out to the hall, holding on to the wall, trying to take deep breaths. The pulse in my forehead beat an insane rhythm, my skin felt hot and clammy.

"Tamara, what's wrong?" was all I heard.

I felt the book fall from my hand and hit the ground with a thud. After that—nothing.

I woke up to find myself staring at a painting of Mary, smiling down upon me in a baby-blue-colored veil. Her thin lips smiling and telling me it was all going to be okay, her hands held out and open as though giving me some invisible gift. Then I remembered what had happened in the bungalow and I sat up with a start. My head felt like it was being crushed, as though the atmosphere was pushing down on me.

"Ow," I groaned.

"Hush, Tamara, you must lie down. Slow down now," Sister Ignatius said calmly, taking my hand in hers and placing another on my shoulder to coax me gently back down.

"My head," I croaked, lying back down and taking in her face.

"That's a nasty bang you got," she said, taking a cloth and dipping it in a dish and carefully dabbing at the skin above my eye.

It stung and I tensed.

"Weseley." I panicked, looking around, and pushed her hand away from me. "Where is he?"

"He's with Sister Conceptua. He's fine. He carried you all the way here," she said with a gentle smile.

"Tamara." I heard another voice, and Mum came rushing over to me and fell to her knees. She looked different. She was dressed, for one thing. Her hair was pulled back into a ponytail and her face was thinner, but it was her eyes . . . despite being bloodshot and swollen as if she'd been crying, her eyes had life back in them again. "Are you okay?"

I couldn't believe she was out of bed so I just kept staring at her, studying her, waiting for her to go into a trance again. She leaned forward and kissed me hard on the forehead, so much it almost hurt. She ran her hands through my hair, kissing me again and telling me she was sorry.

"Ouch." I winced as she grabbed my wound.

"Oh, love, I'm sorry." She let go immediately and moved back to examine me. She looked concerned. "Weseley said he found you in a bedroom. There was a man, with scarring . . ."

"The man didn't hit me." I jumped to his defense immediately though I didn't really know why. "Rosaleen showed up. She was so angry. She kept spouting all of these lies about you and Dad. I ran at her to tell her to stop and she pushed me . . ." I placed my hand on my cut. "Is it bad?"

"It won't scar. Tell me about the man." Mum's voice trembled.

"They were having a fight. She called him Laurie," I said, suddenly remembering.

Sister Ignatius held on to the end of the bed tightly as though the floor were swirling beneath her. Mum looked at her, her jaw tightened, and then she looked back at me. "So it's true. Arthur was telling the truth."

"But it's not possible," Sister Ignatius whispered. "We buried him, Jennifer. He died in the fire."

"He didn't die, Sister," I said. "I saw him. I saw his bedroom. He had photographs. Hundreds and hundreds of photographs all over the walls."

"He loved taking photographs," Mum said quietly, as though thinking aloud.

"They were all of me." I said, looking from one to the other. "Tell me about him. Who is he?"

"Photographs? Weseley didn't mention that," Sister Ignatius said, her face pale.

"He didn't see them, but I saw everything. My whole life was on the walls." The words caught in my throat but I kept going. "The day I was born, the christening." I looked at Sister Ignatius then and an anger came flooding through me. "I saw you."

"Oh." Her wrinkled bony fingers went flying to her mouth. "Oh, Tamara."

"Why didn't you tell me? Why did you both lie?"

"I so wanted to tell you," Sister Ignatius jumped in. "I told you I'd never lie, that you could ask me anything, but you never asked. I waited and waited. I didn't think it was my place, but I should have. I realize that now."

"We shouldn't have let you find out this way," Mum said.

"Well, neither of you had the guts to do what Rosaleen did. *She* told me." I pushed Mum's hand away and turned my face from her. "She told me some ridiculous story about Dad arriving here with Granddad, wanting to buy the place to develop it into a spa. She said he met Mum, and he met *me*." I looked at Mum, waiting for her to tell me it was all lies.

She was silent.

"Tell me it's not true." My eyes filled up and my voice trembled. I was trying to be strong but I couldn't. It was all too much. Sister Ignatius blessed herself. I could tell she was shaken.

"Tell me he's my dad."

Mum started to cry and then stopped, took a deep breath, and found strength from somewhere. When she spoke her voice was firm and deep. "Okay, listen to me, Tamara. You have to know that we didn't tell you this because we believed it was the right thing to do all those years ago, and George . . ." She wavered. "George loved you so much, with all of his heart, just like you were his own . . ."

I yelped at that, couldn't believe what I was hearing.

"He didn't want me to tell you. We fought about it all the time. But it's my fault. It's all my fault. I'm so sorry." Tears gushed down her cheeks and though I wanted to feel nothing, to stare her down and show her how she'd hurt me, I couldn't. I felt everything at once. My world had shifted so viciously, I was spinning out of orbit.

Sister Ignatius stood up and placed a hand on Mum's head as she tried to stop her own tears, and comfort me as well. I couldn't look at Mum, so my eyes followed Sister Ignatius as she then crossed to the other side of the room. She opened a cupboard and brought something back over to me.

"Here. I've been trying to give this to you for some time now," she said, her eyes filled. It was a wrapped present.

"Sister, I'm really not in the mood for birthday presents right now, what with my mum telling me she's lied to me my whole entire life." I spoke with venom and Mum pursed her lips. She nodded slowly, accepting whatever it was I threw at her. I wanted to shout at her more. I wanted to use this opportunity to say all the horrible things that I've ever felt about her, just like I used to do when fighting with Dad, but I stopped myself. Consequences. Repercussions. The diary had taught me that.

"Open it," Sister Ignatius said sternly.

I ripped off the paper. It was a box. Inside the box was a rolled-up scroll. I looked to her for answers but she was kneeling beside me, her hands clasped and her head dipped as though in prayer.

I unrolled the scroll. It was a certificate of baptism.

This Certificate of Baptism is to certify that
Tamara Kilsaney
was born on the 24th day of July, 1991,
in Kilsaney Castle, County Meath
and was Presented to the World
with Love
by
Her mother, Jennifer Byrne, and her father,
Laurence Kilsaney
On this day
1st January 1992

I stared at the page, reading it over and over, hoping my eyes had deceived me. I didn't know where to begin.

"Well, first things first, they got the date wrong." I tried to sound confident but I sounded pathetic and I knew it. This was something I couldn't beat with sarcasm.

"I'm sorry, Tamara," Sister Ignatius said again.

"So that's why you kept saying I was seventeen." I thought back over all our conversations. "But if this was right, then I'm eighteen today . . ." I suddenly thought of Marcus and looked up at Mum. "You were going to let Marcus go to jail?"

"What?" Mum looked from me to Sister Ignatius. "Who's Marcus?"

"None of your business," I snapped. "I might tell you in twenty years."

"Tamara, please," she pleaded.

"He could have gone to jail," I said angrily.

Sister Ignatius shook her head wildly. "No. I asked Rosaleen over and over to tell you. If not tell you, to at least tell the police. She kept insisting he'd be fine. But I stepped forward. I told them myself, Tamara. I went to Dublin to Officer Fitzgibbon and gave him this certificate. There was a breaking-and-entering charge too . . . but bearing in mind the circumstances, it's all been dropped."

"What's been dropped? What happened?" my mum asked, looking at Sister Ignatius with concern.

God, Tamara, if you don't know that by now, then you've far more problems than I thought. Listen, I wish you good luck with everything but . . . don't call me again.

That had been our last conversation. Marcus had known the secret then. I was so relieved for Marcus that my anger subsided momentarily. Then I was fuming again. How messed up was I that

I didn't even know my own age? My head pounding, I held my hand to my wound. They had been feeding me lies, dropping a trail of bread crumbs in their path which I had been forced to follow in order to learn the truth for myself.

"So let me get this straight. Rosaleen wasn't lying. Laurie *is* my father. The freak . . . with the photographs?" I said. "Why didn't anybody tell me? Why did everybody lie? Why did you all let me think I lost my dad?"

"Oh, Tamara, George *was* your father. He loved you more than anything in the world. He raised you as his own. He—"

"IS DEAD," I shouted. "And everybody let me think I'd lost my dad. He lied to me. You lied to me. I can't believe this." I was up then, my head spinning.

"Your mother thought Laurie had died, Tamara. You were only one year old. She had a chance to start a new life. George loved her, he loved you. She wanted to start again. She didn't think you needed this hurt."

"And that makes it okay?" I addressed Mum.

"No, no, I didn't agree with it," Sister Ignatius continued. "But she deserved to be happy. She was so broken when Laurie died."

"But he's not dead," I said. "He's living in the bungalow, eating sandwiches and apple pie every bloody day. Rosaleen knew he was alive."

At that Mum broke down and Sister Ignatius held her tightly in her arms, her face revealing her own heartbreak. I stopped then, realizing that it wasn't just me who'd been lied to. Mum had just found out the man she loved hadn't died after all. What kind of a sick joke had they all been playing?

"Mum, I'm sorry," I said softly.

"Oh, darling," she sniffed, "maybe I deserve it. For doing this to you."

"No. No, you don't deserve this. But he doesn't deserve you either. What kind of sicko must he be to pretend to be dead?"

"He was trying to protect her, I suppose," Sister Ignatius said. "He was trying to give the both of you a better life, one that he couldn't give you."

"Arthur said he was badly disfigured?" Mum looked at me. "What . . . what does he look like? Was he kind to you?"

"Arthur?" I snapped to attention again. "Arthur Kilsaney? He's Laurie's brother?"

Mum nodded and another tear fell.

"It's just one thing after another with you all," I said, but not as angrily this time. I hadn't the energy.

"He didn't want to go along with it," Mum said. "Now it makes sense to me why he was so against it. He said he wanted to always be your uncle. We never said he was my brother. Not until you just assumed it and then . . ." She waved her hand, sensing the ridiculousness of it all.

Weseley arrived in the room then. "Okay, the police are on their way. Are you all right?" He looked at me. "How did he hurt you?"

"No, no, he didn't." I rubbed my eyes. "He saved me from Rosaleen."

"But I thought he . . ."

"No." I shook my head.

"I locked him in his bedroom," Weseley said, producing the room key from his pocket. "I thought he was trying to hurt you."

"No, no." I suddenly felt sorry for the man, for Laurie. He had been defending me. He had been reaching out to me, giving me gifts. He'd remembered my birthday. My eighteenth birthday. Of course he had. And how had I thanked him? I'd locked him away.

"Where's Arthur?" Sister Ignatius asked.

"He's gone to the bungalow, to Rosaleen."

And then I remembered. The diary. "No!" I scrambled to get up again.

"Honey, you should relax," Mum said, trying to coax me back down again, but I jumped up.

"He needs to get away from there," I said, panicked. "What have I been doing here all this time? Weseley, call the fire department, quick."

"Why?"

"Honey, just relax now," Mum said, worried. "Lie down and—"

"No, listen to me. Weseley, it's in the diary. I have to stop it. Call the fire department."

"Tamara, it's just a book, it's only—"

"Been right every single day until now," I responded.

He nodded.

"What's that?" Mum suddenly asked, walking to the window.

Over the treetops in the distance, plumes of smoke were drifting up into the sky.

"Rosaleen," Sister Ignatius said with such venom. "Call the fire department," she said to Weseley.

"Give me the key," I said, grabbing it from Weseley and running from the room. "I have to get him. I'm not losing him again."

I heard them all calling to me as I ran, but I didn't stop, I didn't listen. I ran through the trees and followed the smell, ran straight toward the bungalow. I had just lost the father who'd raised me. I wasn't about to lose another.

CHAPTER TWENTY-FOUR

Dreams About Dead People

When I reached the bungalow there was a squad car parked outside. I could see Rosaleen standing on the grass alongside her mother. Talking to her was a rather impatient policeman, who kept asking her over and over if anybody was inside. Rosaleen was wailing, hands covering her face, and looking back at the house as though she couldn't decide. Beside them was Arthur, who was barking at Rosaleen, shaking her by the shoulders and trying to get her to answer.

"He's in the work shed!" she finally shrieked.

"He's not, I looked!" Arthur yelled.

"He has to be!" she shrieked again. "He has to be. He always locked his bedroom door when he went to the work shed."

"Who?" the officer was saying over and over again. "Who's in the house?"

"He's not there." Arthur's voice was hoarse. "My God, woman, what have you done?"

"Oh my God," Rosaleen wailed over and over again.

Her mother was softly crying.

Sirens were wailing in the distance.

I ignored them all and ran past them unnoticed, down the side passage and in through the back door of the bungalow. Smoke was everywhere, filling the halls, so black and thick that as soon as I inhaled I was choked. It sent me to my knees, retching and gasping, stinging my eyes so badly I rubbed them over and over but it only made them worse. I placed my cardigan across my face. Peering out from one eye, I felt my way along the wall. The plastic beneath my feet was dangerously hot and sticky, so that the rubber in my sneakers was sticking to it. I kept to the sides of the hallway, where it was tiled. I felt my way along the wall to his bedroom door. When I placed my hand on the metal door handle it burned me so badly I let go and cowered over, cradling my hand, coughing, eyes stinging, retching, hand burning. The open door at the end of the hall relieved the hallway of some of its smoke and I knew it wasn't far. I could always run out the door.

I shoved the key in the door, hoping the whole thing hadn't melted, and I turned it. Stepping back, I used my foot to push down the handle and the door swung open. More smoke followed me in and I pushed the door closed. The corners of the photographs were curling with the heat. I couldn't see any fire, just smoke, thick black heavy smoke that hurt my lungs. I tried to call out but couldn't, just kept coughing over and over, hoping he'd hear me, that he'd know I was there.

I felt my way along the bed, then felt his body, felt his face. His beautifully scarred face, ruined just like the castle, which carried such a story I was now drawn to it and no longer repelled. His eyes were closed; I could feel his eyelids. I shook him, moved my hands all over his body to try to wake him. Nothing. He was unconscious. Behind me I felt intense heat, felt fire. It would quickly close in on me, in this little room of my photographs. I pulled at the net curtains, bringing a little light into the gray smoky room. I felt around to try to open the windows. They were locked. There weren't any keys. I picked up a chair, threw it at the window over and over to try to smash it, but I couldn't. I tried to pull at him again to get him to his feet, but he was too heavy. I was getting tired, running out of energy, feeling dizzy. I lay down beside him, still trying to wake him. There was nothing I could do, he wasn't waking, and I felt like I was right back on the floor of my dad's office again, blowing air into his body, trying to get his heart beating. Laurie lay there with his eyes closed, motionless.

I wasn't going to leave him. I held his hand and continued to pull him, but he wouldn't budge. The smoke was now so thick. I was suddenly dizzy, overcome by the fumes.

Suddenly I dreamed of the castle, of a banquet with a long table filled with pheasant and pig, everything dripping with grease and sauces, wine and champagne, the most delicious duck and vegetables. Then I was with Sister Ignatius and she was shouting at me to push, but I didn't know what to push. I couldn't see her but I could hear her. Then the darkness faded and the room was filled with such wonderful light, and I was in Sister Ignatius's arms. Then I was in the field of glass, running, running, with Rosaleen hot on my heels. I was holding Weseley's hand just like before only it wasn't Weseley, it was Laurie. Not as I knew him from today but as I first saw him in the photographs, handsome, young, mischievous. He was turning around and smiling at me, his mouth of perfect white teeth opening and closing as he laughed, and I realized then how alike we were, how I'd always wondered why I didn't look like Mum or Dad, and now it all made perfect sense. His nose, his lips, his cheeks and eyes—they all were like mine. He was holding my hand and telling me we were going to be okay. We were running together, laughing and smiling, not at all worried about Rosaleen because she couldn't catch us. Together we could outrun the world. Then I saw my father at the end of the field, clapping and cheering us on as though I was a child again. Laurie was gone and it was me and Mum for a moment, legs tied together in a three-legged race, just like we used to do when I was young. She looked anxious, not laughing but worried, and then she left and Laurie was back. We were running, tripping, and there my dad was again, laughing and cheering, arms open and ready to catch us when we fell across the line.

Then the glass mobiles in the field exploded all around us, shattered into millions of pieces, and I lost Laurie's hand. I heard Dad scream my name and I opened my eyes. The room was filled with glass, it was all over our bodies, all over the ground, and the smoke was pluming out through the window. I saw a claw, a giant yellow claw, disappear through the glass and the smoke drifted out. But it didn't stop the fire. It continued ravaging the photographs, racing through them with such speed and ferocity. We would be next. Then I saw Arthur. I saw Sister Ignatius. I saw my mother's face, alive, present, terrified. Then there were arms around me and I was outside, coughing and spluttering. I was on the grass. Before I closed my eyes I saw my mother, felt her kissing my head, then saw her embracing Laurie, crying and crying.

For the first time since I'd found my father on the floor of his office, I exhaled.

CHAPTER TWENTY-FIVE

Little Girl

Once upon a time there was a little girl who lived in a bungalow. She was the youngest child, with an intelligent older sister, and an older brother so handsome that he turned heads in the street. The little girl was what some people would call a surprise baby. To her parents, who had long finished having children, she was not just unplanned but unwanted, and that she knew well. At forty-seven years old and twenty-two years since she'd had her last baby, her mother was not prepared for the arrival of another child. Her older children had grown up and moved away, her daughter Helen to Cork to be a primary school teacher and her son Brian to Boston, where he was a computer analyst. They rarely came home. It was too expensive for Brian, and the mother preferred to go to Cork for holidays. The little girl didn't know these two strangers she rarely met and who called themselves her brother and sister. They themselves had children older than she; they knew little of who she was or what she wanted. She'd arrived too late.

Her father was the groundskeeper at Kilsaney Castle grounds, which was across the road from her home. Her mother was the cook.

The little girl loved the position her family was in, so close to such grandeur that the children at school considered her to be a part of it too. She loved that they were privy to bits of gossip that nobody else was. They were always the benefactors of great Christmas bonuses, leftover food, fabrics and wallpapers from recent refurbishings or clear-outs. The grounds were strictly private but the little girl was allowed to play inside its walls. It was an absolute honor for her and there was nothing she wouldn't do to please the family, such as odd jobs around the house, and running messages between her father, Joe, and the groundsman, Paddy.

She loved the days she was allowed to enter the castle. If she was home sick from school her mother couldn't very well leave her at home alone. Mr. and Mrs. Kilsaney were good like that, and allowed her mother to bring the little girl to work. The little girl would remain quiet in the corner of the great big kitchen where she'd watch her mother sweat all day over steaming pots and a roaring stove. She would be quiet, never giving any trouble, but she'd take it all in—not just her mother's cooking but also the goings-on in the house.

She noticed how, whenever Mr. Kilsaney had a decision to make, he'd disappear into the oak room and stand in the middle with his hands behind his back while he stared at the portraits of his forefathers, who grandly watched over him from their great big oil paintings with elaborate gold framing. Then he would exit the oak room, chin high, fired into action as though he was a soldier who'd just received a good talking-to from his sergeant-major.

She also saw how Mrs. Kilsaney, who was so besotted with her nine dogs who constantly ran around the house in a frenzy, failed to notice much of what went on around her. She paid more attention to her dogs, in particular the mischievous King Charles spaniel named Messy, who remained the only dog who couldn't be tamed and who took up most of her thoughts and most of her conversation. She didn't notice her two young boys playacting around the halls for her attention, or her husband's fondness for the none-too-attractive chambermaid Magdelene, who spent much time dusting the Kilsaneys' master bedroom when Mrs. Kilsaney was outdoors with the dogs.

The little girl noticed the one other thing that Mrs. Kilsaney paid attention to: dead flowers. The woman would inspect every vase as she passed, almost as though it were an obsession. She would smile with delight when the nun would arrive every third morning with fresh bouquets from her walled garden. Then, as soon as the nun would leave, Mrs. Kilsaney would pick at them, grumbling, pulling out anything that was less than perfect. The little girl loved Mrs. Kilsaney, loved her tweed suits and brown riding boots, which she wore even on days when she wasn't riding. However, the little girl decided she would never allow so much to go on in her own home without her knowing. She adored the mistress, but she thought her a fool.

The little girl also loved watching the two boys. They were always up to mischief, racing around the halls knocking things over, breaking things, making the chambermaid scream, causing a ruckus. It was the older one, Laurence, or Laurie, she watched mostly, as it was he who usually initiated the plan. He never noticed the little girl, but she was always there on the outskirts, feeling involved without being invited, playing along in her imagination.

The younger boy, Arthur, or Artie, seemed more sensible than his older brother, and would sometimes pay attention to her. He didn't invite her to play, but if Laurie did something silly he'd look to the little girl and roll his eyes or make a joke for her benefit. She'd rather he didn't. It was Laurie she wanted to notice her, and the more he didn't see her, the greater her longing grew. But he wanted nothing from her.

The little girl stayed home from school many times, just so she could spend time in the castle. Summer holidays were the best, having every day free to herself around the grounds without having to pretend to cough or to have a sore tummy. It was during one of these summers, when the little girl was seven and Artie was eight and Laurie was nine, that she was outside in the grounds playing alone when her mother called her into the castle. Mr. Kilsaney had gone foxhunting with their cousins in Balbriggan. The little girl's mother was in charge for the day, helping Mrs. Kilsaney in her room, and when Rosaleen reached the front of the castle she could tell from the look on the boys' faces that they were in trouble.

"It's a beautiful day, so play outside and get some fresh air and don't be getting under my feet," her mother said. "Rosaleen will play with you too."

"I don't want to play with her," Laurie sulked, but at least Rosaleen knew that she wasn't invisible to him, that he could see her after all.

"Be nice to her, boys. Say hello, Rosaleen."

"Hello, Rosaleen," they both mumbled, Laurie looking at the ground, Artie smiling at her shyly.

It was as if the little girl had no name before that. When she heard her name pass his lips, it was as though she had been christened.

"Now off with you," her mother said, and the boys ran off. Rosaleen followed.

Once they were deep in the woods, they stopped running and Laurie went to study an ant hole.

"I'm Artie," the younger one said.

"Don't talk to her," Laurie huffed, picking up a stick from the ground and waving it around as though he were in combat. He concentrated on poking the stick in the hole of a tree trunk. Suddenly they heard voices and Laurie, ears pricked, followed the sound. He held his hand up and the three of them stalled and spied through the trees and saw the groundsman, Paddy, on his knees, sorting through some brambles. Beside him, in the wheelbarrow, lay a little girl aged about two. She had white-blond hair.

"Who's that?" Laurie said, and his voice sent warning signals straight to Rosaleen's heart, but excited for their first conversation she replied, with a pounding in her chest, conscious of her voice, wanting to be so perfect for him.

"That's Jennifer Byrne," she said, ever so prim and proper. "Paddy is her dad."

"Let's ask her to play," Laurie said.

"She's only a baby," Rosaleen protested.

"She's funny," Laurie asked, watching the baby lazing about in the wheelbarrow.

So from that day on it was the four of them. Laurie, Artie, Rosaleen, and Jennifer played together every day. Jennifer because she'd been invited, Rosaleen because they'd been forced. Rosaleen always remembered that. Even when Laurie kissed her in the bushes or when they were boyfriend and girlfriend for a few weeks, she always knew that little Jennifer was his favorite. She always had been. For some reason, she captivated him.

Jennifer grew even more beautiful year by year, though she was completely unaware of her beauty. Without a mother since she was two years old, she was quite the tomboy, hanging out of trees, racing both Artie and Laurie, stripping off her clothes and diving into the lakes without a care in the world. She always tried to get Rosaleen to join in but never understood why she wouldn't. Rosaleen, on the other hand, was biding her time. She knew that the tomboy act would wear off with the boys. They'd lose interest. They'd want to find a real woman someday and she was going to be that woman. She could be like Mrs. Kilsaney, she could keep the castle, cook the food, train the dogs, make sure the nun brought her nothing less than perfect flowers. She dreamed of Laurie someday being hers, that they could live together in the castle, looking after the dogs and the flowers while Laurie received inspiration in the oak room from his forefathers on the walls.

When the boys went off to boarding school, Laurie wrote only to Jennifer, while Artie wrote to both of them. Rosaleen never let Jennifer know this. She would pretend that she had received a letter from Laurie too but that it was too personal to read aloud. Jennifer never seemed to mind, and it made Rosaleen even more jealous. Then when the boys went off to college, Rosaleen's mother's MS was deteriorating, her aging father was ill, and they needed money. Rosaleen's brother and sister were too far away to help, so Rosaleen's parents relied on the child they never wanted in the first place. Rosaleen was forced to leave school and take over her mother's job at the castle, while Jennifer continued to prosper, taking trips to Dublin to visit the boys.

Those were the worst days for Rosaleen. The weeks were long and boring without the others. She lived in her head, dreaming of all that was past and creating all that could be in the future, while the three others were off in the city doing exciting things—Laurie at art college, sending home his glass work; Artie studying horticulture; Jennifer being offered modeling jobs every time she stepped outside the door. When they returned home during the breaks, Rosaleen's life couldn't be happier, except that she yearned for Laurie to look at her as he did Jennifer.

She didn't know how long the romance between Laurie and Jennifer had been going on. She could only assume it started in Dublin while she was at home plucking pheasants and gutting fish. She wondered if they were ever going to tell her, if it hadn't been for that embarrassing day when she brought him to the apple tree to finally tell him how she felt, showed him the carving in the tree, "Laurie and Rose." She was so sure he would finally see her for who she really was, how she had been keeping the castle going without him, for him.

But it hadn't worked that way. It hadn't gone at all like she'd imagined for all those years and for all those months alone in the kitchen in the castle. So life became dark and cold then. Her father passed away, her older sister tried to take her mother away with her to Cork. But without her mother, Rosaleen had nothing, so she promised to look after her. Jennifer offered her a firm friendship and Rosaleen accepted it while all the time hating her. Hating everything she said, everything she did, hating the fact that Laurie had fallen for her.

Then, one autumn, Jennifer fell pregnant, and Rosaleen's life fell apart. Jennifer was welcomed into the Kilsaney household with open arms. A delighted Mrs. Kilsaney showed her her wardrobes, the family wedding dress, everything that should have been Rosaleen's. Jennifer and her father were invited to the weekly dinners that Rosaleen cooked for them. The humiliation was beyond repair.

The child was born two weeks early and with not enough time to get to the hospital, so Rosaleen had run through the dark night to fetch the old nun. They had a little girl. They called her Tamara, after Jennifer's mother, who'd passed away when Jennifer was a child. The couple weren't yet married but living in the castle. Rosaleen and Arthur were godparents. The christening was in the castle chapel.

Meanwhile, life in the castle had been getting harder. The Kilsaneys were finding it difficult to keep the castle going since money wasn't coming in, so they were becoming desperate. All those rooms to keep, to heat, to maintain—it was all too much. They would meet at dinner to talk about it all with Rosaleen eavesdropping.

Perhaps they would open the castle to the public. Every Saturday allow the public to trample through their home, taking photographs of their eighteenth-century writing desks and the oak room filled with portraits, at their chapel, at their age-old letters from generations ago between lords and ladies, politicians and rebels, during times of great unrest.

"No," Mrs. Kilsaney would cry, "I can't let them visit us as though we're a zoo. And still how will we afford the place? A few pounds admission fee per adult won't fix the roof, it won't pay Paddy's wages, it won't pay the heating bills."

They soon found a solution, though. Developers Timothy and George Goodwin arrived in Kilsaney in their Bentley on the most beautiful day of the year, and the two men couldn't believe their eyes when they saw the grounds, the view, the lakes, the deer, the pheasants. It was like a theme park to them, and they saw money everywhere they looked. Timothy Goodwin, a dapper but rude old gentleman in a three-piece suit, with a checkbook in his inside pocket, fell in love with the property. George Goodwin fell in love with Jennifer Byrne. This was the happiest day of Rosaleen's life. While serving them during their banquet meal in the great dining room one evening, she couldn't help but observe how George Goodwin had eyes only for Jennifer, how he had little to say to Laurie and a lot of time to play with the child. Everybody at the table saw this, certainly Laurie.

The Goodwins returned over and over with builders, architects, engineers, surveyors in tow. George returned far more often than his father, taking over the project. One night Rosaleen overheard George offering Jennifer the sun, the moon, and the stars. While

Jennifer found George Goodwin a pleasant and kind man, she rejected his advances.

But Rosaleen still saw her opportunity to get Laurie back.

Laurie caught her in the scullery crying her eyes out. She wouldn't tell him at first, she didn't want to hurt him. It was none of her business, she said, Jennifer was her friend. But he gently coaxed her into telling him what she'd seen. She'd felt bad for causing the hurt that went through his eyes. So bad that she almost took it right back, but then he'd taken her hand and squeezed it, given her a hug, and told her what a great friend she'd always been, how he hadn't always acknowledged that. Well, how could she take it back then?

It was a long night, a long argument. Rosaleen allowed them to fight it out between themselves, their own words doing more damage than hers ever could. Laurie didn't tell Jennifer that it was Rosaleen who had told him. And Rosaleen let Jennifer cry on her shoulder while she gave her halfhearted advice. Later, Jennifer came to Rosaleen with a letter. A letter that Rosaleen read and, though she rarely cried, it made her do so. Jennifer's wish was for her to pass it on to Laurie. But Rosaleen burned it. As she did, the child wandered in, the toddler who looked so like her father. So Rosaleen shook out the letter until the fire subsided and she threw it in the bin before taking the child to bed.

That was the night of the fire. She can't be sure if it was the burned letter that caused it, though they say it came from the kitchen. Still, nobody ever blamed her. The child was saved that night by Laurie. Then he went back in to fetch some valuables. As far as Jennifer knew, he died in that fire. After he survived, Laurie didn't want Jennifer to take him back just because she felt she had to. As far as he was concerned, George Goodwin had her heart and could offer her more. Though it was his own decision, a little prodding from

Rosaleen helped Laurie to decide this was the best thing. Laurie had no castle, and he'd lost the use of an arm and a leg. He was badly burned, beyond recognition. Ugly as though he'd rotted away. Artie didn't agree, but he couldn't talk his brother out of the decision to deceive Jennifer. The brothers never spoke again, not years later even when living across the road from one another.

For months Jennifer mourned Laurie, refusing to leave her house, refusing to live. But there's only so much of that you can take, particularly when there was a handsome and successful gentleman knocking on her door, wanting to rescue her and take her away. Rosaleen once again was at the helm of that decision. She engineered it all so wonderfully. She hadn't meant to start the fire, hadn't meant to hurt poor Laurie like that, but it had happened and it all worked in her favor. Artie moved in with Paddy and they worked the grounds together. Laurie moved into the bungalow where Rosaleen could care both for him and for her mother. While he thanked her every day, he still couldn't give her what she wanted. He didn't love her. She realized then that she'd never have him exactly the way she wanted. She'd never become a Kilsaney.

It was when Paddy died and Artie was living in the gatehouse alone that she finally returned the attention Artie had been giving her ever since she'd been a little girl. Rosaleen eventually became a Kilsaney, though they never used their titles.

That was seventeen years ago and it was all going well, not perfectly, but well, until George Goodwin messed up her plans and that awful child who looked so much like her biological father, and who should have been hers, had come back into their lives to throw it into turmoil again. It would all have been all right if Jennifer had just healed so that she and Tamara could both move on with their lives in Dublin. But she had reverted back to her time grieving for

Laurie somehow, and she was confused; she was grieving for the wrong person.

Rosaleen couldn't cope with losing anything else. She loved Laurie more than anyone in her life, but the lie he had forced her to keep had led to so much unhappiness for so many people. She could see that now. And she was tired. Tired of fighting for her marriage to the wonderful, lovely Arthur. Her beautiful, kind husband who was torn apart every day by the lie to Jennifer and Tamara, who deserved more. She was tired of keeping the secret, tired of running back and forth, tired of being unable to look anybody in the eye in the village for fear of them knowing what she had done, guessing what was going on in the bungalow and in the work shed, where smoke funneled out night and day. She wanted everything to go away. She wanted this bungalow, which had always felt like a prison to her, which had become one for Laurie and her mother, to be gone. She was going to release them all. She made sure her mother was safe before she struck the match.

Why, Rosaleen, why? They asked her over and over outside the burning bungalow. *Why?* They still didn't know, they still had to ask her. All that she had been through, her silent torture. But that was why. That was always the reason why. From a little girl to a grown woman, she had loved one man too much.

CHAPTER TWENTY-SIX

What We Have Learned Today

Friday, 7 August

I heard Mum and Laurie talking until the sun came up. Sister Ignatius has been helping them talk through everything. It's like anything bad or scary that happens, when you finish it or get through it you're so relieved you forget how terrifying it was or how miserable you were and you just want to remember the good parts, or you tell yourself it's helped you get to the new part of yourself.

All is not well in this household. All is not perfect. But then again, it never has been. Gone is the elephant from the room, though. He's been released and is running riot down the roads, while we all try to tame him. It's just like when a card dealer shuffles the pack—he messes them all up and ruins the order, just so he can deal them and find some order again. That's what had happened to us. A long time ago things were shuffled, we were all dealt our cards. Now, we're tidying them up, trying to make sense out of them all.

I don't think Mum or I will ever forgive Laurie, Rosaleen, and Arthur for keeping such a secret from us, for propelling such a lie for so long. All that we can do is try to understand that Laurie did it because he wanted the best for us, no matter how misguided it was. He believed it would give us a better life. It's not forgivable, but we have to try to understand. Maybe when I understand it properly I can forgive it. Maybe when I can understand why both Mum and Dad lied to me about my real father, I'll be able to forgive them. I think that's all a little too far off for me to imagine right now. But I can thank Laurie for giving me such a wonderful dad. George Goodwin was a good man, a good father, thinking of us until the end. He fought his father all the way to the end of his father's life about developing Kilsaney. He knew it was the one thing that my biological father could have left behind for me, had things gone the way they should have, had he not perished in the fire. It was also Mum's home. Where she grew up, where she carried all of her memories, and when the banks came knocking, he couldn't let it go. I would rather have my father than Kilsaney, but it's a reminder of how much he loved us, what he was attempting to do. Both of my fathers gave up so much for us. I can only thank them and feel fortunate to be loved so much by two people.

Arthur goes back and forth to Rosaleen in the hospital every day. She's been the luckiest person in the world to have him and she never knew it. She'll know it now, when everybody else has turned their backs on her. I find his loyalty to her unfathomable, but then again, I've never been in love. It obviously does crazy things to people. He just wants her to get better but, between you and me, I don't think she'll ever get out of that place. Whatever is wrong with Rosaleen is so deep-rooted that it has reached up from her past life and is growing far into her next one, already uprooting whatever is sprouting there.

Arthur and Laurence have been reunited. Arthur will never forgive Laurence for making him promise to be a part of this entire thing. But I think he'll forgive him quicker than he'll ever forgive himself. He tormented himself every single day about not having stepped forward, for allowing the lie to grow, watching me grow up and my mother grieve while my father was across the road in a room. I suppose it's easier to see the way out of anything when you've found your way out of that maze. When you're stuck in the middle, in a series of dead ends, making circles, it's difficult to make any sense of anything. I know that feeling.

Me? I'm a little wobbly but oddly, I feel stronger. I've said good-bye to Zoey and Laura completely after they asked for photographs of my burned hand for their Facebook pages. I'm planning on inviting Fiona, the girl who gave me the book at the funeral, to this house very soon. When things have calmed down, at least a little.

So that's the story. The whole story. As I said at the beginning, I don't expect you to believe it but it's the truth, every single word of it. All families have their secrets, most people would never know them, but they know there are spaces, gaps where the answers should be, where someone should have sat, where someone used to be. A name that is never uttered, or uttered just once and never again. We all have our secrets. Ours are unearthed now, or at least they're beginning to be. I constantly wonder how much of my life would have stayed a secret if it hadn't been for the diary. The diary definitely led me here. It helped me discover the secrets, but it also made me a better person. That sounds really slushy, I know, but it helped me to realize that there are tomorrows. Before, I only concentrated on today. I would say and do things in order to get what I wanted right then. I never gave a second thought to how the rest of the dominoes would fall. The diary helped me to see how one thing affects another. How I can actually make a difference in my life and in other people's lives. I always think back to how I was drawn to the diary in Marcus's traveling library, almost like it was there just for me that day. I definitely think about books a lot differently now.

When I was in primary school, the teacher used to tell us to write a paragraph at the end of every day titled "What I Learned Today." I feel in this circumstance it would take far less to say "What I Haven't Learned," for what haven't I learned? Nothing. Absolutely nothing. I've learned so much, I've grown so much, and I know this is not the end.

I thought this whole thing—finding out who I am—was the purpose for the diary. I thought after the fire the diary would become a notepad again and I would have returned it to the traveling library and replaced it on the nonfiction shelf and allowed somebody else to benefit from it. But I can't do it. I can't let it go. It continues to tell me about tomorrow and I continue to live it, to try to live it better.

I closed the diary, left the castle, and made my way toward the orchard where I'd arranged to meet Weseley by the apple tree with the engravings.

"Uh-oh," he said, eyeing the diary under my arm. "What now?"

"Nothing bad." I sat down beside him on a blanket.

"I don't believe you. What is it?"

"It's actually about you and me," I said with a laugh.

"What about us?"

I raised my eyebrows suggestively at him.

"Oh no!" He threw his arms up dramatically. "So now, as well as saving you from burning houses, I have to kiss you?"

I shrugged. "Whatever."

"Where does it happen? Here?"

I nodded.

"Okay. So." He looked at me seriously.

"So," I replied. I cleared my throat. Readied myself.

"Does it say that I kiss you or that you kiss me?"

"You definitely kiss me."

"Okay."

He was silent for a moment before leaning in and kissing me tenderly on the lips. Then he opened his eyes and pulled away.

"You just made that up, didn't you?" he asked, eyes wide.

"What do you mean?" I said.

"Tamara Goodwin, you made that up!" He grinned. "Give me that book." He swiped it from my hands and pretended to hit me over the head with it.

"We have to make our own tomorrows, Weseley," I teased. I fell back on the blanket and looked up at the apple tree that had seen so much over the years.

Weseley leaned over me, our faces close together, our noses almost touching.

"What did it really say?" he asked softly.

"That I think it'll all be okay. And that I'll write again tomorrow."

"You always say that."

"And I always do."

"Are you ready?" he asked, studying me closely.

"I think so," I whispered.

"Right." He sat up and pulled me up with him. "I brought this."

He took a clear plastic bag from beside him and held it open. I dropped the diary in—reluctantly at first, but I soon knew it was the right decision.

He wrapped the diary up in the plastic bag and handed it back to me.

"You do it."

I looked up at the apple tree, at the engravings of the names of my mum, Laurie, Arthur, Rosaleen, and the dozens of others who had so many hopes for tomorrow under this tree, and then I knelt down and placed the diary in the hole that Weseley had dug, and we filled it again with soil.

I didn't lie when I said I couldn't let it go. I can't let it go. Not completely. Maybe someday when I'm in trouble again I'll dig it up and see what it has to say. But in the meantime, I'll have to find my own way.

Thanks for reading my story. I'll write again tomorrow.

Acknowledgments

David, Mimmie, Dad, Georgina, Nicky, Rocco, and Jay (and Star, Doggy, and Sniff)—I feel like I couldn't wake up in the morning without you, never mind write a book. Thanks for holding my hand all the way along this long, exciting, and intriguing path. "Carry you . . . ?!"

For the yesterdays and todays, and the tomorrows I can hardly wait for. Thank you.

The Kellys (somebody will write a book about you lot yet), Aherns, Keoghans, and my dear full-time friends and part-time therapists. Thank you.

Marianne Gunn O'Connor. Thank you.

Vicki Satlow, Pat Lynch, Liam Murphy, Anita Kissane, Gerard O'Herlihy, Doo Services. Thank you.

Lynne Drew, Claire Bord—my books wouldn't be what they are without your comments, advice, and guidance. Thank you, thank you.

Amanda Ridout—there's an empty chair at the anything-is-possible table and you'll be missed. For all your encouragement and belief in me, thank you.

The entire army at HarperCollins—for working so hard on so many fantastically new and exciting ideas. I'm extraordinarily lucky to be a part of the team. Thank you.

Fiona McIntosh, Moira Reilly, and Tony Purdue—I do enjoy our road trips! Thank you.

I do want to pay tribute to Killeen Castle. While this book is certainly not about Killeen, I was looking for a setting for this story and suddenly came across this extraordinary place. Something clicked in my head and an entire world for Tamara and her family began to form. Thank you to those at Killeen Castle for, although unknowingly, unlocking the world for *The Book of Tomorrow*.

The booksellers—for your incredible support. In *The Book of Tomorrow* I share my belief in the magic of books, how I believe books must contain some sort of homing device, which allows them to draw the correct reader to them. Books choose their readers, not the other way around. I believe that booksellers are the matchmakers. Thank you.

About the Author

Before embarking on her writing career, CECELIA AHERN completed a degree in journalism and media communications. At twenty-one she wrote her first novel, *P.S. I Love You*, which became an international bestseller and was adapted into a major motion picture starring Hilary Swank. Her successive novels—*Love, Rosie*; *If You Could See Me Now*; *There's No Place Like Here*; *Thanks for the Memories*; and *The Gift*—were also international bestsellers. Her books are published in forty-six countries and have collectively sold more than twelve million copies. The daughter of Ireland's former prime minister, Ahern lives in Dublin, Ireland.

In 2010, Ahern became the youngest recipient of a Nielsen Book Platinum Award, for achieving more than a million sales in the UK for *P.S. I Love You*. For more information, go to www.cecelia-ahern.com.